About the Author

David J. Godden practiced medicine in the UK. He undertook many laboratory studies and clinical trials in the UK and Canada and, as a clinical professor, directed a successful academic research unit. He has published and lectured widely in North America and Europe. He left clinical research in 2011 to pursue interests in travel, music, and writing. He lives in the Scottish Highlands.

CURE

THE

DAVID J. GODDEN

Matador
9 Priory Business Park,
Wistow Road, Kibworth Beauchamp,
Leicestershire. LE8 0RX
Tel: (+44) 116 279 2299
Fax: (+44) 116 279 2277
Email: books@troubador.co.uk
Web: www.troubador.co.uk/matador

ISBN 978 1783061 778

British Library Cataloguing in Publication Data.
A catalogue record for this book is available from the British Library.

Typeset by Troubador Publishing Ltd, Leicester, UK
Printed and bound in the UK by TJ International, Padstow, Cornwall

Matador is an imprint of Troubador Publishing Ltd

To all those individuals, past, present and future, whose unselfish participation in clinical research studies enhances medical knowledge and improves the lives of others.

ACKNOWLEDGEMENTS

My heartfelt thanks to Jean for her support with this novel and for all the years of love and companionship. Alan and Ann McKay provided invaluable comments on earlier drafts of the novel. Steven and Fiona Godden commented on presentational issues. Any residual errors are mine. Particular thanks to the wonderful singer songwriter Allan Taylor who gave generous permission to reproduce the lyrics of his song "Roll on the Day" (Chapter 18).

CHAPTER 1

The rumble of applause in the auditorium rose to a crescendo. At first a few ... then more ... then all 2,000 people in the room rose to their feet.

Ray was bemused. He'd never seen, or heard, anything like this at a medical conference before. Now they were applauding him. As he scanned the audience, he saw a few familiar faces. Gerard Carter, his boss, was in the front row, accepting handshakes from distinguished-looking men and women and smiling broadly. Towards the back of the lower tier, a tall beautiful African American woman rose, slipped quietly towards the side door of the auditorium and disappeared from view. Ray's eyes lingered on the closed door for a few seconds, until he was abruptly brought back to the present by the chairman's voice.

"Well, Dr Shepherd, I think you will realise that congress is more than impressed with your work. In the interests of time, we'll have no questions just now, although I'm sure that many colleagues will want to catch up with you over coffee later. We'll look forward to hearing the next stage of your work as it progresses".

Ray made his way from the stage in a daze. Next thing, Carter was introducing him to some of the greybeards he had noticed from the stage. He didn't fully catch some of their names, although a number of them were familiar to him from his reading: Sven Pedersen from the Karolinska Institute, Oleg Fedorov from St Petersburg, Masashi Saguro from Tokyo, and Sir Albert Smithfield from Queen Square, London. There was no real need for Ray to say much, as Carter was in full flow, describing how they would be moving ahead to a full-scale clinical trial shortly and, with a note of smugness and no small amount of grandstanding, how he fully expected that this would be the biggest advance in neurology in any of their lifetimes. Ray began to feel oppressed by the whole place and, after a polite interval, he made his excuses and headed for the main door under the enormous banner '5th Pan-European Congress of Neurology – Barcelona'.

He moved quickly through the concourse and headed down to the Metro, buying a ticket en route and heading into the familiar underground station. After a couple of stops and a change of train, he emerged from the labyrinth into the sunshine again and immediately saw, at close quarters, the fantastic spires of La Sagrada Familia. Although he had seen it before, the sight of the Gaudi cathedral never failed to take his breath away. He marvelled at the scale of Gaudi's imagination, surpassed only by his ability to have his plans converted into bricks and mortar. The spires, rising to over 100 metres, had an unearthly appearance with rivers of stone cascading from them. In the more modern section of the building, where an attempt was being made to preserve the Gaudi tradition, garish colours had been used to adorn the structures. Within the seemingly random icons, a definite pattern of symbols was to be found, though this might be obscure to the casual observer. In some ways, there were parallels with the processes of scientific research, he thought.

As he moved along to his favourite tapas bar, he heard a familiar voice.

"Well, Dr Shepherd, how does it feel to be curing multiple sclerosis?"

As he had expected, she sat at their old table, looking every bit as stunning as when she walked through the door of the auditorium. She was, if anything, even more beautiful than when he had last seen her. Her long black hair was about shoulder-length and hung around her wonderful face. Her cheek structure was bold and her make-up subtly applied. She wore a grey tailored two piece suit and white shirt, carried a smart briefcase and was still wearing her conference name tag

Liz Washington MD PHD
Senior Research Fellow, Harvard University

Her overall appearance was that of a highly intelligent, slightly forbidding professional, perhaps a lawyer or high-ranking executive. However, as she looked across at him, her face suddenly transformed into the most amazing smile and he felt the envy and admiration of the other men in the bar transmit to him.

"Ray, I hoped you might turn up here. I realised that I'd have no chance of reaching you at the conference, and I didn't want to distract you from all your new eminent friends."

"Liz, you distracted me without even reaching the stage," he said, pulling her towards him and sharing a long and warm embrace. "Anyway, Carter was loving all the attention, you know how he is! From the stage, I thought it was you, but the suit and the briefcase? I wasn't sure if my eyes had deceived me after staring into the hall lights. I guess this is the Harvard uniform? I thought you had given up on me when I didn't get a Christmas card last year."

She looked a bit sheepish, if that was possible. "I moved last year and I forgot to send you my new address. I'm faculty now, you know, though all it gives me is a smaller office and less time for music. Hey, I really enjoyed your talk; and so confident too … I always knew the big one would come your way one day. Prions to treat disease? Well, I'll be damned, as we Americans are supposed to say. You must tell me more."

Ray pulled up a chair as the waiter approached.

"Dos cervesas, si us plau," said Ray, attempting the order in halting Catalan. "I hope the smart suit doesn't mean you stopped drinking beer."

Liz and Ray had shared many beers and much more besides, including two visits to Barcelona and this very tapas bar, when they were both junior research fellows at the Massachusetts Medical Research Centre in Boston some years before. Their work then had been on blood supply to the brain, trying to develop a method of predicting strokes. Like many research projects, the work had been ultimately unsuccessful, as had their relationship. His time in the US had done wonders for his confidence, but at the end of his eighteen month secondment, Ray had returned to the UK to a clinical training post in care of the elderly, while Liz had obviously moved on to greater things at Harvard. They had kept in touch by Christmas cards, at least until last year's failed attempt. Now his mood of slight deflation after his presentation was lifted by the sight of her.

"I'll tell you about my work in minute. What about you first? You look great, and sexy as ever, if I may be so bold."

"Oh, you English guys are always so formal. 'If I may be so bold' indeed – You've been reading too much P.G Wodehouse!"

"Wait a minute – how many English guys do you know?"

"Well, there's Sean Connery, Richard Burton, Liam Neeson …"

"That's a Scotsman, a Welshman and an Irishman so far" Ray laughed.

"OK. Point taken," said Liz, laughing. "Anyway, one Englishman I do know, purely professionally of course, is Martin Downey. He came out to Boston from Nottingham last year about two years after you left and we resurrected some of that work on stroke prediction. He has a technique for estimating clotting factor activity and we have been able to show that the activity changes about twenty-four hours before the stroke in an animal model. There is still a long way to go, but I think it's got potential. I managed to interest the NIH and we got a grant of about $2million to develop the study, hence the elevation to faculty ..."

"... and the smart suit" joked Ray.

"Well no, that's not such a happy story," said Liz. "My parents were driving up to Boston from New York last December. There was heavy snow ... the car ... they were both ..."

Tears began to well up and she opened her briefcase to get some tissues.

Ray took her arms firmly in his hands. "I'm so, so sorry," he said. He knew the pride that Liz's parents had in her achievements and how close they had been, even though they had never really approved of her relationship with him.

She gradually began to regain her composure.

"Anyway, the result of all that is that I have come into some money and I don't need to check the door each night for signs of the wolf. Now tell me about you. How did you find the cure for MS?"

"Not so much to tell really ..."

As he began to speak, time rolled back ...

CHAPTER 2

Ray walked up the paved path between rows of cheery flowers as the bright sun warmed his back. The houses on either side of the path were small, with a white emergency light beside each door. Most of them had access ramps or bars by the side of the door to assist elderly and disabled folk. He was looking for number thirty-two.

Normally, he didn't get out of the hospital much, but today his boss had asked him to visit Eric, a young man who had multiple sclerosis and was having some difficulties. Dr Ahmed, the consultant in charge of Eric's case and also Ray's current boss during his attachment to the Rehabilitation Unit, would usually have done such visits himself but today he was feeling unwell.

"Could you visit Eric Strother today? I don't think you've met him before. His wife called today saying that he's got a fever and is very lethargic. Usually means he's got a urine infection or similar. Anyway, see what you make of him. It'll be good for you to see a bit of medicine outside the hospital."

The front door of number thirty-two was like most of the others, the steps replaced by an access ramp. A few wallflowers were in the border below the window and the grass was neatly trimmed. Ray rang the bell and, after a few seconds, the door opened. A young woman, dressed in an open neck shirt, jeans and sandals, stood there. She had blonde shoulder-length hair and there was something about her face that grabbed Ray's attention, thought he couldn't quite put his finger on what.

"Oh, you must be Dr Shepherd. Dr Ahmed said that you'd be coming today. He's such a nice man, I'm sorry to hear he's not well himself. Anyway, thanks for coming. Eric's having a bad day, I'm afraid – he'll be glad to see you. By the way, I'm Susan."

She walked through the small hallway into the main room of the small house. Immediately, Ray felt that he was back in the hospital. The room seemed particularly dark, given the brightness of the day. As his eyes accustomed to the light, he looked around.

In the right-hand corner by the window was a large TV set. On-screen, a young couple appeared to be searching for a house in some sunny Spanish resort. On the mantelpiece above the gas fire were a couple of photographs. Across the room was a sideboard, the top of which was covered with a range of surgical supplies, dressings and wipes. The flooring in the room looked to be the same sort of stuff that covered hospital floors and the skirtings were rounded off for cleaning purposes, he supposed. A large hoist for lifting a patient was parked in the corner. In the centre of the room was a hospital-style bed. In the centre of the bed was Eric.

"Hey, doc. Thanks for coming. I've been a bit rough for the past couple of days and Susan thought she should call for the cavalry."

Eric had a thin pale face topped by wavy black hair which had obviously been washed a little earlier. Even with the bed covers pulled up, Ray could guess that he was probably very emaciated. His arms lay outside the covers, slightly turned in towards his body. Like his face, they were pale and thin with very little muscle evident. His fingers were slender and it crossed Ray's mind that he might have been a musician, or perhaps that was just another sign of muscle loss.

"So what's been the problem, Eric?"

"Last couple of days I've been more knackered than usual. I feel a bit sweaty and Susan tells me that my pee's been a bit cloudy – usually means I have a urine infection."

"Have you had any pain passing your water?"

As soon as he asked, Ray realised this was a stupid question.

"I haven't been able to pee normally for about five years, doc, and I've got a catheter in. I don't really feel anything from that department."

"OK. What about your chest?"

"It's been OK, I think. I haven't been coughing much and I'm not breathless."

As he spoke, Ray noticed that Eric's voice seems to be weakening a little.

"All right," said Ray. I'd better have a look at you."

As he pulled back the covers, the full extent of the problem became more obvious … and shocking. Eric was incredibly thin, his ribs sticking out above a flat belly with very prominent hip bones. From his penis, a green tube snaked over the edge of the bed towards a bag which contained a small amount of cloudy fluid. At first look his knees seemed swollen, but Ray quickly realised that was just due to the wasting of the muscles in his legs causing the ends of his thigh bones to stick out. There was no indication that he could move his legs much, if at all.

As he took in this first impression of Eric, Ray's eyes briefly glanced again at the mantelpiece. One of the pictures showed a handsome young couple: a blonde girl in a white wedding dress; by her side a tall muscular lad in full Highland dress – kilt, sporran, black jacket and white shirt with black bow tie. The other picture showed the same young man, this time in rugby kit and holding aloft a trophy with a huge grin on his face.

Eric caught Ray's eye as he turned back from the pictures.

"Aye, I couldn't lift that trophy now. Don't you think that Susan looks stunning in the picture though? That was at Stirling – it was a beautiful day too."

In that moment, Ray began to realise what he was witnessing here – the inexorable decay of a young man's body and also of his hopes and plans for the future. The contrast between the wasted body lying on the bed in front of him, the strapping young athlete in the picture, and the other young couple still visible on the TV screen looking for their dream home in the sun, was almost too painful to bear.

Susan had moved back into the kitchen doorway and, as he looked at her, the odd feeling he'd had at the doorway clicked into place. Her face was still the beautiful one of the young girl in the picture, her body looked in great shape too; she obviously loved Eric just as much as she had done on that wedding day in Stirling, but there was an emptiness in her eyes. It was as though while Eric's world contracted from all its early possibilities into the reality of these four walls, the hospital bed, the hoist and the surgical supplies, so her world had contracted with it. Not for them the place in the sun, days climbing hills or running along the beach, nor the joy of children or even of sex. The flaccid penis was reduced to being a conduit for a rubber tube to drain waste from this otherwise wasting body, not even capable of normal peeing, never mind an erection.

Ray pulled himself back into professional mode and set about examining Eric. His chest and heart sounded fine, although his heart rate was a bit fast and he felt a bit hot and clammy. In his abdomen, Ray felt a fullness rising up from his pubic bone, just above the penis, and extending up close to his belly button. He tapped over the area with one finger on the back of his outstretched hand, and sure enough, the note was very dull up to about the same level. Ray gave no sign that this felt uncomfortable, or indeed that he felt anything at all there.

"Your bladder is pretty full, Eric. I suspect the catheter is blocked and that you've got a urine infection as a result. How long has that catheter been in?"

"Better ask the boss," said Eric.

"I think it's about two months since it was last changed. The nurse comes in to flush it from time to time, but she was last here ten days ago," added Susan.

"OK," said Ray. I'll put a new one in now, and send off a sample, but I think I'll just give you a prescription for some antibiotics to start in the meantime. If the lab tells us you need a different one, I'll let you know."

Ray inspected the surgical supplies on top of the sideboard. There were some sterile packs and two replacement catheters, so he set about the process of changing the catheter. First he cleaned the area, then he removed the water from the small balloon that held the old catheter in the bladder. He then took hold of Eric's penis and pulled gently on the catheter. As is sometimes the case when it's been in for a while, it needed a fairly strong tug to remove it. At this point in the proceedings, it was probably a bit of a blessing that Eric was numb in that area. As he took the old catheter out, he again noted how wasted Eric's muscles were. He must have had virtually no movement in his legs and very little in his arms, yet, as Ray had turned him over to listen to his back, he had noted that Eric's skin was in good condition, with no signs of pressure sores. This was obviously down to the great care that Susan took of her husband, as he knew that she had only relatively infrequent visits from the district nurse. Even with the benefit of special mattresses and other things, she must have kept changing Eric's position regularly and cleaning the inevitable sweat and faeces from his body. Surely not the life she had intended for herself, but one lived with great love and tenderness.

Ray removed the new catheter from the packaging and gently

slid it into Eric's penis and up into the bladder, inflating the balloon with sterile water once it was in place. Almost immediately, cloudy urine began to flow down the new catheter into the new collection bag. Ray took care that this process happened only slowly, knowing that it was possible to cause the patient to faint if the drainage occurred too rapidly.

"There we go," said Ray. "That should hopefully let things settle down now."

He cut the tip from the old catheter to send to the lab with a urine sample to check which bugs might be causing the infection, and once he'd satisfied himself that everything was working OK, he pulled the bed cover up.

"Is there anything else I can do for you?" said Ray.

"No, thanks doc, that's been great." said Eric.

"Yes, thanks very much for coming out so quickly," said Susan. "You can let Dr Ahmed know that he's got a good subs bench," she laughed. In that fleeting moment her eyes lit up before falling back to their previous state. "I'll see you out."

As she opened the front door, the sun streamed in, the day seeming even brighter than before he had gone in.

"I'll let you know if the antibiotic needs to be changed," said Ray. "Give us a call if you've any worries."

"Thanks, doc, have a good day," and with that the door closed on Eric and Susan's world.

As he walked back down the path, emotions raced through Ray's head. He felt some pride that he had handled the situation professionally, given his lack of experience of treating people in their own homes. However, a profound sadness also came over him. Eric was only a little older than Ray; he had obviously had great potential, found himself a beautiful and loving partner, and then gradually had his world taken from him by this disease. Sadness started to give way to anger and frustration in Ray's head. How could this disease do this to a young man … no, to a young couple; as surely as Eric's horizons had narrowed and disappeared, so had Susan's. What was her life now – full-time carer and amateur nurse for her young man? What was the eventual outcome? Slow decline and, eventually, death. When would that happen? Would she still be young enough to find another partner? Would she ever have children? If not, would she come to resent the years that multiple sclerosis had taken from Eric and her? Would she come to resent Eric himself, perhaps after he was gone?

Ray realised that in the face of this, despite all his so-called professionalism and skill, he was virtually impotent. The stupidity and irony of his throwaway question came back to haunt him.

"Is there anything else I can do for you?"

…. Well doc, maybe you could give me back the feeling and strength in my legs; maybe you could let me pee and shit normally; maybe you could let me play rugby again; maybe you could let me go to that house in the sun in Spain; maybe you could let me make love to my beautiful Susan like any other man would; maybe …

"Is there anything else I can do for you?"

… No, actually there's fuck all …

CHAPTER 3

Later that night, as on many others, Ray sat down with a dram and a ready meal in his small apartment. He liked this room, although there wasn't much to it, just a settee, a couple of big cushions, a small coffee table, some bookshelves and his guitar propped in the corner.

He felt more drained than usual, as his thoughts replayed the scene in Eric's house and the look in Susan's eyes. His mind drifted to what he had been taught in medical school about MS: a disease of unknown cause, commoner in temperate countries, commonly affecting young adults, more females than males, a varying type of progression; in the lucky ones a single attack of loss of vision, sensation or power in some part of the body which improved spontaneously and never happened again; in others, recurrent attacks which gradually lent to permanent loss of function, so-called relapsing and remitting disease; and, in the really unfortunate ones, an inexorable progression of loss of function which could affect sight, balance, coordination, power and sensation, with eventual loss of bowel and bladder control, recurrent chest problems and death often from general debility and infection. At least that was a précis of the textbook. It didn't focus so much on the loss of optimism, destruction of hope and enjoyment for the sufferer, or, of course, for the family and loved ones.

Ray thought about some of the famous and not so famous who had suffered this disease. It seemed to him particularly savage when it affected sports people or musicians, stripping away their talent. Often in the early stages of the disease, when coordination could be affected, people would think that the sufferer was drunk or drugged. Stuart Henry, a 1970s BBC disc jockey was one who had described this in interviews before his death. Ronnie Lane and Clifford T Ward were other pop musicians who had succumbed, while the most famous sufferer in the UK was probably Jacqueline du Pré, the beautiful cello virtuoso whose hands were rendered useless before she died at an impossibly young age.

Ray knew something of current thoughts on the pathology and pathogenesis of the disease. It was called a demyelinating condition, referring to the sheaths of myelin material which covered each nerve fibre … a bit like the insulation on an electrical wire but, unlike simple insulation, these myelin sheaths were essential to allow a signal to pass along the nerve. In MS, the myelin was destroyed in patches along the length of the nerve, so that the nerve would lose its ability to carry a signal. If it was a sensory nerve, the patient would lose that particular sensation; for example, they might cut their finger or burn their foot and not feel it at all. A lot of the real damage in MS was due to these kinds of trauma. If it was a motor nerve, then the affected part of the body would become immobile. In Eric's case, for example, the young, previously fit, rugby player could now no longer move his legs at all and had very little power in his arms. He had also lost the feeling of when his bladder was full or bowels needed to move and was doubly incontinent, hence the need for the catheter. As well as that basic loss of function, a really distressing symptom for lots of sufferers was the occurrence of paraesthesia: episodes of shooting pains or numbness along the lines of particular nerve fibres which could disturb sleep and cause distress during the daytime. Many MS sufferers found that marijuana would relieve these symptoms, although in the UK using the drug remained illegal.

There were many theories, but no firm knowledge, about why and how the condition would start in any patient. Among the most recent ideas was that there might be some sort of gene-environment interaction, where people who were for some reason genetically susceptible would develop the condition when exposed to an environmental trigger such as an infection or a dietary deficiency. Ray was aware that some recent work suggested that vitamin D might be important, given that the disease was common in latitudes such as the northern British Isles, where there was a lack of sunshine in the winter (and in the summer too …), vitamin D levels tending to fall in people who lack exposure to the ultraviolet component of sunlight. There was some research on this going on in his medical school and he knew that Gerard Carter had an interest.

Carter was an interesting character. He had risen through the ranks of this medical school with apparent ease, becoming one of the youngest consultants and clinical professors ever. Ray didn't know a lot about him, except that he had a reputation for self-importance, not that uncommon among senior clinical academics, that he had supported the careers of some of his juniors very well, but in other cases had proved not only unsupportive, but positively vindictive. There was a hint that those people who stood up to him and who displayed independent thought were the ones whom he would attack, often a sign of an underlying insecurity, thought Ray. He had certainly published a lot of books and papers and many people sought to work with him, first and foremost to further their careers.

Ray was different, though. He had never been much of a one for self-aggrandisement, although to any external observer, his career to date was a true success story. Brought up by his dad, a coal miner on a council estate in one of the large towns in the north of England, he had been the first and so far only family member to go to university. His school's career service had actually tried to put him off studying medicine, clearly thinking that someone from his background was not cut out for that particular profession. Of course that had served to make him more quietly determined to take this on. Academically, he was towards the top of the pile, though not a medal winning student. It was only after graduation that his determination and methodical thinking began to really benefit his career. After his basic training in surgery and medicine, which all junior doctors were required to do at that time, he had gone on to a smaller district hospital where he had rapidly gained the Membership of the Royal College of Physicians, a requirement to progress in hospital medicine. He had then moved to a professorial research unit in Cambridge for a short period, before gaining a scholarship to go to America where he had worked with Liz. After that was over, and returning to the UK, he felt that he needed more clinical training and so he moved into Dr Ahmed's unit as a clinical registrar. All of these jobs he had more or less planned himself. Many of his colleagues at medical school came from large medical dynasties and could seek advice from parents, aunts, uncles, family friends and others 'in the business'. Ray had no such informed advice to seek, which was in some ways an advantage, as he was free to choose his own path, unencumbered by family history and expectations.

There had been an added challenge though. Ray had always been a quiet thoughtful type, though not especially prone to worrying about things at school. However, about halfway through his medical course he had his first panic attack. He'd been due to give a talk at a seminar for his fellow students on the causes and symptoms of heart attacks. He'd stayed up late the night before and was well prepared. He went to bed around 2 a.m. and fell asleep quickly. Suddenly, about a quarter to five, he woke up with a start. His heart was racing, there was a tight feeling in his chest and he knew he was going to vomit. He ran through to the bathroom and just made it in time. After he had thrown up, he sat partly kneeling over the toilet pan. His first thought was that he had maybe eaten something bad. He wondered how he was going to make the seminar later in the morning. Gradually the sick feeling settled and he was able to take a shower. He made himself some tea and toast and listened to the radio for a while. Then he took out his notes and began to read quietly through them. As he read, he could feel the chest tightness slowly building up again. He was sweaty but felt cold, his palms were clammy and his heart was racing again. He thought he might be sick again, but after a few waves of nausea it settled. 'This is crazy,' he thought, 'Why am I getting worked up about this?' Of course he made the seminar and gave a good presentation, but this was just the first of many similar episodes. Later, as he took the psychiatry module, he began to recognise the significance of his own symptoms. He certainly was prone to periods when he felt great energy and creativity and other times when he found it hard to motivate himself. These were the typical features of the so-called cyclothymic personality. When taken to extremes, this could spill over into bipolar disease, alternating periods of depression and mania. It would be some time before his first real episode of depression but it was to colour much of his life over the next few years.

Despite, or maybe because of, his psychological problems he had until today settled to the idea that he would become a good and caring physician, probably in a general hospital, for the rest of his career, but the sight of Eric and the realisation of his own impotence in the face of this illness had sparked something new in him. While a good doctor was worth his or her weight in gold to their patients, the person who could come up with a major medical advance could serve many more people whom they would never meet. That meant getting involved again in medical research. Ray decided that he would have to speak to Carter as soon as possible, although only after he had squared it with Dr Ahmed.

CHAPTER 4

Ten days later, Ray was sitting outside Carter's office, awaiting his appointment with the great man. Since the meeting with Eric, Ray had firmed up more of his background reading and had a helpful meeting with Dr Ahmed, who, as he had suspected, had proved hugely supportive.

"Of course you must look into this, Ray, and if you think it's right for you, then go for it. We'll be really sorry to lose you from here; good ones like you don't come along every day, but I know that you have to follow your heart and I am sure you have the ability and the right sort of mind for it. The only thing I would ask of you though is that you don't forget the patient. So many people in medical research become obsessed with the laboratory or the clinical trial, the grant-getting, the writing, the papers, the conferences, the international travel and so on, that they forget the real reason for doing it. I would have loved to be a researcher myself, but I didn't really have the aptitude for it and I realised early on that my skill, such as it was, lay in talking to people, in supporting them through the crises, looking after them at the end of their lives. Don't get me wrong, I also do my best to make the right diagnosis, provide the best treatments and so on, but the real thing about being a clinical doctor is to deal with the person in front of you at the time as if they were the only thing that mattered to you in the world. It's tough to keep that up all the time, and sometimes it doesn't work out, but when it does, it's just about the best thing in the world. But, as you already know, that limits you to helping only these people that you see and their families, whereas the new knowledge you might come up with could have much wider influence. Just promise me that you'll stay true to your patients and your principles and you'll go with my blessing."

"Thanks, Dr Ahmed. I'll do my best on both fronts and I'll certainly remember a lot of the clinical and ethical messages that I have taken from you. I see how much your patients appreciate the care they get from you and, if I do move on, it will always remain a privilege to have worked here."

Just as he replayed this conversation in his mind, the door opened and strains of classical music wafted out from the office.

"Come in, come in!" an impatient voice called, and Ray got up and walked into the room. If Dr Ahmed's room had been a shrine to clinical work, piled high with case records, textbooks, post-it notes about calls to be made and, somewhere among the clutter, a photograph of a smiling wife and three attractive teenagers, this office was something else entirely.

The room had heavy oak panelling up to about four feet high round each wall. Against the left wall was a large bookcase, which contained a few books but was mainly populated with artefacts from all over the world, many of them with plaques or inscriptions along the lines of:

'A gift to Distinguished Professor Gerard Carter from the Medical Society of the Philippines'

'Awarded to Professor Carter on the Occasion of the Suarez Memorial Lecture, Brazil, 2001'

... and so on ...

To Ray's right, the wall was covered with a mix of photographs, many obviously taken at overseas conferences, and an array of awards and diplomas to Gerard Carter, starting with his intercalated BSc degree and moving through undergraduate and postgraduate medical awards. All were in frames of varying quality and colour, some more expensive than others. From his own perspective, Ray wasn't entirely sure where his own medical school graduation diploma was ... maybe at the back of his sock drawer, he thought with some irony. Straight ahead was a large window. Although it wasn't a particularly bright day, it took a moment for his eyes to accustom to the light streaming in and to realise that the music, Beethoven maybe, was coming from a Bose iPod docking station in the corner, while a seat and a large, amazingly tidy desk were directly in front of him. Behind the desk sat a smallish man with glasses, neatly trimmed reddish hair, and a smart suit and tie. There was a hint of expensive aftershave, similar to that Ray had experienced when meeting individuals from the pharmaceutical industry, but never worn himself.

"Well, Dr Shepherd, have a seat," said Carter, gesturing towards a chair, which turned out to have a rather soft cushion, in front of the desk.

Ray knew something about room design as they had been taught about it in clinical skills training. From a clinical point of view, the objective in room design was to set your patient at ease by avoiding placing objects such as desks between you and the patient, by ensuring that you sat at a comfortable angle to the patient, allowing them to make or avoid eye contact at different stages of the consultation, and, importantly, ensuring that you sat at approximately the same level as the patient. Most consulting suites were designed with these thoughts in mind.

Carter's office, on the other hand, came from the corporate school of domination of the visitor: light shining into their face, desk interposed and visitor's seat made soft to ensure that he looked down upon them. For a brief moment, Ray imagined that Carter might be stroking a cat and would say "Welcome, Mr Bond ..."

There were no preliminaries to the conversation, no offer of tea or coffee, and no pleasantries. Carter, as Ray came to learn, was straight to the point.

"So Dr Shepherd, you're interested in joining our research group. I've had a look at your undergraduate record, not outstanding but not bad, and I've had good reports from my friends in Boston. I was slightly surprised that you came back to work for Ahmed, but I imagine that you've seen the light now ..."

"Well, Professor Carter ..." began Ray.

"I do have a potential position for you," interrupted Carter. "As you probably know, I've been doing some interesting work on the role of vitamin D in MS, and we've got a good mouse model that we've developed here. I've had significant interest from the Peploe's Food Company and they are willing to sponsor a clinical research fellow post to continue and develop that work. The post would include about one day per week of clinical work covering my ward and doing a general neurology clinic on a Friday. That would keep your hand in, and would count for clinical training accreditation. The full details of the proposed study are in the brochure here," he said, pointing to a large pharmaceutical company folder lying on his desk. "When can you start?"

Ray was slightly taken aback by the speed of all this. For a start, he had envisaged that he might have some say in the type of research they were going to do, rather than simply being given a study protocol already worked out by someone else to deliver. He was aware that there had been some controversy over the Peploe's Food Company marketing of breast milk substitutes in sub-Saharan Africa, though they were a pillar of the British commercial establishment. He also rapidly put two and two together with the pictures and trinkets on the walls and the expectation that he would 'cover the ward'. For that read: Carter will be out of the country a lot of the time and needs a junior to whom he can delegate clinical work with only very nominal cover from one of his consultant colleagues. Ray also had not had any time to read the study document and see whether it was something he might be interested in. Finally, he was irritated by the not so subtle put-down of Dr Ahmed, obviously someone not rated by Carter, or, Ray suspected, by any of Carter's senior academic buddies. However it was a definite job offer in the clinical area that he wanted to work in, so maybe the thing to do was to accept it and then try to change things from the inside.

"Well, thank you, Professor Carter. I'll need to give a month's notice in my current job, so would a start date of August 1st suit? Also, how long will this post last?"

"August 1st is fine, though I'd like you to read the research brochure before then, so that you can hit the ground running. You'll also need to get your animal licence, so you should speak to Fiona Graham at the animal house about that. This post is for three years, but we always have a good stream of income so if all goes well, we could find you more after that. You should think about writing an MD thesis on the work too, never does any harm on the CV. Take this copy of the brochure with you and we'll send on particulars. Speak to Barbara on the way out and she'll sort that for you."

"Thanks very much …" began Ray, but noted that Carter had opened the desk drawer, pulled out some other papers, and was already on to something else.

Ray let himself out and went across the corridor to the secretaries' office. Three of them shared this room, each one working for one of the three senior professors in the department. Unlike their bosses, whose dislike for each other was intense, the secretaries got on really well with each other and with all the other staff. As in many large organisations, it was probably these people who kept the show on the road.

19

"So, Ray, are you going to be joining us?" said Barbara.

"Yes, he's offered me a post funded by Peploe's …?" said Ray, partly framing his reply as a question.

"I thought so," said Barbara. "I'll need to get an up-to-date copy of your CV and HR will need some other details from you, I'm sure." Ray winced slightly at the use of the 'Human Resources' term. He couldn't see what was wrong with old fashioned 'Personnel'. Human resources always conjured up an image of piles of broken spectacles and gold fillings in a concentration camp …

"I've said I should be able to start on August 1st," said Ray, "I just have to give notice to Dr Ahmed first."

"He'll certainly miss you," chipped in one of the other women in the room. "He's such a nice man and a great doctor," as all three nodded their agreement.

"I need to go and see Fiona Graham at the animal house too. I think I'll head down there just now and get the ball rolling."

Ray took the paperwork that Barbara had offered, tucked it inside the trial protocol folder and headed out the back of the building to a large, windowless white building behind. He pressed the entry phone and said : "Dr Shepherd to see Fiona Graham."

After a short pause, a female voice said "Come on up," and with that there was a loud click followed by a buzzing noise and Ray was able to push the door open and go inside. Immediately, there was a smell of small animals that he recognised from when he had kept a hamster as a child, although in this case, it was mixed with the scent of disinfectant. Everything seemed spotlessly clean both in the stairwell and in Fiona's office as he went in and took a seat. This time a cup of coffee was on offer, so he took one, black with no sugar, and sat down. He realised that he had seen Fiona before at a distance in the canteen, though he hadn't known then who she was. She was dressed in a plain green top and trousers, similar to theatre scrubs from the hospital. Her name and job title was embroidered over her right breast. She had shortish black hair, cut in a bob, and an attractive face, lightly tanned and free of make-up. She looked like her off-duty time must be spent mostly out of doors. She smiled a lot, Ray would come to learn later.

"So you're coming to join the Carter Family," she said with just a hint of a smile. "He contacted me last week to say you'd be along so I've started some of the paperwork. Have you done any animal studies before?"

"Not in the UK," said Ray, "only in Boston."

"Well, you'll probably find the paperwork here even more demanding, but we'll get you through it. We'll also need to take you through all of our SOPs ... Standard Operating Procedures," she clarified, catching the fleeting hint of confusion across Ray's face at this bit of jargon.

Most of the general public, and especially animal rights activists, seemed to carry a notion that scientists could do all manner of unpleasant things to animals more or less as they please in the name of research. In fact, especially in the UK, nothing could be much further from the truth. Almost more than in research involving humans, animal work was very strictly regulated. Every step of every potential study had to be specified and justified; all sorts of procedures to ensure minimum distress for the animals had to be in place; and anyone doing this type of work had to be strictly vetted, to undergo training with regular updates and approvals and so on. Any changes to protocols or procedures had to be approved by an Ethics Committee and by a government appointed inspector who was usually a fully trained veterinarian; all laboratories had to be accredited and could be closed down immediately and permanently if they breached any procedures. Strict protocols also had to be in place to protect staff, mainly from the development of allergies to animals which could result in occupational asthma or eczema, which could in turn trigger a significant compensation claim against the institution. Ray knew all of this in outline and had been through something of these procedures in Boston, but, as became obvious during the next two hours in which he and Fiona sat completing his application form for a licence, the UK procedures were much more rigorous than anything he'd encountered before.

"OK. We'll get all that sent off today – usually takes a few weeks to process ..." said Fiona. "Do you want to have a look around now?"

"Sure," said Ray, "if you've time."

Fiona handed him a set of protective gear, including gown, mask, gloves, overshoes and hat, while she herself pulled out a large helmet with a face visor and air pump attached to it. As she went to put the helmet on, she explained: "I have allergies, so I have to wear this air filter any time I'm in the animal areas. It makes a bit of noise, but actually it's quite comfortable once it's on and probably doesn't look any sillier than your paper hat!"

"That's for sure," laughed Ray, warming to this woman who was clearly efficient and obsessional about procedure, as her job demanded, yet obviously had a sense of humour to go with it. Although he had never worked in the animal house and had only now put a face to the name, he was aware through the grapevine that she was a popular leader of that section and he could immediately see why.

As they walked through the various sections where access was allowed to visitors of his type, the same air of calm efficiency, pride in their work, and genuine enjoyment of the job seemed to emanate from everyone he met. There were sections devoted to different types of animals, ranging from fruit flies and worms up to rats, mice and rabbits. Funding and administrative restrictions meant that his university no longer worked with cats, dogs, or monkeys, and indeed over the entire medical research field, strong efforts were being made to reduce the amount of animal experimentation to a minimum, but there were still things that could not be tested in test tubes, or even in cell cultures, since the response of a whole organism to a drug or dietary intervention couldn't necessarily be predicted from what happened in single cells or in plates of cell culture.

Eventually, they reached a room labelled 'Prof Carter – MS mice – study numbers GC54092 and GC68145' and Fiona led the way in. The room contained rows of cages, each with groups of six mice, many of which clearly had some problems with normal movement.

"These are Carter's knockout mice," said Fiona. "We've managed to breed a strain which develops symptoms like those of progressive MS in humans. The pathology looks the same too – loss of myelin, etc. I'm not an expert on that, of course, Dr Simpson is the one for the neuropathology. I guess you'll get to meet her soon. We can set up the room to provide different diets for the mice but keep everything else the same, so that we can look for any effect of the dietary intervention. You'll see that each mouse is wearing a numbered identification disc and there's a camera above each cage that records movement. One of the computing science research fellows had developed an algorithm that can quantify the amount of spontaneous movement of each mouse and automatically log that. We can also test sensation by seeing how the mouse reacts to changes in the temperature and texture of the cage floor. Upstairs, we've got an MRI scanner that we can use to image their brains and spinal cords, and finally, when they're killed, Dr Simpson can look at the pathology. So we can build up a picture of the structure and function of their nervous systems in life and after death, and can look at how treatments might change that. Pretty cool, eh?"

"Yeah, that is pretty cool, Fiona. Thanks for showing me round. I think that reading that protocol is going to make a lot more sense to me now. I guess the one thing we can't do is to ask them how they're feeling?"

"No. we can't do that, but we nevertheless try to treat them with respect as other living beings, even though we recognise that we are creating illnesses in them and that ultimately they are being used for our studies. However, I don't see it as being that much different from breeding cattle or pigs for beef and bacon."

Once again, Ray warmed to the quiet professionalism of this woman. He felt that he was going to enjoy working with her.

"OK. I should get off now and let you get on with your work." said Ray. "I have to go back and let Dr Ahmed know that I'll be leaving his unit soon. I'm looking forward to coming here, though, so I'll see you soon. Once the initial paperwork is through, I'll arrange to come over for some of the training."

"Don't worry about that. We'll set up an induction week for you at the beginning of August. We'll have you dreaming SOPs by the end of that …" she laughed, as she took his protective clothing for disposal and led him to the door.

CHAPTER 5

Ray donned his leathers and helmet and climbed aboard his pride and joy, a Triumph Bonneville copy. It was the weekend after his trip around the animal house. He'd had another helpful and very supportive chat with Dr Ahmed as he had handed in his notice, and it was now time to go a break the news of his next career shift to his dad.

Joe Shepherd had spent his working life in the coalmines and lived on in the house where Ray had been brought up. Mary had died when Ray was only four years old, leaving Joe to bring his kids up by himself. Life had delivered a few tough blows to Joe, not the least of which was the legacy of years in the mines and of smoking about thirty cigarettes a day. Chronic obstructive pulmonary disease, or COPD, is a disease that, unlike MS, medical science largely knows how to prevent by avoiding smoking and air pollution, but still struggles to treat in those who have developed the progressive cough, phlegm and breathlessness. Joe had given up the fags, but too late. His life was now dominated by the need for continuous oxygen, delivered from an electric concentrator sat in the corner of the room, and by the repeated courses of antibiotics and steroids that the COPD nurse would deliver to his house. Despite that, he was still determined to live in his own home and to look after himself as much as possible. He enjoyed his visits from Ray, but, like most men of his time, he wasn't really given to overt shows of emotion.

The world in which Ray lived was also a mystery to him. When Ray had applied for medical school, Joe had been bursting with pride, although again he didn't make a great deal of that with his pals down the pub. They all assumed that one day Ray would become the local GP, to their minds the pinnacle of achievement in the medical world. As time had gone by, and Ray had worked first in hospitals then gone off to America, it had begun to dawn on Joe that there was more to medicine than he first thought, although he still couldn't really understand why Ray didn't just become a proper doctor. Now that he was back in the UK, Ray generally visited about once a month, depending on what his on call schedule allowed. According to the usual routine, Joe wouldn't have been expecting a visit today so when Ray had called to say he was coming, he guessed something was up. Surely it couldn't be another change of job? Ray had seemed to be really enjoying working with that foreign doctor and Joe knew that Ray thought a lot of him. Was he having some other problem? Ray had never told Joe about any kind of stress or mental problem, but Joe knew that there had been times when things had not been quite right. Or could it be a girlfriend …? That was another area of Ray's life that Joe couldn't fathom. At Ray's age, he'd been married with one child already and another (Ray) on the way. Joe knew that there had been somebody in America who had been a bit special, though he'd never met her and that seemed to all be a bit quiet now.

As this ran through his head, he heard the familiar roar of the bike engine as Ray pulled up. He burst through the door, swinging his helmet in his right hand. Joe thought to himself that he had raised a good 'un. Ray was about six feet tall, probably about twelve stone and obviously looked after himself, taking regular exercise and not smoking. Just the same, his dark hair was already showing a few strands of grey, though Joe could imagine that in a few years that would make him look quite distinguished.

"Hi, Dad! How are you doing?" Ray strode into the room and threw himself down on the settee. As ever, there was no physical contact, handshake or embrace between them. That wasn't the northern way, except maybe at Masonic meetings or funerals.

"Oh, doing away son, just the usual." The effort of that short phrase triggered a bout of coughing ending up in Joe putting a small dollop of spit into a tissue which he threw into a carrier bag by the side of his chair. As the coughing subsided, Ray looked concerned and said, "How's the breathing going, Dad?"

"Oh, it comes and goes, son. You know how it is. The last few nights have been quite good, managed to sleep through with only a couple of coughing fits. It's a bugger when that Billy Connolly comes on the telly though."

"What?" said Ray.

"You know, Connolly, the Big Yin. He's doing that trip round Australia on the telly at the moment. The bugger gets me laughing, and then I can't get my breath for about five minutes, even with the oxygen. I think I'm going to have to stop watching him. Anyway, what about you?"

"Well, Dad, I'm changing jobs again, but not moving away, so I'll definitely be around here for the next three years."

"More than I'll be," said Joe.

Ray looked straight at his father, but said nothing. There was no point in offering some platitude or false reassurance, as Joe was probably right. At his advanced stage of the disease, it was very likely that he would be dead within three years and nothing Ray could say or do would change that. The only treatment that could change things would be a lung transplant and Joe was beyond the age that would be considered, at least in the UK. If truth were told, Joe wouldn't have wanted it anyway – he would have felt that any available lungs should go to some more deserving person, perhaps someone who hadn't smoked themself into this position … although something to relieve the paroxysms of coughing and breathlessness would be good.

"Anyway, what about this job?" said Joe, moving the focus away from himself as usual.

"Well, I'm going back into research. I'm going to be looking at ways to help treat multiple sclerosis."

"That sounds good," said Joe. "Do you remember young Angela, Albert Tait's youngest? She started it when she was just about twenty-one. I'm not sure how she's doing, although she moved out to live in Australia, and the last I heard from Albert, she was doing okay. That was a couple of years ago, right enough."

"Well," said Ray, "it is possible that moving to Oz was a good thing for her. That's partly what our research is about, whether vitamin D, which you get from sunlight, helps to prevent and treat MS."

"I'm sure there'll be no shortage of volunteers for the sunshine treatment," said Joe.

"Oh, we're not working on people at this stage. I'm going be working with mice."

"Jesus Christ, I didn't think I was raising a vet … Does that mean you'll not see any real people?"

"Oh no, dad, I'm going to be doing some clinical work too, about one day a week plus some on call. So you can tell your mates I'm still a proper doctor!"

"What about these animal rights nutters? Do you have to bother about them?"

"Well, we do have to take some precautions. I can understand that they feel strongly about it, but when it gets round to sending messages like 'we know where your kids go to school – keep an eye on them', then it has gone a bit too far. That happened to a mate of mine, you know."

"I'd stop them all from getting any treatments when they get sick. That would fix 'em." said Joe.

"Well, I'm not sure it's as simple as that, but anyway, I'll keep a lookout."

Ray spent another couple of hours with his dad and made them some dinner, although Joe didn't eat a great deal these days. He got too breathless when his mouth was full, so it was a slow process having a meal with him. Still, Ray was happy to spend the time with him, and, as always, felt a tinge of guilt when it came time to put on his leathers again and head back up the road.

"I'll be on the phone and I'll try to get down again in a couple of weeks, if my rota's OK," said Ray.

"That's fine son. I suppose I'll be here, unless that lottery comes up or Elle Macpherson phones to invite me down to St Tropez," said Joe, before collapsing into another fit of coughing and wheezing, preventing any further conversation.

As Ray made his way home, he thought again about the opportunities that life had offered him, compared to his dad. Joe was a clever man, and in another time might have followed a path more like Ray's, but when he was young, leaving school at fouteen and going down the mine was what you did. The rest of his tough life was devoted to making sure that his kids didn't have to do the same, or at least to make sure that they had some choice. Ray's older brother had thought about becoming a miner too, but had trained as an electrician and now had his own small business, which was just as well, given that the coal mining industry had been more or less finished off by Maggie Thatcher. Understanding and appreciating the opportunity he had been given only made Ray more determined to make a success of this new job.

CHAPTER 6

August 1st came around pretty quickly and Ray found himself rapidly immersed in the steep learning curve of animal house procedures and SOPS. The technical staff were superb and, as ever, Ray found himself slightly embarrassed that, as a clinical doctor, he probably earned three or four times as much as these people who were patiently taking him through all the steps of animal husbandry, techniques for injecting drugs into mice and so on. He had done a bit of this in the USA, but of course there were local variations in how things were done in order to meet the strict requirements of the government licensing agencies. There were regular visits from the inspectors, who could call at any time, unannounced, and carried the authority to shut down a facility at no notice if they felt things were not right. However, in practice, Ray found that the relations with the inspectors were a bit more constructive than that. As well as inspecting and monitoring, they offered advice on how they expected things should be done, as they also felt that they were in the business of supporting medical advances, albeit from the perspective of making sure that things were done with utmost rigour.

During this period, Ray had a lot of dealings with Fiona, who was responsible for the overall supervision of his training and for signing off his various competencies when he had reached the required standards. He had also spent a great deal of time looking at the study protocol, such that he had more or less memorised the details. The study had a fairly simple design which involved randomising mice into one of four groups, each of which could receive up to two types of treatment. One group was given a standard diet and normal living conditions; a second received a diet supplemented with high levels of vitamin D and normal living conditions; a third group were exposed to ultraviolet light for four hours per day and received a standard diet; while the fourth group received both the ultraviolet exposure and the supplemented diet. The animals all suffered from the multiple sclerosis syndrome and were monitored from the outset of the experiment by a combination of movement and sensory studies using the specially designed cages and cameras that he had seen on his first visit to the lab. They also had MRI scans at regular intervals to study the progression of any lesions in their nervous systems, and at the end of the experimental period, which was set for six months, the mice would be killed and have detailed post-mortem analysis of their nervous system anatomy. The purpose of this experiment was to determine whether in mice that already had symptoms and signs of the disease, either of the treatments alone could halt or reverse the disease process, and, if so, whether giving both together gave any additional benefit. In humans, exposure to ultraviolet light enhances the production and metabolism of vitamin D in the body, so it seemed reasonable to include that environmental stimulus as well as the dietary manipulation.

In order to prevent interference from any other external influences, it was very important to control the environment in which the mice were living. One of the ever-present threats in the animal house was the introduction of viral or bacterial infections that could spread rapidly through a mouse population and would mean that the experimental data had to be discarded. The analysis of the movement and sensory data and the interpretation of the scans were also complex processes which had to be undertaken by researchers who were unaware which type of conditions each experimental animal had been brought up in, so as to avoid any bias in the study. Ray's job was to be in charge of the overall study conduct and coordination. He held the data key as to which animal had been exposed to which conditions and was in charge of the final analysis and writing up of the results, working with one of the departmental statisticians, Andy Turner. Andy had also been involved at the beginning to work out the sample size for the study. This was a very important part of the design, since it was essential to make sure that enough animals were included so that any changes observed were unlikely to be due to simple chance variation, while at the same time ensuring that the number of animals studied was kept to the minimum so that no unnecessary suffering was caused. Ray spent many hours with Andy, learning about these concepts of clinical trial design, which applied to more or less any study of a potential new medical treatment. Although maths had never been his strongest suit at school, he found that he actually quite enjoyed this part of the work, and it helped his understanding of many other clinical papers that he would read in the course of his work with patients.

The study got up and running relatively smoothly. As Ray would learn later, one advantage of working with mice was that, once ordered from the supplier, they would generally turn up on the appointed day and the study would begin. Recruiting humans into clinical trials was a whole other ball game as they would often, as was their right, take a long time to decide to take part, or withdraw at an early, or worse still, late stage of the study with no requirement to give any reason. In general, data from people who withdrew would have to be discarded and destroyed, in some cases meaning that a study might become uninterpretable. With mice, that wasn't an issue, although the development of infections and so on certainly was.

Over the next weeks, Ray settled into the rhythm of the job. As he had suspected, he saw very little of Professor Carter apart from a brief fortnightly research meeting when Carter was in the country, and the hospital clinical meetings when Carter and the other greybeards sat in the front row, attempting to score points off each other by the erudition of their comments on some obscure clinical case while the junior staff were put through the ringer in terms of their presentation and understanding of the case. However, this was an environment in which Ray felt strangely comfortable, having now been exposed to it on both sides of the Atlantic; when his turn to present came round, he dealt with the inquisition in a thoroughly professional way, at least as far as the external observer was concerned. There were still times when he would feel stressed beforehand, although he comforted himself that many experienced entertainers never really lost their stage fright and in many respects this was just another form of entertainment. He was also much better at controlling it since his time in America.

After three months in the job, Ray felt that he was sufficiently in control to be able to take a holiday. The study was running well, all the baseline measures on the animals had been completed, the randomisation had taken place, and the various dietary and exposure protocols established. Joe was much the same as ever, although neither the lottery win nor the phone call from the supermodel had happened. Ray opted to head up to rural Perthshire with his bike, even though the beginning of November could be a dodgy time for weather and road conditions. He decided to stay at a B&B in one of the small villages and spent a pleasant two weeks riding around the country roads, having a few beers in front of a warm fire in the pub, and taking his guitar along to a couple of impromptu music sessions in other pubs around the area. He had left no note of his whereabouts, except a message to his brother in case of problems with Joe, and his mobile phone remained firmly off. Bliss!

CHAPTER 7

Ray arrived home late on a Sunday evening in mid-November. The weather on the ride home had been hellish, wet and windy, never a good combination on a motorbike, especially not when you have a guitar strapped to your back, catching every gust of wind going. Once he had showered and dried off, he sat down with a dram and turned on the late night radio show, which often played good stuff from up and coming singer-songwriters. He looked at his mobile, but decided tomorrow morning would be soon enough to re-engage with the world, so left it off along with his e-mail.

After a great sleep, during which the pub session seemed to go on and on and to involve some of his heroes such as James Taylor, Dick Gaughan and Ray LaMontagne, he woke refreshed and ready for the new week. It was always a good sign when you looked forward to going back to work, excited to see how your patients, and now the experiments, were going. He turned on the phone.

Six missed call messages all came up from a number he didn't recognise. There were also two voicemails. He listened to the most recent. A tearful and anxious voice, which he vaguely recognised, but couldn't place at first, came on.

"Oh Ray … can you please call me as soon as you get this message. Something terrible has happened at the lab, and I don't know what we should do. Professor Carter's in Malaysia and I haven't been able to contact him yet. I can't explain this on the phone. I'll be in the lab at 7 a.m. Can you come straight there?"

Now he had placed the voice, but it wasn't the Fiona he knew. The quiet professionalism had gone and she sounded truly panicked. He guessed it wasn't something wrong with one of the staff, but, whatever it was, it was major. He dressed quickly, turned off the kettle before it boiled, and headed straight for the animal house.

The car park was quiet so he found a space close to the animal house building, tapped in the security code, and headed straight up to Fiona's office.

She was behind the desk, eyes red-rimmed and looking like she hadn't slept for a week, which more or less turned out to be the case.

"What's happened, Fiona?" said Ray.

"Something terrible – nothing like this has ever happened before. Your experiment is ruined and I think it will cost me my job."

"Hold on," said Ray. "Slow down and tell me what's happened."

He was used to dealing with clinical emergencies and, remarkably, considering his past problems with depression and anxiety, over the years he had trained himself to deliberately stay calm when others around him were panicking. In any case, compared to dealing with a child who'd been run over by a car, a much loved husband who was suffering a major heart attack, or the distraught partner of a woman who had just killed herself, most other things paled into insignificance, or at least into a different perspective.

"Ten days ago we took a delivery of prion-infected mice for the study upstairs from yours. For some reason, the cage numbers were correct but the floor numbers were wrong. Young Siobhan assumed that they were additions to your experiment and put them into the matched cages in your room. The whole experiment is wasted. It's not her fault of course, it's my responsibility to supervise these deliveries, but we were having some problems with the rabbits on level five that morning and I was dealing with that. I haven't been able to contact Professor Carter – he's on his way back from Malaysia – but he should be back this afternoon. What are we going to do?"

Prions sounded like bad news. During recent years, they had come to be recognised as the probable cause of Bovine Spongiform Encephalopathy, better known to the wider public as BSE or mad cow disease, and of Creutzfeldt-Jakob disease, degenerative brain diseases which remained untreatable and fatal in humans. These tiny mis-folded proteins could be transmitted between animals and humans by contaminated material from an infected animal and had led to widespread bans on movement of animals and meat across Europe and a whole range of other restrictions in medical practice. Ray wasn't sure how easily prions would transmit, but people working with prion-infected animals had to take strict precautions to reduce risk to themselves and to other laboratory animals. However, he stayed calm.

"Ok, let's not panic. What have you done so far?" he said.

"Well, I've left everything as it was. I've continued the feeding protocols and so on, and the monitoring is still in place. I've contacted Dr Oldham, and he'll be here later this morning."

"OK, that all sounds good; especially that Oldham is on at the moment. Let's go up to the lab and have a look at things."

As they walked up to the lab, Ray began to try to work out what to do. Obviously, dealing with the animal inspectorate was going to be a priority. John Oldham was one of the senior animal inspectors and a very interesting character. Although Ray had not been in animal research in the UK for long, he knew all about Oldham, whose reputation preceded him. He had trained initially as a vet and had then gone to medical school with the intention of becoming a surgeon. However, a tendon injury to his hand, ironically sustained while cutting a joint of meat at home, had put an end to his surgical ambitions and he had entered the animal inspectorate. Lesser people in his position would have remained bitter and most likely become very difficult, jobsworth types. Amazingly, he seemed to have risen above all that. He regarded his role as facilitator as well as regulator, and put a huge effort into supporting young researchers and helping studies develop. However, he also expected high standards, so would take this breach of procedure very seriously.

At first sight everything in the lab looked much as usual. Only on closer inspection could Ray see that a number of the cages had extra mice, and that the new ones looked even less healthy than the MS variants that he was studying.

"They look like poor little guys," said Ray.

"They were meant for another study that Professor Gillingham's group are doing, looking at prion disease – a sort of mouse model of BSE or mad cow disease. They tend not to live very long. Already they're not eating and losing weight compared with our guys."

With that, Ray's attention was drawn to the MS mice in the cages.

"You know, if I didn't know better, I'd say our guys were looking the better of their new lodgers. Of course, I haven't seen them for a couple of weeks, so I'm probably imagining it, or it might just be relative to their pals here."

"To be honest, Ray, I haven't been able to be that objective since this happened. I've spent most of last week writing and re-writing my resignation letter in my head. Carter is going to go ballistic. We've got a site visit from the Peploe's Food Company people next week, and I think all we're going to be able to show them are some empty cages and an empty animal house supervisor's office ... but now that you mention it ..."

"Let's have a look at the motion data," said Ray.

For the next three hours, Ray and Fiona pored over the data. There was plenty of it. Each mouse had recordings for total distance travelled, average and range of speed of travel, number of changes of direction, total time spent in motion, average and range of duration of sedentary periods, and so on. There were also recordings of how quickly each mouse reacted to changes in temperature or consistency of the cage floor, giving some indication of sensory perception.

Ray checked the data once, then again, and then a third time. There was no doubt about it. For the first four days that the mice had had their 'visitors', there was no change in their patterns of behaviour compared to the previous week, apart from the usual slow deterioration that was typical. However, from day four onwards, there was some suggestion that their movement was better although the sensory responses hadn't changed appreciably. The changes were tiny and could have happened by chance, or maybe just due to the presence of the visitors.

"We need to discuss this with Dr Oldham. Let's not do anything too rash just yet," said Ray, "... and not a word about this to anybody in the meantime ... not even to Siobhan."

At 1 p.m, the buzzer went and John Oldham's familiar tones came over the intercom. Fiona pressed the door release and he came upstairs to the office. Ray had met him a couple of times during his first few months, but remained on fairly formal terms with him. He was a small man with curly fair hair and glasses. He was smartly dressed and carried a document case. As he held out his right hand to shake hands, Ray noticed the scars and the two fingers that couldn't straighten properly. Ray decided that he should begin the discussion.

"Thanks for coming, Dr Oldham. I'm afraid we've got a bit of a problem to tell you about."

"Yes, it happened while Dr Shepherd was on leave, it's really my problem," chipped in Fiona, her voice trembling slightly and several tones higher than usual.

Oldham looked serious, but there was also a slight twinkle in his eye as he spoke.

"Well, how about a cup of coffee and you can tell me all about it, then we'll go and have a look at the lab."

"Sorry, of course, I'm a bit flummoxed at the moment," said Fiona, heading across to the coffee machine in the corner of the office.

Once they were settled with coffee and some biscuits, Fiona started to outline the events of the past days. Ray noted that she was at pains to take full responsibility for the error, even though she knew that this was potentially a career-ending situation. Although the mistake had been made by Siobhan, Fiona stressed that she should not have been left on her own to deal with the delivery. Misplacing the mice had rendered both experiments invalid, although the prion experiment could be re-started with a new batch without adding too much delay. Ray's experiment, however, was completely invalidated, with the resultant loss of several months' work and substantial costs to the company and the university. Fortunately, no infection control rules had been breached as both experiments were subject to the same high levels of isolation and infection control, so there was no added risk to other animals in the facility, or to the staff.

Throughout the story, Oldham remained inscrutable, although he was writing detailed notes. Once Fiona had finished the tale, including specific details of batch numbers which would be required for the final write up, Oldham turned to Ray. His tone remained formal.

"What about you, Dr Shepherd – have you anything to add?"

"Well, obviously the primary experiment has been invalidated and will have to be repeated at some time in the future, subject to the appropriate approvals etc. However, there is one thing I wanted to discuss with you. When I looked at the animals this morning, I had the impression that the mice from our experiment that were exposed to the prion-infected ones seemed to be moving better than when I last saw them before I went on holiday. We've had an initial look at the data, and it seems to bear that out. He pulled out a couple of activity graphs he had hurriedly prepared and pushed them across the table to Oldham, who nodded almost imperceptibly.

"Well?" he said.

"Well," Ray repeated, "the changes are small and might be due to chance or a whole host of other reasons, but the fact is that Fiona and her colleagues have never seen anything like this before. I wonder if it is possible that the prion infection has passed across to these mice and begun to reverse the demyelination process. If that's the case, it could be significant." Ray wasn't keen to push it any further than that at this stage.

Oldham was an inspector, but he was also a trained clinician and had research experience himself. He recognised that the essence of research was to make detailed observations, to develop hypotheses from these observations and then to test these rigorously. He also knew that historically, many advances in research had come from chance observations, the significance of which wasn't always immediately clear, the most famous example, of course, being the discovery of penicillin. He could see the potential opportunity here but did not want to be proactive in this. However, inwardly he was inclined to try to support this earnest young man if possible.

"So what would you like to do, Dr Shepherd?"

"Of course this is Professor Carter's study and we haven't had a chance to appraise him of any of this yet. He's on his way back from an overseas conference and has been out of touch since this happened. However, I would like to have your permission to continue the observations on these mice for another month at least. If the movement profiles continue to improve, then I would like permission to repeat the MRI scans at two weekly intervals and to carry our post-mortems on them for quantitative analysis."

"What would you do with the data?" said Oldham.

Ray realised he was being tested here.

"Well, since this would now be an open-label study in that we know which mice have been exposed, it's not going to prove anything definitively. But the findings could be used as pilot data to design another study to formally test the hypothesis."

Oldham said nothing initially. Eventually, he spoke. "Well, let's go up to the lab and see what's what. I'll also need to see all the study documentation, both before and after the mistake. I'll need to talk to Siobhan later as well, but don't worry, I'll go gently with her," he said with a nod of the head to Fiona.

Fiona led the way and proceeded to take Oldham meticulously around the lab, pointing out the cages where prion-infected mice had been added by mistake, and showing all the laboratory notes and logs of procedures carried out. After what seemed like an eternity, Oldham stopped in the corner of the lab and drew a long breath.

"This has obviously been a serious breach of protocol, and I'll have to make a full report. I can't give you the final results of that just yet, but I think that you can take it that I will be recommending some further training and appraisal for all the staff involved with the perpetration of this error." Fiona bowed her head slightly. "However, one mistake is not a hanging offence and I know that this is generally one of our best run labs, so from my point of view, that will be the end of the matter, I think." He caught Ray's quizzical look. "With regard to your proposal, Dr Shepherd, I agree that it seems reasonable to continue observation of these animals on condition that I receive a detailed protocol. You'll also need to have approval from the Ethics Committee, of course. However, the first thing you've got to do is to get approval from Professor Carter and from the company sponsoring the study." Ray took it from the look on his face that Oldham knew that that might be a more difficult conversation than the one they had just had with him.

CHAPTER 8

An hour after the meeting with Oldham found Ray and Fiona sitting on the familiar seat outside Carter's office, the strains of music emanating as usual from the inner sanctum. Eventually, a voice called out.

"Come in, both of you."

Carter looked tired and a bit tetchy, probably jet-lagged, and definitely not a good starting point for the conversation about to take place.

"Professor Carter ..." began Fiona, but Ray decided to interrupt as he felt this was his problem and that he should try to offer Fiona some protection if at all possible.

"Professor Carter, I'm sorry that we've had to interrupt you this afternoon. I'm sure you must be tired from the journey, but I'm afraid that this couldn't wait. I'm afraid that we have a problem with the vitamin D study which is going to need immediate action. While you were away, there was a mix up in the lab. Some new mice were delivered which were intended for another study looking at prion disease. These mice were inadvertently added to some of the cages of our study mice."

"What?" said Carter, his voice raising an octave and suddenly jolted into a new state of wakefulness.

"How in the devil's name could that happen? Don't we have procedures to prevent that sort of thing? Who was responsible? What have you done about it so far? Who knows about this? We've got a visit from Peploe's senior execs next week, how are we going to deal with that? What will we tell them?" He paused only momentarily to draw breath. "What about the animal inspectorate? They're going to come down on us like a ton of bricks? Never in my life have I been involved with anything like this ... Jesus Christ ..."

Ray was acutely aware that Fiona was tensing up beside him. The tirade that she had expected was beginning to unfold and she sensed that Carter's anger was going to focus on her any minute. Ray noted the tone of some of Carter's questions with some surprise but remained calm and continued to take control of the conversation.

"What happened was a simple human error, although there was obviously a breach of procedures. I'll go into the details in a minute. However, there are some other developments that you need to know about too, which could turn out to be very important for our research."

Carter looked like he was about to explode. He stood up from the desk, turned his back to them and looked at the window. Ray could see that his fists were clenched and he was holding his shoulders in a very rigid position.

"I think you'd better tell me the story from the beginning. We are going to have to do some very sharp thinking," said Carter.

Again this struck Ray as a slightly odd choice of words but he put it to the back of his mind. He resolved to tell the story from the beginning. During the next few minutes he recounted how the mice had been mistakenly placed in the cages by one of the junior technicians while Fiona was busy dealing with a problem in another part of the animal house. He explained how Fiona had opted to keep the animals in the cages until he and Carter had returned as neither of them had been contactable at the time. The animal inspectorate had been notified and Dr Oldham had visited earlier that day. He was preparing a report which was likely to highlight the breaches of procedure, but he had expressed an opinion that while there would be some recommendations on retraining and audit, the lab work could continue and the lab would not be closed down.

"Well, thank God for small mercies …" blustered Carter, "… but the study is ruined. This is going to cost us money and reputation …"

"That's not quite the end of the story though, sir," said Ray, considering that a bit of deference at this point might not be a bad thing. "You see, Fiona, rightly in my opinion, decided to leave the rogue mice in place until she had guidance from you and from the animal inspectorate. When I got back from leave, I thought that the MS mice were looking a bit more lively than when I left, so we've run a quick preliminary analysis of the movement data, and it does seem that they are improving. We've not seen anything like that in any of our previous studies, and Fiona agrees that she's never seen anything like it."

There was a slight but definite change in Carter's tone of voice. He might be angry, but he was also a clinical scientist. "Are you trying to tell me that exposure to the prion-infected mice has made our mice improve? That could be interesting. Who knows about this? "

That odd question again.

"Well," said Ray, "so far only the three of us in this room and Dr Oldham, the animal inspector."

"What did he make of it?" said Carter.

"We suggested to him that we should carry on the observations for a bit longer. Of course this could just be chance, but it does seem like nothing we've seen before. I asked him if we could extend the period of observation of the mice, carry out some follow-up MRI scans, and get some post-mortem data from them at the end of the observation period. He has agreed that if we can produce a protocol and get it approved by ethics, he'll look favourably on it. Of course it would be an open-label study, so the results probably wouldn't be publishable, but it could give us pilot data to inform a definitive study."

"Good thinking," said Carter, his shoulders relaxing a little as he resumed his seat, still casting a slightly disapproving look at Fiona. "What do you make of that?" he said, addressing her directly for the first time.

"First, I should say that the original mistake was my responsibility and I am prepared to offer my resignation," said Fiona, somewhat to Ray's horror.

"That shouldn't be necessary," said Carter.

"I will have to tell Peploe's what happened. They might take a different view," said Fiona.

Carter looked a little irked, having regained his composure. "They don't run this laboratory, I do," he said curtly.

"Since the mistake was made," she continued, "we've carried on treating the mice according to the protocol. As it turns out, some of them that have been contaminated are from the enhanced diet and UV exposure group, while some are controls. So we might be able to see some effects. There's no problem with infection control, as we've been adhering to highest levels of isolation from the beginning. There might be some implications if they go to post-mortem, I suppose."

"That's right," chipped in Ray. "We're going to have to get the radiologists and pathologists involved as soon as possible."

"The important thing here is to keep the number of people who are aware of this to the absolute minimum at this stage," said Carter. "I'll arrange a meeting tomorrow morning with all of those who need to know. You can work on the protocol and ethics application for the committee and for Oldham, and I'll have a word with the Ethics Committee chair. Ten o'clock tomorrow, my office."

With that, the audience was over. Ray noted that Carter did not offer to come to the animal house, though to give him his due, he was probably very tired after the journey. As they walked back to the animal house, Ray reflected that it could have been worse.

"I'd better get back to my office now. It's midnight oil for me," he said.

"Sorry," said Fiona. "This is all my fault." Her shoulders had dropped and a hint of a tear appeared at the corner of her eye. Ray put his arm around her; it felt good ...

"Fault?" said Ray, raising a bit of a grin. "Don't feel too badly. We might just have stumbled on the cure for MS! See you tomorrow ..."

CHAPTER 9

"Good morning, sorry I'm a bit late," said Ray. That wasn't actually true. Although he was the last person into Carter's office, he was still ahead of the official start time by about thirty seconds. He had been up until 5 a.m. writing up the protocols for ethics and for Oldham, and as he pulled up a chair, he took five copies of the documents from his briefcase. For this meeting, they were in the other corner of Carter's office, seated around the small circular meeting table.

Carter was there of course, looking as though he was back to his normal manicured self. Fiona too was looking a little more composed than she had been the previous day. She blushed a little as she caught Ray's inquisitive eye. Also at the table were the other two key players in any potential further study.

Dr Sarah Simpson was a neuropathologist who had trained at some of the best centres in Europe and America, including London, Stockholm and San Francisco. Although she did some clinical human neuropathology, her special interest was in experimental neuropathology, specifically in quantitative methods which could be used to determine the amount of injury to brain, spinal cord or peripheral nerves, and to link that to the functional abnormalities seen in life and on scanning.

The fifth person making up the group was Paul Schmidt, a neuroradiologist, who again split his professional career between clinical and experimental work. Neuroradiology was a field which had changed out of all recognition in the past thirty to forty years. At the time that Carter had trained, patients were still undergoing tests such as pneumoencephalography, in which a needle was put into the cerebrospinal fluid either at the back or at the base of the neck, and air was injected to allow plain X-rays to outline, very approximately, the shape of the brain. Such techniques were not only very limited in terms of the quality of image that could be produced but were also dangerous, carrying risks of displacement and damage to brain tissue, and of introduction of infection leading to potentially fatal meningitis. Fortunately, the development of computerised axial tomography, better known as CT scanning, had rendered the old tests obsolete. Slightly later came magnetic resonance imaging, or MRI scanning, which originally showed static images of the brain similar to CT, but had been developed further to study the function of the brain. Dynamic images could now be produced which would, for example, show the area of the human brain concerned with speech light up on the scan when the patient spoke. Since MRI was relatively non-invasive, it could be repeated in the same individual several times over the course of an illness, and could be used to evaluate the effects of treatment. Paul was one of a network of neuroradiologists internationally at the forefront of this type of work. Recruiting both Sarah and Paul into his team had been one of Carter's greatest coups of recent years.

Coffee was on offer, perhaps reflecting the audience, or the importance that Carter assigned to this meeting. As Ray stepped over to help himself, Carter called the meeting to order.

"I've asked you all along today to discuss an intriguing development that has come out of the vitamin D study, albeit unfortunately as the result of an error. However, having looked at the data, we could potentially be on to something very important here, so before we go into any detail, I would ask that you all keep what you are about to hear strictly and absolutely confidential," said Carter, looking pointedly and Sarah and Paul, slightly to their irritation, Ray thought. He and Fiona had of course already had this message the day before.

"Ray, could I ask you to fill in our colleagues here on the story so far?"

Once again, over the next few minutes, Ray recounted the events of the past days. Of course, Paul and Sarah had no knowledge of what had happened, as the mice in the study had not been scheduled for MRI studies or pathology during that time.

"… so the upshot is that we have Dr Oldham's blessing to submit a protocol to continue to study these mice with a view to giving us pilot data for a potentially definitive study if our suspicions are confirmed. I've worked up an application for ethics and a further proposal for Dr Oldham's department, spelling out what we might do," said Ray, inviting people to open the documents in front of them.

"That's an incredible story," said Sarah, "and you must have been up all night drawing up these documents, Ray."

"Well, it wasn't quite so bad. On Dr Oldham's advice, I've treated the application to ethics as a major amendment to the existing protocol, since most of the assessments, including the MRIs and the quantitative pathology, would be done using similar operating procedures to the original protocol. That meant that I could focus most of the discussion on the background to the prion question and on the proposal to use this as a pilot for a possible future definitive study. Of course, these are just drafts, and I'd be very grateful for your input, particularly in your specialist areas, but also to the overall thrust and the detail of the proposals. I'll definitely need help on the protocol for post-mortem studies, given that the mice have been exposed to prions."

Carter chipped in: "I would suggest that we read these documents during the rest of today, that we send any revisions to Ray by first thing tomorrow. I've spoken to Braithwaite, the chair of the Ethics Committee, to alert him that we have a highly unusual, but hopefully not contentious, proposal coming his way, and he has agreed to add it on to next Monday's agenda, given the need to make a rapid decision on the fate of these mice."

A brief meeting of eyes around the table indicated acknowledgement, but not major surprise, that Carter had been able to engineer this departure from usual Ethics Committee procedure. Normally the meeting agendas were made up well in advance and were sacrosanct. Carter, however, was obviously more equal than others in his dealings with such bodies, and in this particular case, Ray suppressed his egalitarian ethic to allow relief that Carter had forced it on to the agenda and that they might be able to pull this off.

Paul, who had been quiet up until now, then asked the question they had all been silently considering.

"What about Peploe's? What are they going to make of this?"

"Well," said Carter, "I've been giving some thought to that. Obviously the primary study that we have been doing with them has been compromised, and we'll have to see what they want to do about that. If we decide to repeat the study, we'll have to start again from scratch, which means we've lost about three months on the time frame. We have a meeting coming up with them very soon, as you know, so I'll have to discuss that with them. Ray and Fiona, I'll need both of you at that meeting. Obviously this prion thing doesn't really bear any relation to the type of commercial work they're involved in, so they might not be that interested in what we're doing with the mice from the failed study."

"But we'll have to tell them," chipped in Fiona, her voice again rising with anxiety.

"Of course," said Carter. "I'll discuss that with them at the meeting. I want you and Ray there for any points of information for them."

'Speak when you're spoken to and leave tactics to the grown-ups', thought Ray.

"Right," said Carter. "I think that's all for just now."

"How are we going to fund these additional studies on the mice? Scans and quantitative neuropath don't come cheap," said Paul.

"I think we can legitimately draw on endowment funds for that, given the importance of the project … unless anyone has any objections …" said Carter.

Ray knew a little about the world of endowment funds. They had generally been built up over years by departments, often from bequests or one-off donations from grateful patients. Most departments and departmental heads guarded their endowment funds closely, and, as such, it was difficult for the average researcher to have any idea what amount of funds he might be talking about.

Perhaps sensing this, Carter immediately followed on: "I can assure you we have sufficient funds to cover the work."

With that, the meeting was over and they all headed off on their separate ways, with promises to get back to Ray by close of play that day with any revisions. That they were all willing to put aside other pressing work to look at this at zero notice was an indication that they all recognised the potential importance of the study.

On the way back to his office via the animal house, Ray walked with Fiona.

"Well, that wasn't so bad. I hope that you've been able to reassure young Siobhan. Actually it's quite exciting, don't you think?"

"Dr Oldham was very good with Siobhan. He told her to treat it as a learning experience, and not to be put off by it. He also said that we would organise some further training for her, and that we would be requiring further training ourselves. I think he made her feel that it was the system, not just herself, that had led to the mix up, so she feels a bit better about it now. I think we were lucky to get him and not one of the others. I think I was also lucky to be working with you."

She let her hand brush against his, but then moved off without saying more towards the animal house.

CHAPTER 10

The next couple of days went by in a blur. As promised, Ray had received annotated copies of his documents from all of his colleagues by the end of the meeting day. Sarah, in particular, had re-written the section on the post-mortem protocols to cover the strict infection control procedures required for dealing with prions. Another evening and the best part of the night went by incorporating the comments, which greatly improved on his first draft, he thought. By 3 a.m. the documents were ready for submission and he crawled into bed, sleeping almost before his head hit the pillow.

The shrill tone of his alarm took him from his recurring dream of losing his way in a large building (what was all that about?) back to the reality of the morning. He stretched over and pressed the snooze button, then lay back looking up at the cracks in the ceiling and following a spider as it made its way into the corner of the roof. For the first time since this whirlwind began, the enormity of what might be started to sink in. Could they really be on to something here? Was it even conceivable that anything could rebuild myelin and restore function, especially at the rate that it seemed to be happening in these mice? If it was true for the mice, could something similar work in humans? Often researchers become so tied up in the minutiae of their work that they can't see the wider significance, but in this case, it didn't take a great deal of imagination to work out the potential consequences.

The ride into work that morning seemed different – colours seemed brighter, noises sharper, the gardens more attractive, and people happier than usual. Of course, he realised that this was something to do with perception and heightened awareness on his part, but there was no doubt he had never felt anything quite like this in all of his life so far, except maybe on the day when he heard about his acceptance for medical school.

When he arrived, he made straight for Carter's secretary's office and arranged for the necessary thirty copies of the papers to be submitted to the Ethics Committee and five copies to Oldham's department. That done, he headed up to the animal house to check on progress.

"Hi, Fiona, how are things today?"

"It's all quiet in the lab," she said, sounding relieved.

"How are the little guys? Sorry, not very scientific …"

"Everything looks OK. I think they are moving better every day."

"Great. I've submitted all the papers, so fingers crossed that we get the go ahead. I'm off to do some more background reading."

"OK. By the way, I've had a call from Professor Carter's secretary … seems like the meeting with Peploe's will be on Friday."

"That's weird, she didn't mention anything to me."

"Oh, she called just before you came in. She probably just heard from them as you were on your way over. I guess there'll be something on your voicemail."

Sure enough, when Ray got back to his office, there was a message confirming 10 a.m. on Friday for the meeting with Peploe's. Later that afternoon, Dr Oldham called.

"I've had a look at your papers. I think the application is fine, but I'll have to clear it with my colleagues and superiors. I understand that the Ethics Committee are going to consider it on Monday. Our procedures are totally separate, but given the time critical nature of this, I will be able to give you a definitive answer by next Wednesday. I imagine you should hear from ethics by then too. Of course, given the circumstances, and if the formal approvals are given, I will be closely monitoring the progress of this study, so you can expect regular and unannounced visits."

"Thank you, Dr Oldham. I really appreciate your understanding on this. Of course we'll redouble efforts to ensure that there are no more slip ups in laboratory protocol."

"There had better not be, or our department will come down on you like a ton of bricks."

Ray thought he sensed some lightness in the way in which the last remark was delivered, though he was equally sure that the inspectorate would not hesitate to carry out the threat if circumstances dictated.

Friday came around impossibly quickly, it seemed, and he once again found himself on the now familiar chair outside Carter's office with Fiona seated next to him. Today the door was closed although they could hear voices from within. Neither he nor Fiona had known how to prepare for this meeting, but they had decided over coffee the previous day that they should take the lead from Carter as he had previously ordered, and that they should only contribute when asked for information or maybe an opinion. That didn't come altogether naturally to Ray, who was usually pretty forthright in offering opinions on science, politics, music, and most other things, but then this was going to be like no other meeting he'd ever attended. How would Carter approach it? Ray guessed they'd know pretty soon ... with that the door opened.

"Dr Shepherd, Ms Graham, do come and join us. You've met Dr Lassky before, but I don't think you've met Dr da Cruz, International Vice President for Research at Peploe's. This is Dr Shepherd, the research fellow in charge of the study and Ms Graham who is in charge of our animal facility," he explained to the visitors.

Ray shook hands and quickly scanned the faces of the two visitors. Lassky was probably in his early forties, wore the commercial uniform of expensive suit and shirt but no tie, and looked as though he was a regular visitor to the gym. His hair was cropped short and he wore neat square-framed specs, through which shone eyes that suggested a sharp intellect. Ray had met him before at some of the set-up meetings for the study. His handshake was firm but relaxed, from which Ray concluded that Carter had not yet let the cat out of the bag about their study. Dr da Cruz was a strikingly tall woman wearing a smart business suit, moderate heels, and an elegant, understated, but most likely expensive necklace with matching earrings. She had rather a long face and aquiline nose with shortish dark hair. She also stood to shake hands with Ray.

"Pleased to meet you," she said in an accent which, somewhat to Ray's surprise, suggested a Home Counties English upbringing. He noted the wedding ring, which suggested there might be a señor da Cruz. However, this lady was clearly a serious careerist who had risen to a very senior position in the company. Ray wondered if Carter had invited her especially to this meeting, as she would not normally attend project meetings at this level. His deliberations were brought to a sharp stop when Carter suggested they sit and begin the meeting.

"First, can I welcome you all to this meeting," he began. "I'm especially pleased that Dr da Cruz could be here today. She's attending a conference in London and decided to take some time out of her busy schedule to join us here."

So she hadn't been asked, but had just turned up. That would make things doubly interesting.

"We have some important issues to discuss in relation to the dietary study that we are working on together" Carter began. "I'm afraid that we have to report a problem with the study." Lassky and da Cruz both tensed a little, and da Cruz leaned forward in her seat. "About ten days ago, we had an irregularity in lab procedure" he continued, "and some animals intended for another experiment were brought into the laboratory in error. Some of them were caged with the experimental group, which of course invalidates any findings that we might take from these animals. I'm afraid it means that we will have to restart the experiment with a new cohort of mice, which probably sets us back about three months."

Dr da Cruz was the first to reply. "That really is very disappointing, Professor Carter. As you know, we have a lot invested in this study and we have not had any lapses of this type with other research partners." In other circumstances, this could be construed as a threat to take the work elsewhere. However, as everyone in the room knew, Carter was speaking from a position of strength as he had the only population of mice of this type in the world, so the study could not be replicated elsewhere.

"Of course, Dr da Cruz, I am as disappointed as you, and you can be assured that internal disciplinary action has been taken to ensure that nothing of this sort happens again. In the circumstances, I think it is only reasonable that we bear the cost of this unfortunate delay. I would therefore suggest that my department underwrites all costs to date, together with a contribution for the inconvenience caused to your company. I would suggest a total compensation payment of £400,000 from our departmental funds."

'Wow!' thought Ray, almost blurting it out. There must be a lot more in Carter's endowment funds than we thought.

"That seems an appropriate gesture," said Da Cruz. "But are you sure that your department can meet those levels of expense? I thought academia was just about bankrupt these days."

"Well," said Carter, "I think in the circumstances it is only appropriate and we do have the funds to meet it, although as you say, times are quite hard in academia."

Ray wondered if he was now going to try to negotiate the figure down, but even as this thought ran through his head, Carter began again.

"There is one thing I would like to confirm with you. Of course, the data from the animals that we have used to date is going to be of no value. We would like to retain these animals however, for our own internal studies. We won't release or publish any of the data from them, but it would be very helpful to run through the protocols with them. We'll bear the costs of that."

Suddenly, Carter's true intentions exploded into Ray's consciousness and, judging from the sudden tensing of Fiona's knee which was touching Ray's under the table, into Fiona's mind too. 'He's not going to tell them …. He's going to keep the data for himself.'

"If that's agreeable to you, I'll have our Research and Innovation people draw up an agreement to that effect and we can get it signed in the next couple of days. In the meantime, we'll set up another lab and prepare a new experimental run. We should be able to begin that on Monday week, shouldn't we, Ms Graham?"

Fiona just nodded, apparently struck dumb by this turn of events.

Dr da Cruz pulled herself forward in her seat and looked first at Lassky and then at Carter. "That is agreeable to me. Of course, I am disappointed about the delay. I was hoping on my visit today to be able to see progress in the study, but obviously this problem does set us back. However, if we can get things moving again ASAP, then we shouldn't be too disadvantaged. I'll have to feed this back to our board. I would also like to visit the labs myself this afternoon just to get a feel for your procedures."

"Of course, I'd be delighted to take you round myself," said Carter. "I am sure that Fiona will accompany us. In the meantime, Dr Shepherd will update the timetable for the study, and we should have things underway within the next few days."

Ray almost took all of this in, though things were just about moving too fast for him. Could it really be that Carter wasn't going to tell them anything about their discovery, or at least their potential discovery?

As they walked over to the animal house, Carter and da Cruz took the lead, leaving Lassky to fall behind with Ray and Fiona. Fortunately, Lassky decided to chat about weather, politics and the most recent results from the Asian golf tour, leaving Ray more than a little relieved that he wasn't going to be quizzed further on the fate of the existing study mice. In the animal house, da Cruz commented on the poor condition of the prion-infected mice, but made no specific observations about the study mice. Carter moved them all through briskly, ostensibly not to interfere with their busy schedules, though Ray imagined that Carter didn't want them observing the study mice too closely. In a fairly short time, he found himself shaking hands with the visitors at the door of the animal house, reassuring them that they would have the new experimental groups set up as soon as possible and heading back upstairs to Fiona's office, Carter having rushed off to another important faculty meeting.

Fiona and Ray sat for a few minutes before either of them spoke. Eventually she said "I can't believe that just happened."

"Ours not to reason why …" joked Ray, before remembering the second part of that old aphorism and hoping that they wouldn't have to 'do or die'. "I guess we better get things moving for the new studies. I'll speak to Paul to provisionally arrange scanning appointments for our mice, assuming that we get the go ahead from all the necessary bodies. How about a quiet beer at the pub later?"

"That would be nice – see you about 5.30 at the Old Mill? I think we need it." She laughed, for the first time in a few days.

CHAPTER 11

Two weeks later, Ray found himself in the animal MRI suite with Paul Schmidt, about to begin the first follow-up scans on the mice from the corrupted study. The plan was to scan all the animals, both those infected with the prion and those not infected. Since the study was now 'open label', blinding of the observers as to which study group the animals came from was less important, but Paul had decided that he should remain blinded before interpreting the scans, so each mouse being put through was identified only by a study number which had no specific meaning to Paul. However, even before the scans commenced, there was little doubt in Ray's mind about what they were likely to show ...

A lot had happened since his visit to the pub with Fiona, which was very pleasant but remained on a professional colleague footing – just as well thought Ray, given all the other stuff going on just now, but also slightly disappointing? The approvals had come through as hoped from both the government inspectors and from the Ethics Committee. The latter had included some critical comments about the circumstances leading to the application but had agreed that the ethically correct course of action was to proceed with the further observations, bearing in mind the caveats about the use of the data. Meantime, the new experiments for Peploe's had been set up, with baseline measures made on new batches of mice which were housed in a different laboratory to prevent any risks of cross-contamination. A schedule had been agreed for the follow-up observations, of which today's scans were an important part. Carter had gone off again to southern Spain for a conference, having left some dire warnings about the consequences of any further errors, together with a reminder of how much this had cost his endowment fund to date. However, he was obviously excited about the potential importance of findings arising from that initial error.

Ray's optimism about the likely scan appearances was not simply wishful thinking. He had continued to observe the mice

54

during the past fortnight and the improvements in those that had been housed with the prion-infected mice, most of which had now died, were nothing short of miraculous. Many of them were now moving normally, their responses to sensory stimuli were similar to those of normal healthy mice, and indeed in some cases you would have been unable to tell that there had been anything wrong with these mice at all, at least from the point of view of clinical observations and measurements. Would the scans show something similar? It seemed almost inevitable that they would.

The scanning procedure itself took about twenty minutes for each mouse and the images that could be produced were of amazing quality. The whole structure of the nervous system could be clearly seen and areas of damage to myelin and secondary effects on nerve fibres could be quantified on a simple visual grading scale, but also on much more detailed computed figures which calculated areas of affected tissue compared to normal tissue. Since MS is a patchy condition affecting the nervous system at multiple sites but sparing other parts, then the distribution, as well as the area and volume of affected tissue, was important to record and this was also automated. Ray sat spellbound as the first few of the infected mice went through. Although he was not a neuroradiologist, he had seen enough scans by now to be able to pick up quite subtle abnormalities and it was immediately plain on looking at the live scans that these mice had little, if anything, abnormal to find on scanning – they were cured! Ray was desperate to tell someone, but he knew that he had to wait for the official results, and even then, the findings would have to be kept confidential among the very small group of investigators who knew what was going on. However, it did seem likely that they wouldn't have to wait much longer before killing these mice and carrying out detailed post-mortem examinations. A meeting of the group was planned for the following Monday, but it did look as if they would have enough data to begin to design a more detailed trial in a new batch of mice to confirm the findings.

The assumption was that the prion-infected mice had somehow passed on the infection to the MS mice and that, for reasons as yet completely unknown, the prions had allowed the MS mice to rebuild the missing myelin sheaths around the nerves, allowing the nerves to regenerate normal function. Nothing like this had ever been seen before, and it somehow seemed counterintuitive that agents that were associated with damage to the nervous system, i.e. prions causing conditions like BSE, could in other circumstances confer a healing process on nerves damaged by a different type of pathology. However, that seemed to be what they were seeing and the history of science, medical science in particular, was littered with chance discoveries which initially seemed implausible but ultimately proved true. From additional reading that he had done, however, Ray was now aware that prion proteins were thought to cause disease by propagating their abnormal structure to other proteins in the nervous system. Therefore, perhaps it wasn't so crazy that this particular prion, if indeed that was the cause of what they were seeing, could propagate its effects to allow the proteins in nerve sheath cells to regenerate. The other amazing thing, however, was the speed at which this was happening. In the well-recognised prion diseases like BSE and CJD, the incubation period was usually very long and the process of degeneration was slow, but this regeneration process was staggeringly quick. To test the hypothesis properly would require setting up a new experiment where MS mice were randomly assigned to be exposed to prions or not and to repeat the functional and pathological studies that these mice were undergoing.

One issue was clearly going to be to find a more appropriate way to expose the mice to prion infection. Since pure solutions or cultures of prions were not yet possible, it seemed that they would have to inject a solution containing tissue from prion-infected animals into the target mice. There were precedents for this in human medicine. For example, the Kveim test had long been used to help diagnose a condition called sarcoidosis. Small quantities of a solution of ground up tissue from a patient with sarcoidosis were injected into the skin of a suspected sufferer. A later biopsy of the injection site would show the typical appearances of sarcoidosis if the patient had the condition. This had been a very useful test for many years, but, ironically, had been abandoned when people had recognised the potential risk of transmitting prions, or other infections such as HIV, with the injection. Ray guessed that for their study the injection would be into the peritoneal cavity (the belly). This was a relatively common way of injecting drugs and other test substances into mice. The exact details of all of this would need to be discussed and agreed by the research team in due course, before once again submitting another application to the animal inspectorate and to the Ethics Committee for permission to do the study. Ray made a mental note to discuss the details with Fiona, before drafting a proposed plan of action to present to their next research team meeting. At last, he thought, this is why I went into research. His planning and daydreaming were interrupted by Paul, who had left while the scans were performed.

"Well, that's them all completed now," he said. "I'll need a day or so to review and score the scans, so I'll touch base with you tomorrow. I'll also tee up another set of follow-up scans in two weeks."

"Thanks, Paul," said Ray, trying to remain as inscrutable as possible and giving no hint that he had already done some amateur diagnostics on the scans. "I'll accompany the mice back to the lab. See you tomorrow."

With that, he headed off with the precious cargo, and after seeing them re-housed in their cages, he went on to Fiona's office. He felt that his chest was going to burst with excitement as he knocked on the door and waited to be called in. "Kettle's on," she said, trying to remain calm. "How's your day so far?"

"Well, we have to wait for Paul's reports, but let's just say that I think we need to be putting together a draft protocol for a more definitive study to take to the meeting next Monday."

"So, I guess the scans mirror the activity data," she said, breaking into a grin as he filled the cups and sat down.

"Well, I'm no expert of course, but I would say the little chaps are more or less cured, a bloody miracle as we scientists would call it. Of course we need to keep this confidential, but I'm sure I've already seen enough to start drafting that protocol. I've begun thinking about how we expose the mice to the prions for that study, but I thought I should talk it through with you first before we put something together."

Fiona leaned back and took a long sip of her coffee. "I don't suppose we can just bung some infected mice into the cages again like we did this time," she laughed.

Ray was silently pleased to see that she could now make light of the near disaster that had precipitated all of this, but he also knew that she had redoubled all efforts to ensure rigorous adherence to protocols throughout the lab. However, as he would have expected, she had done this in a sensitive way with all the staff, particularly young Siobhan who now seemed to have returned to her usual bright self about the lab.

"I would have thought that we need to prepare some sort of suspension from neural tissue of infected mice and give it intraperitoneally," she went on. "Of course, we've no idea of how much, but since prions are thought to be highly infectious only a tiny inoculum should be needed. It will need to be prepared and administered with the highest levels of biosecurity, but it should only be a one-off treatment, so I don't see that as too much of an obstacle. I would imagine that the disease progression monitoring would be similar to what we've just done, but perhaps at shorter intervals since this recovery process seems to be remarkably fast."

"Great minds," joked Ray. "I think I just said most of that to myself on the way over here. I can't believe we're actually talking about this, but it does begin to seem real now."

"Don't get carried away. I've seen one-offs before that couldn't be repeated."

"One for the JIR then," said Ray. Fiona looked puzzled. "There used to be a journal in America called the *Journal of Irreproducible Results*. Scientists would send in spoof papers and it also had great cartoons along the same lines ... the great breakthrough that wasn't, and so on. Not the sort of publication you'd want to quote on your CV, of course, although they were very cleverly written by very bright people."

"Well, I hope we might do better than that," said Fiona. "Will you not be thinking of *Nature* or the *New England Journal*?" As Fiona knew, scientific journals have a hierarchy, and academic credibility increases with the quality of journal in which a paper is published. This can in turn determine future research funding, promotion and job security for scientists at all levels. So although she wouldn't be doing the writing or even be a co-author of any papers, she did have a stake in where studies were published.

"If we're in one of these two, I'll buy the drinks," laughed Ray.

Fiona returned rapidly to business. "What I'll do in the next couple of days is to draw together all the SOPs that you'll need to put in the protocol for the new study. Are you going to have it ready for next Monday's meeting?"

"I think that would be jumping the gun a bit, given that we haven't completed these observations or got any pathology yet, but I think we need to be ready to discuss it, so the more that's already on paper for inclusion in the final draft, the better."

"OK. Message received. Now, if you'll excuse me, I've got a load of other work to do. Yours is not the only study on the block." There was a twinkle in her eye as she pointed him towards the door.

CHAPTER 12

During the next couple of days, Ray put a lot of effort into writing up the draft protocol for the new study. He could barely contain his excitement, especially when drafting the section on 'Anticipated Benefits of the Research'. This was always a very important section for the Ethics Committee and, increasingly, for all types of research, no matter how esoteric, they expected to see some articulation of the benefits to society as well as the purely scientific outputs of the work. For many studies, that could be quite a difficult section to write without either understating the potential of the work by applying very a conservative attitude, or overstating the impact of something which would really advance knowledge by only a small degree. In this case, however, the potential impact of the work was huge and that could be justified easily in the submission.

Friday, Ray's clinical day for that week, came round quickly and served, as it always did, to bring him back to earth with a bump. The morning was spent in the ward while in the afternoon he had a general neurology clinic to undertake. One of the great fascinations of the specialty for previous generations of neurologists had been the quest for a diagnosis in any particular patient. The nervous system is probably the most complex 'organ' of the body with its multiple functions controlling sensation, movement, coordination, special senses such as sight, hearing and smell and then the higher functions of thought, reasoning etc. at which point it begins to merge with philosophy and other disciplines. When someone presents with a symptom, it is very important to get a detailed history and examination in order to localise the site of any pathology and, if possible, the nature of that pathology. Over the years, the battery of specialist investigations at the doctor's disposal had increased and improved in quality and many conditions could now be diagnosed with a fair degree of accuracy and confidence. However, having established what the problem was, there were still very few neurological conditions which could be treated satisfactorily and even less which could be cured by means of medicines, surgery or other interventions. Much of Ray's time in his clinical work was therefore spent in helping people to understand the nature of their condition and its likely prognosis, and to cope with its effects in their everyday lives. This was very intense and stressful for the doctor as well as the patient.

Today, there was another concern for Ray to deal with as he approached Jo's bed in the ward. Jo had very severe, long-standing multiple sclerosis that meant she now had very limited use of her hands, no power in her legs, no control over her bladder or bowels and had various problems with digestion and with palpitations which were assumed to be related to abnormalities of her autonomic nervous system which controls functions such as gut motility and heart rhythm. Her treatment was mainly delivered by physiotherapists and occupational therapists who were trying to get her as fit as possible to allow her to get home to her husband and two teenage children. Despite all of this she remained remarkably cheerful – Ray was never quite sure whether this was part of the neurological abnormality or whether she just chose to put on a particularly brave face.

"Hi, Jo, how are things today?"

"Oh, I've just been down to the gym. I had a really good session this morning. Mary's thinking that I might get home at the end of next week, but she's going to go round to the house first to see if there are any more modifications that could be added."

"Are you getting some sleep?"

"Well, you know what it's like in here … never the quietest. These pins and needles in my arms are also still pretty troublesome during the night. I don't get any problems with them in my legs now though – I think they've just shut up shop altogether. Anyway, how are you? Have you got a cure for me yet? Don't worry, only joking …"

Ray bit his lip. He had this same question from Jo, and many other patients, on a regular basis. As usual it was delivered in a jokey way, as most people with Jo's level of disease had long ago given up any hope of a cure. So far as she was concerned, it was a bit like asking if he'd done time travel yet. Or was it? Actually, all of these people still harboured a dim hope somewhere that one day Ray or someone else would just say yes and take them back into the normal world.

"You'll be the first to know," said Ray, again his stock response to this question. But today, maybe …

The afternoon clinic followed the usual pattern of some patients newly referred by their family doctors for assessment by a specialist, and 'return' patients who had a range of chronic neurological diseases which required ongoing treatment and monitoring. In the course of the afternoon, he saw people ranging from age twenty-one to eighty-six, with conditions such as epilepsy, Parkinson's disease, motor neurone disease, Wilson's disease and others, as well as a number of regulars with MS, mostly those with the relapsing/remitting type who were being given interferon or other treatments to try to prevent relapses. With each patient, Ray was methodical and frank, but kindly, and he had rapidly become one of the most popular doctors in the clinic. However, he always ended the afternoon exhausted and a little depressed that he had seen so many people for whom he could offer relatively little. Paradoxically, those who had the most severe conditions were often the least complaining, but Ray realised that could be because they had lowered their expectations to a point where they wouldn't be disappointed by some other setback. This had been shown for people with asthma, where those with mild disease often find their symptoms more intrusive and depressing than those with severe disease who have long since given up ideas of playing football, skiing or dancing through an all-night party. A key part of his role as a doctor was to help people manage that balance of expectation and function.

That evening, he collapsed on his settee with a carry-out curry and a beer and put on a Ladysmith Black Mambazo CD. This was music he always found uplifting, born as much of it was out of adversity, yet carrying those soaring harmonies and echoes of an older Africa mixed with contemporary themes. There was something about harmony singing and group music; the bringing together of a number of people, each of whom adds a small part but the sum is way more than the individual constituents. He wasn't sure if his love for this type of music was partly a reaction to the solitary nature of his work and the lonely struggle that each of his patients seemed to endure with their illness. Whatever the reason, he found his heart lifting and he slept well that night.

He woke early on Saturday to the phone ringing … 7.45 a.m.

'Who the hell's phoning at this time? I'm not on call. Hope it's not dad,' he thought as he struggled to find his mobile among the wreckage of last night's meal.

"Ray? Sorry to ring so early, but I've been up all night working through the final analysis of these scans."

Ray recognised Paul's voice, and realised that in the heat of yesterday's clinical work, he'd forgotten that Paul hadn't reported back yet. "Yeah …?" he said.

"I've never seen anything like it, Ray. When I saw the dramatic changes in some scans I decided to break the code for myself. These prion-exposed mice are as near normal as you might get. They've completely rebuilt their myelin. I've checked the data over several times, as I'm sure people will think it's too good to be true, but there's no doubt."

Ray was now wide awake. "OK. That fits with all the functional data we've got too. How do you think we should present it?"

"How are you fixed today, Ray? It would be good to collate everything we've got to date and maybe make up a PowerPoint presentation for Carter's meeting on Monday. I could get in to the lab by ten o'clock, I reckon we could have it done by five and maybe have a couple of pints then? Unless, of course you've got other plans …?"

"No, sounds good. I can get a jog in before then and the prospect of the pints at five will help the day shoot by … See you then …"

He loved his early morning runs when time allowed. As well as keeping him in good physical shape and reducing his stress levels, he always found this was a great time to think, and would rehearse ideas and presentations in his head as he went round the park. He could never really understand the folks who ran with earpieces in and music blaring in their heads. He liked to hear the birds, children shouting and all the other sounds of normal people going about their normal lives. Sometimes when clinical work was proving particularly stressful, he would go swimming at the nearby championship pool just to remind himself that not everyone in the world was sick or disabled. Today he felt particularly energised, he seemed to be running smoother than ever, ten years younger even.

Back in the flat, he showered, took some cereal and a coffee, gathered together the printouts of activity data and his laptop, and slipped on his leathers. Today felt like a day to take the bike to work.

Six hours later, Ray and Paul had assembled the data on all the animals and prepared a presentation for the next week's meeting with Carter. Ray plotted the activity data for the exposed and non-exposed mice along a timeline from the start of the original experiment. For each of the activities measured, he used a different coloured line to represent each mouse. All of the mice showed the same pattern – essentially no change or a slight deterioration in activity up to point where the prion-exposed mice were accidentally introduced into the cages, then a progressive improvement in function to the point where the activity was really no different from a normal mouse. Paul similarly went through the scans in sequence for each mouse. Often scientists presenting data would choose what they would refer to as a 'representative example'. Most knew however that they had usually chosen the best example to demonstrate their point and that not all subjects studied would necessarily show quite such striking changes. In this case however, Paul really could have chosen any of the mice that had been exposed to the prions, since the improvements were identical and spectacular in all cases. He decided to group the images for all the mice on two slides, one before exposure and one after exposure, taken from the most recent run of scans. The 'after' slide again looked like an assembly of scans of normal mice.

Although the history of recent events would be well known to all who would be at this meeting, Ray decided to add a few introductory slides briefly summarising the background, followed by the data, followed by one or two 'next steps' slides. Clearly to complete the present study they would need to have the post-mortem pathology studies on these mice. Ray felt a little sad that, having been brought back from a debilitating illness to a healthy state, they would now have to be killed to have their nervous system anatomy studied in detail, but rigorous science demanded it. He would then need to design the follow-up randomised experiment. Although Ray was not a statistician, he did know enough to realise that these changes were so dramatic that they would not need to include a large number in the next study, as in general the bigger the size of an effect, the fewer subjects were needed to prove that a result was not likely to have happened by chance. The main purposes of the follow-up study would be to use a proper randomised protocol, to develop a method for administering the prions, assuming that they were the active agents, that could be adapted for future human studies, and to examine the timeline of any response, again with a view to future human studies. He would need to consult the statistician for the sample size calculation, so decided that he should be invited along to the meeting with the rest of the team.

By 4.30, the presentation was complete and Paul and Ray headed for the pub, having agreed that any conversation there would be about anything other than MS research. This was partly for reasons of confidentiality but mainly because they were talked out about work and needed to relax. However, for Ray, Monday couldn't come soon enough.

CHAPTER 13

This time there was no background music in Carter's office as the team gathered for probably the most important research meeting that any of them had ever attended. Round the table, as well as Ray and Paul, were Fiona, Sarah Simpson, Andy Turner, the statistician, and, of course, Carter himself, who was looking serious though even he couldn't hide some of his excitement. Coffee and buns were available this time, a sure sign of the status of this meeting. Carter began proceedings.

"Thanks to all of you for coming along this morning. I'm sure we're all looking forward to an update on the experiments. May I remind you again that all of this morning's proceedings are to be treated in the strictest confidence ..." Ray sensed that this time, the caution was mainly for Andy's benefit, Carter looking in his direction as he gave his instruction. "Dr Shepherd, could you bring us up to date with the findings?"

"Thanks," said Ray. "Paul and I spent Saturday looking at the data. I thought for everyone's benefit it might be useful to give a short PowerPoint presentation going over the background, the current findings and some thoughts about the next steps. Apologies to those who know all this already, but it seemed sensible to ensure that we're all on the same page."

"Excellent" said Carter, and leaned back in his seat with his coffee in hand.

Over the next fifteen minutes or so, Ray went through the sequence of events from the initial accidental exposure of the mice to the prion-infected animals; through some of the thinking about how prions might be capable of reversing the changes of MS; on to the activity data, the images of the mice before and after exposure to prion-infected mice; and then his own thoughts about the next, more definitive study. Mostly his small audience was quiet, spellbound by what they were seeing, but even Carter and Sarah couldn't suppress a gasp when the scans were put up. Andy, as befits a statistician, was inscrutable throughout, realising in part that his role in all of this was relatively minor but nevertheless sensing the excitement of his clinical research colleagues.

"… and that's the state of play to date," said Ray completing his presentation and leaning back in his chair, exhausted by the adrenaline rush that had gone with seeing the data and scans again.

"Thank you," said Carter "an excellent summary … thoughts, everyone?"

Sarah was the first to speak. "This is astonishing – I've never seen anything remotely like this in my life. Of course the pathology is going to be interesting, but judging from the scans, I suspect I'm going to be hard pressed to find anything wrong in these mice. I suppose we might get some clues on the mechanism of repair with some detailed work, especially some electron microscopy. I think, according to the protocol, we need to wait until the next set of scans before sacrificing the animals for the pathology studies, so it will be another six weeks or so before we have the data from that part of the study."

Ray smiled inwardly at the use of the word 'sacrifice'. This was common practice among many laboratory scientists, although to his mind it was simply wrong, implying some sort of religious or spiritual sense to the killing of the animals, and he always avoided the use of the word, preferring to use the more prosaic 'kill'. However, he knew what she meant, and maybe in this case sacrifice was a more appropriate term since they were going to be killing mice that were to all intents and purposes healthy now.

"There's no question that we have to stick rigidly to the protocol here," said Ray. "Apart from being good practice, Dr Oldham would have our guts for garters if we digressed from the protocol at this stage. However, I don't think that should hold us up from drafting the outline protocol for the more definitive study, as it will be important to get that moving as soon as we have the final data from this one."

"Agreed," Carter clearly felt it was time for him to assume command again. "It seems inconceivable that the pathology is going to show much more than normal findings, given the scan appearances. However the next study is crucial to demonstrate that we can replicate these findings in a randomised trial and that we can find a more convenient and widely applicable way of administering the prions. We may only need a small number of animals, given the magnitude of the changes?" The last sentence was part statement, part question, directed at Andy, who spoke next.

"That's right. I can work out a sample size now. Of course we'll have to allow for some potential dropouts due to intercurrent infections and so on, but I think we're going to be looking at no more than tens of mice."

"That should help to keep the cost down too," added Ray, who was immediately admonished by Carter.

"Given the importance of this work, I don't think we should be constrained by costs."

Again Ray wondered just how much money Carter had stashed away in his endowment accounts. Anyway, it was helping to pay his salary and possibly funding the most important piece of work in neurology for decades, so there was no need to complain.

"I think we need to move towards a timeline," continued Carter. "As soon as the pathology is available, we need to be submitting our ethics and licensing protocols. If that is in six weeks, then we could have started the new exposures within ten weeks, assuming ethics and licensing move quickly. I'll have a word with the relevant people at ethics, and I think given Oldham's interest and facilitatory attitude to date, we might hope that licensing moves equally smoothly. That could give us data for the next major European congress in Barcelona. I'm sure we'll also get a publication in *Nature*." He had already moved beyond the experimental stage to consider how the work might be presented for maximum impact. Although he was slightly uncomfortable with this level of confidence about something that hadn't already been done, nevertheless Ray couldn't help but feel a tingle of excitement at the back of his neck, even at the mention of the dissemination phase of the work.

Fiona, having now fully regained her confidence and professionalism after the blow of the initial debacle, pitched in.

"I'll have to look at scheduling of space in the labs for the studies. I would suggest that we designate a specific lab for this study. We'll need to operate at the highest levels of infection control and we need to ensure that there's no cross-contamination of exposed mice and controls. I'll get the protocols and SOPs drawn up within the next two days. The timing is good actually, as we have one of the gastroenterologist's studies coming to an end, which will free up the space for this study. I'll work closely with Ray on that."

Ray allowed his heart a minor skip on that prospect.

"I'll expect to be kept in close touch with all developments," said Carter. "I suggest that we avoid using the regular e-mail channels in case of infiltration. We need to also ensure that any of our staff who is involved, for example in the animal house or the pathology labs, is aware of the highly sensitive nature of this study and the proposed one. I am sure we'll all brief them appropriately." Nods all round. "If no one else has anything to add, I suggest that we re-convene at fortnightly intervals to discuss progress. Same venue and time suitable for everyone?" Again nods all round. "We'll need to have a separate meeting about the Peploe's study. Can I take it that it's progressing satisfactorily?"

Fiona was the first to speak. "All going smoothly … of course it's early days but we're not seeing anything like the effects in this study."

"No …" said Carter, tailing off and indicating that this meeting was over for now.

"When do you want to come over to discuss the plans?" said Fiona as they left the meeting. "I'll need until the early part of next week to draw up the protocols, SOPs and floor plans for the cages. Would next Tuesday do? Of course you're welcome to come over anytime," she added quickly.

"I hope so" said Ray, smiling. "Wild horses wouldn't keep me away."

"We don't do large animals," laughed Fiona.

CHAPTER 14

The next few weeks went by in a blur. Fiona and Ray worked out the protocols and SOPS for the studies as she had indicated. Andy fairly quickly came up with a power calculation indicating that they could do the study with only a small number of animals in each group and with a randomisation schedule that indicated which animals should have which treatment, either injection with a solution containing the prions or with a sham solution containing no active agent.

The exposure period of the infected animals from the first study was completed and the animals were killed or 'sacrificed' as planned. As everyone had expected, the initial pathology showed no significant abnormality of the nervous system, and the electron microscopy again seemed to be within normal limits. It was as if the mice had completely healed.

"I can hardly believe what I'm seeing," said Dr Oldham. Ray had convened another meeting, this time involving Fiona, Paul, Sarah, once some slides were available and just before submitting the application for the randomised study. Oldham had agreed to come along and they were sitting round the meeting table in Sarah's office this time, to allow her to project the images on screen.

"We're all in that boat," said Sarah. "We've never come across anything like this. We don't know what the molecular mechanism is, but there is no doubt that these mice have been able to completely repair their myelin sheaths, both functionally and anatomically, apparently after exposure to the prion-infected mice. We've come up with a new protocol that Ray, sorry ... Dr Shepherd, will have submitted to you that should allow us to inject mice with a prion solution that we have prepared from the central nervous system of some infected mice. We think that if we inject it intraperitoneally, into the belly of the mice, they should absorb it and demonstrate any effects. Our statistician has made a sample size calculation that suggests we could use a fairly small number of mice in a randomised study, assuming the effect size is the same as we've seen here, to demonstrate that this really works.

"Yes, I've had the paperwork from Dr Shepherd, which is going to my committee with an urgent consideration label, so we should have an answer for you soon. Incidentally, I've been more than impressed with the general standards throughout the lab, and with the way in which you seem to have rehabilitated and supported your young technician who made the original error, so keep up that good work."

Fiona allowed herself a little inward smile at that, as did Ray.

As Oldham had indicated, approval for the new study came through within two weeks, as did Ethics Committee approval and the study began.

On day one, Ray and Fiona worked methodically through all the mice allocated for the study. According to the randomisation schedule, half were injected with 3 ml of a solution that contained material harvested from the nervous systems of infected mice, assumed therefore to contain the active prions. The other half received a solution with similar material harvested from non-infected mice, assumed therefore to contain no prions. Each mouse had a code number. Ray remained 'blinded' as to which mice were receiving the active solution. Only the statistician had a record of that and the code would only be broken after the study had been completed and all the activity data and pathology studies had been carried out. As before, the mice were subject to regular recording of activity data and response to various stimuli, to functional MRI scans of their nervous systems, and ultimately were killed and detailed pathology studies performed.

Very soon into the study, it became apparent that once again some of the mice were making dramatic improvements in their response to stimuli and activity data, while others were unchanged or slowly deteriorating. By the end of the study, some of the mice appeared to have returned to normal while others were unchanged or worse. Excitement mounted among the research team that the results of the first study were no fluke, but of course they all had to wait for completion of the study, for Andy to break the code, and for the data to be analysed according to whether the mice had received an active or sham exposure.

The Sunday before the meeting at which the results would be revealed was warm and sunny, so Ray decided to take a run on the motorbike to visit his dad.

71

"Hiya, how are you doing?" he shouted as soon as he opened the door to his dad's small place. The door was rarely locked to allow friends and carers easy access.

"Is that you, Ray?" His dad's voice sounded distant or weak, and his initial shout was followed by a loud bout of coughing.

As Ray came into the room, his dad had grabbed the small pot that he kept beside his chair and was in the process of trying to cough a thick string of greenish phlegm into the pot. The effort was puffing out his neck muscles and there was a decided blue tinge around his lips, bluer than normal, Ray thought. Eventually, he was able to free the spit from his lower lip and looked up to see his son.

"Sorry about that, this cough's a bugger ... Not pleasant to watch, I suppose," he said.

"Don't worry, I've seen worse stuff, Dad. How are you feeling?"

"Knackered. Ready for the blue pill, I think. Don't suppose you've got a cure for me yet?" That question again.

"Sorry, Dad, I really wish I had."

"Never mind son, mainly my own fault I know, or maybe Mr Benson and Mr Hedges. Or maybe that bloody mine. Anyway, the nurse has been in and I've got the old antibiotic and steroid pills again so I suppose I'll be right as rain in a couple of days, though each time I feel a bit weaker after one of these. I suppose that's how it goes. I guess you've seen it often enough."

There was no way that Ray could lie to his dad. They both knew what was happening and how it would end. The main thing now was to keep it as painless as possible.

"I know, Dad. It's pretty grim. You need to let us know how you're feeling at any time. The doc can give you tablets to help the breathlessness, though they might have other effects that aren't good for you overall. I'm thinking about morphine, for example. It would ease the breathlessness, but it might shorten your life."

"I know that son. I'll be ready for it soon I think, but not quite yet. Just promise me one thing ..."

"What, dad?"

"I won't have to stick my head down the lavatory like that boy in Trainspotting!"

With that, he burst into another prolonged spasm of laughing/coughing, but there was a look in his eye which said to Ray that he wasn't finished yet. Eventually, he could speak again.

"Anyway, how's your work going?"

"It's great, dad, I think. I can't tell you much about it yet, sworn to secrecy by the boss, but it looks like we might have made a very important discovery about treating a major illness … not yours though."

"That's OK, there's plenty worse than me out there. You just keep at it and I'll try to hang around till the secret's out …" The glint in his eye was unmistakable.

After supper, which was a prolonged affair since his dad could only eat very slowly without being breathless, Ray headed back to his flat and settled down with a dram and some Tracy Chapman. As on many occasions before, he had a deep inner feeling of helplessness. Here he was, potentially on the verge of one of the biggest breakthroughs in medicine of the century, yet he could do nothing to help his dad who had given him so much … well, life for a start … and asked for nothing in return. Is this what we do, he thought, succeed on some sort of large stage but fail where it really matters? But even as the thought went through his head, he knew that his dad would have none of that attitude. Who was he to be feeling sorry for himself? His dad would say that he had had his life and was fulfilled and ready to leave when the time came. He would expect his son to make the most of the opportunities presented to him and to leave the stage in due course (hopefully a long time hence, thought Ray) with dignity and a sense of achievement. The lyrics of the old Sean Keane song about a 'Satisfied Mind' came to him and he slept OK that night.

Twelve hours later found him again in Carter's room gathered with the familiar team. During a pre-meeting, Andy had broken the code for the study and the results were now displayed on a composite slide projected on the back wall of the room. It was as they has hoped, dreamed … and expected.

The prion-exposed mice had completely restored function and structure in their nervous systems as demonstrated by all the different modes of data collection, while the sham exposed mice were all showing progression of their disease to varying degrees.

"Colleagues," said Carter, "I believe we may be seeing a cure for multiple sclerosis in the making. Congratulations to all of you. The next step is to get the work written up. I think we should go for a plenary presentation at the Barcelona conference and a paper in *Nature* to begin with. There will be other supplementary presentations and papers and we'll have to manage the publicity. I'll speak to colleagues about the conference and ensure that we get the major plenary presentation without giving them any specifics at this stage. Again I would stress that we must keep this strictly confidential at present though we will have to bring in the university press office and the research and innovation team to ensure that we maximise the value to the institution."

"I've already begun work on the conference abstract and the paper," said Ray "and I would suggest that Sarah, Paul and I continue to work on the first draft before passing it on to you, Professor Carter. We will need to think about authorship too."

This was always a thorny question in academic work. Being listed as the author of a paper was an important measure of academic standing, and in many cases, the position of one's name in the author list was also important, the first and second authors carrying most weight. Some senior scientists would insist that their name went first in any paper coming from their group, others would agree that the person who did the bulk of the work and the writing should come first, yet others would always appear last, considering this to reflect their position as the group leader. Increasingly, journals asked all authors to outline their specific contributions to the work. In this case, assuming the paper included data on study design, conduct, and outcomes including radiology and pathology, then the four authors that Ray had mentioned would be the right ones, with acknowledgements for Andy, whose role was relatively minor, and for Fiona, who, although she had done a great deal of the practical work on the study, was not in an academic career track and would not expect to be included as an author.

"Ideal," said Carter. "The deadline for abstract submission is in two weeks, so if we have the first draft circulated this week, we can meet again next Monday to discuss and finesse it."

"That's no problem," said Ray. In fact preparing a paper such as this was easier than it first appeared, since the rationale, the design and execution of the study had all been written for the original proposal; what was required was to add the results and a discussion of their significance.

"We also need to make plans to move immediately to a human

study, so I would be grateful if you could also bring some draft ideas on that to next week's meeting."

As they left the room, Carter motioned to Ray to stay behind.

"I've been very impressed with your work on this study, Ray. The Barcelona conference will be a big stage for us, but I'm sure that you will handle it well. Of course, I'll be in the audience if there are any questions that you are uncomfortable with. I've also been giving some thought to protection of our intellectual property and patenting of the prion solution should it be effective in a human study. The research and innovation team will help with that, but I think it is our duty to ensure the potential of a financial reward for the university, should this prove successful. There will also be a share of that income due to the investigator. Anyway, you don't have to worry about that at this stage, but I'll keep you informed."

At the mention of the conference, Ray felt a brief surge of anxiety, though he had it under much better control these days. As to financial gain from the studies, Ray hadn't even considered this. It was alien to him to think that medical advances should somehow generate profits for individuals, although he did see that some return to the university was probably justified to support future research activity. It began to dawn on him how Carter might have amassed the endowment funds that he had raided for this study. Anyway, none of that was his concern at present.

"Thanks, Professor Carter. It is pretty exciting, I have to say."

"Yes, yes ..." said Carter, as Ray was dismissed.

CHAPTER 15

As Ray had expected, writing the abstract and the paper proved not too difficult, and during the next week he met with Paul and Sarah a few times until they had acceptable drafts of both documents ready for Carter on the following Monday.

The protocol for the human study was a different kettle of fish. He hadn't much experience of writing this kind of thing although he had read a number of different human study protocols and been involved in some clinical studies over the years. The biggest initial questions were what kind of patients to include in the study and what to use as a 'control' treatment. In general, where there was an existing and established treatment for a condition, then any new treatment would be compared against that, usually by taking a group of patients with a similar degree of illness or disability and randomising them to receive either the established treatment or the new one, delivered in such a way that neither the patient nor the doctor knew which was being given until the study period was complete and the outcomes recorded. This was the classic 'double blind randomised trial'. If there was no established treatment for the condition, then the new treatment would be compared against a dummy or placebo, for example a pill or injection that contained no active ingredient.

In the case of multiple sclerosis, there were some treatments that had been shown to be effective in reducing the frequency or intensity of relapses of the illness, though overall progression of the disease still took place. Most patients eventually developed a progressive form of the illness that was resistant to treatment and led to deterioration and eventual death. The nature and speed of that decline was very variable between patients, but it was generally accepted that there was no effective treatment for people once they were in that category. Over the years, claims had been made for many weird and wonderful treatments to help people with progressive disease, but none had stood up to scrutiny. Ray's own view was that this might be the group of people to target in the study. After all, it seemed from the mouse experiments that the prions could somehow repair previously damaged tissue and if this treatment could cure or even improve people with the most advanced disease, surely it would help less severely ill people who could be studied at a later date. The other advantage of tackling these people with very severe life-threatening disease was that, ethically, the risk of side effects, which were as yet largely unknown for this type of treatment, could be better justified, given that their life expectancy and quality was very poor anyway. Often, when new treatments such as drugs became available, they would be given initially to normal volunteers to test for possible adverse effects, but of course that was completely inappropriate in this situation, when an agent being given was of a type that was known itself to cause a progressive fatal illness in humans.

Another dilemma was how many people to include in the study. As in the animal studies, it was important to ensure that enough were included to demonstrate effectiveness of the treatment, but given the animal findings, which were dramatic and unequivocal, it was likely that only a few subjects would be required for the initial study. Ray decided, pragmatically, that they would aim to recruit 26 people of whom half would receive randomly allocated active treatment and half placebo. That allowed for a few dropouts and still a good chance of having 10 in each group at the end of the observation period.

The length of that observation period was another unknown. If humans did respond as the mice had done, how quickly would their nervous systems recover? As much larger animals, with longer nerves and nerve sheaths, common sense would suggest that any repair procedure in humans would take much longer than in mice. At least, since the treatment was to be given as a single injection, there was no issue about when to discontinue active treatment, as there would have been, for example, with a course of pills or repeated cycles of injected treatment. Again, pragmatically, Ray decided to draft in an observation period of one year, with standard questionnaires, activity and function scores measured at monthly intervals and functional MRI scans at two monthly intervals.

Last, but not least, were the crucial questions of how patients would be recruited into the study and what information they would be given. It was an absolute requirement that patients volunteering to take part in the study should be fully informed of potential risks as well as benefits, that they should be free to withdraw at any time and that if they did withdraw, no data that had been collected about them would be used further in the study. Again, in the case of a course of injections or pills, should a patient choose to withdraw, then the treatments could be stopped, but in this case, once the prions had been injected, there was no way of removing them. All of this had to be made clear to the patient and their carer, by way of a patient information sheet and accompanying consent form. The thought of carers brought Ray's mind right back to Eric and Susan, where all of this had started for him. Suddenly the whole thing became a bit easier. He began to write the information sheet as he thought Eric might have wanted to read it – straightforward, plain language, realistic about the many risks and potential unknowns of this treatment, not overambitious about the potential benefits although making it clear that substantial improvements might take place. He thought about how Eric might react to this opportunity. Of course, by agreeing to take part in the trial, Eric (or any of the Erics who might take part) was signing up to the possibility he might be getting an injection of salty water or similar with no active ingredient, and then being subject to repeated observations and scans over a year when he would likely be deteriorating and less fit for the rigours and psychological distress of all of that. On the other hand, if the active treatment caused some horrific unexpected side effect, then those who had received the placebo might prove to be the lucky ones. That was the reality of taking part in such a study. Despite all that, Ray had little doubt that, given any prospect of improvement, most Erics would jump at the chance to take part.

By the end of the week, Ray had managed to prepare a first draft of the study outline and protocol, the seventy-five page ethics application, patient information and consent sheets and some outline costs for preparation and administration of the prion solutions, patient assessments and scans.

On Sunday, he even found enough time to take a premiership match at the local pub. As he watched the game, he realised that he had almost no social life and seemed to be working sixteen to seventeen hours a day. Not exactly a party animal ... but maybe next year.

CHAPTER 16

"Good, good ..." said Carter, leafing through the drafts of the paper and the conference abstract. "I've a few minor edits to add. I'll get my secretary to type them up tomorrow and you can get the abstract off later this week. I'm sure we'll draw a good crowd for the plenary in Barcelona. I've spoken with the press office and they'll help us draft a release once the conference papers come out. I think we're going to have some significant issues with expectation management once the news is out."

Ray spoke. "I've also made a first attempt at the human study protocol, but I'd appreciate your help with that, Professor Carter. I haven't written a human protocol before, but I have prepared a draft of all the documents. I've suggested that we go for a small-scale randomised study in people with severe, end-stage disease. I think that makes it easier to handle the ethics questions, given the uncertain nature of potential effects and side effects. I'm not sure how potential subjects will take to the possibility of being allocated to the placebo arm of the trial particularly, as you say, once word gets out on the dramatic effects in mice." Ray looked quizzically at Carter.

"Thank you, Ray. I'll give all that some thought. One option might be to form a trial monitoring committee."

The look on Ray's face indicated that the he wasn't sure what that entailed.

Carter continued, "An independent monitoring committee will oversee the study and have access to the data accruing as the study proceeds. If it becomes obvious that the treatment is either overwhelmingly effective or is causing unacceptable side effects, then they can stop the study. If the treatment proves as effective as we think, those patients who have had the placebo could be given active treatment as soon as the study stops."

"That sounds ideal," said Ray "but I'll have to describe that in the ethics application and in the patient information."

"I'll read what you've written so far and make some edits in respect of the monitoring committee and so on. I think it would be useful to hold off the final submission until after the conference. We might get some useful input from colleagues to inform the final draft. We can also recruit members for the trial monitoring committee there. I'm sure there'll be no shortage of volunteers." Carter stretched back in his chair, looking rather pleased with himself.

"Incidentally, I've asked Barbara to book travel and accommodation for Barcelona. I've seen an early draft programme for the conference and it looks as if all the big hitters will be there from the USA and Asia as well as Europe, so we should have a good audience for the work. I've also been speaking to the university lawyers about copyright protection and patenting. Of course once the work is published, that element of it is in the public domain, but we can certainly patent the prion solution and the mode of administration, which we could licence on to a pharma company or create a spin-out in due course."

Ray had some idea of what he was talking about, although his idea of a spin-out was more to do with events at Brands Hatch or Silverstone than anything to do with his clinical work. He thought he would continue to leave that part of proceedings to Carter.

A few weeks later he was on the plane to Barcelona, the conference and that meeting with Liz ...

★★★

As he finished his story, she smiled that smile again. "That's quite a tale. I guess working with Carter hasn't been a picnic?"

"To be honest, we don't see that much of him. Although he does have an uncanny knack of knowing what's going on even though he's not often there. It's not like our group was in Boston though. The atmosphere there was brilliant. It was really good for me you know. You were really good for me. I always thought ..."

"I know. I did too."

"You always seemed so confident, Liz. Remember when I used to waken up at 3 or 4 a.m.? You always calmed me. I guess I didn't realise the strain I was putting on you. Living with some sort of psychological cripple couldn't have been easy."

"Hardly that ... I know you got stressed out sometimes. But you had an illness ... OK at a low level, but an illness just the same, although I didn't realise it then. I thought it was all to do with you being in the States, with everything being unfamiliar. I thought I was partly to blame. That's one of the reasons why I thought it was good for us to split and for you to go back to England. I see now that it was more of an intrinsic thing. But you seem different now, more content, more optimistic, more focussed. If I met you today ..."

"So there's no one else, Liz?"

"No one significant ... not right now anyway. After my folks passed I was pretty busy sorting out their affairs and then getting this new project up and running. All work and no play, you know ..."

"Maybe I could come out to see you again then sometime? Unfortunately with this project I'm not going to have much free time ... I'll have to do all the assessment visits. Or maybe you could come over to the UK?"

"Well, I'm going to be busy too, though it is a nice thought. We do have this afternoon though ... my place?"

"I don't know ..."

"Sorry, Ray, I should have realised ... there's someone else for you ...?"

"No ... well, not really ... there is a woman ... but we've not, you know ... actually we've not even been on a proper date ... and I don't know ..."

"OK then, my place ... no strings ... no commitment ... for old time's sake?"

She stood up and took his hand firmly. He followed her to the door. Somehow it seemed right.

Part 2

CHAPTER 17

The letter box clicked open and three letters fell on the carpet. The tired-looking middle-aged man shuffled through in his pyjamas and slippers.

"Is that the mail, dear?" A woman's voice came from the bedroom.

"Yep, three today. Let's see … bill, bill, … and one for you from Dr Booth."

"Me? I hardly ever get mail, and certainly not from the quack. You'd better open it."

Jim Bush slit open the brown envelope, which was quite thick and marked 'Private and Confidential'.

Dear Mrs Bush,

I am writing to inform you that a group of doctors at the University are planning a trial of a new treatment for multiple sclerosis. They are looking for patients who have quite severe symptoms to volunteer to take part in a study of a new injection which has appeared in laboratory tests to improve symptoms. To date, this treatment has not been tested in humans, but it may have potential benefits. The trial will involve volunteers agreeing to receive a single injection which may contain the active ingredient or an inactive solution (placebo), and then undergoing monitoring over a one-year period. The monitoring will require monthly visits from the doctors undertaking the study, when you will be asked about symptoms and will be examined, together with visits to the hospital at two-monthly intervals for brain scans. Some blood tests may also be required.

You are under no obligation to volunteer for this trial. However, if you wish more information about it, I will pass your name and address on to the doctors undertaking the trial who will contact you directly with much more detailed information to help you decide whether you wish to take part. All your information will be treated in the strictest confidence and will be available only to the doctors, nurses and hospital staff undertaking the trial.

I enclose a reply slip which should be returned to me in the enclosed envelope (no stamp required). It is entirely your choice whether or not to take part. If you decide that you do not want details passed on to the study team, that will in no way influence your current and future treatment from the NHS.

Yours sincerely,

Dr William Booth

General Practitioner

Elsie Bush tried to pull herself up in the bed as Jim sat down with the letter in his hand, looking slightly dazed. Nothing like this had ever happened to them in the ten years that Elsie had suffered this hellish disease. It had begun innocently enough with temporary blindness in one eye, which, although it had been frightening at the time, had recovered over a few weeks and Jim and Elsie had assumed that might be that. "Optic neuritis," the doctor had called it then, "quite often just comes as an isolated event and doesn't happen again," he had said, although he did mention that it could be a sign of something "more serious". Well, the something more serious hadn't taken too long to show its hand. Within a couple of years, Elsie had several more attacks of temporary malfunction of various nerves, including her eyes again, hands and feet. Then it had moved into a more progressive phase, such that now she was unable to stand or walk, had lost control of her bladder, needed a permanent catheter and had very little movement of her hands. It might have taken her an hour or so to open the envelope. Instead, in the space of the seconds that Jim needed to open it, it seemed that a lifeline had suddenly emerged from the little brown package. If Elsie was surprised, Jim was even more stunned. He had long since given up any hope of a treatment for Elsie, never mind the possibility of a cure. Did the letter mention cure? No it didn't, but on the other hand, no offer of any treatment had ever been forthcoming since she had gone into this phase of the illness.

Elsie was the first to speak.

"What should we do, love?"

Jim couldn't say anything at first, so Elsie chipped in again …

"I think we should find out about it. Can't do any harm. I mean, I'm not getting anywhere with anything that's been done up till now. I suppose I shouldn't get my hopes up, but I don't think Dr Booth would have contacted us if he didn't think there was something in it."

Jim finally pulled himself back into the present. For so many years, he had watched Elsie gradually weaken, her life become more and more restricted, his own life become more and more tied up in just doing the basic things for her. He had long since given up any hope that she would ever improve, and so his first reactions to the letter were mixed. Of course, something that could help her would be fantastic, but what if it was just another disappointment? There had been others in the earlier phases of her illness … hyperbaric oxygen, interferon, various homeopathic treatments, other refuges of the desperate – none had worked, and although Elsie had accepted each failure with equanimity, each one had been like another spear through Jim, and each time his already depleted stock of optimism had taken another sharp fall. It was almost as though he couldn't bear to tempt fate again. But it wasn't really his decision.

"You're right, love. Of course, it's up to you. But I guess we should find out about it. I think I did read a bit in the paper a few weeks ago about some treatment they were talking about … in Spain, I think it was, but I didn't pay much attention, coz we've heard a lot of it before."

"I know, Jim. But for Dr Booth to actually write to us … Can you tick the 'yes' box on the reply slip and we'll find out what they have to say. Now I guess it's time for my wash, if you don't mind."

The usual morning routine began again, although Elsie somehow looked at her wasted legs with a new curiosity. Would it really be possible that they could work again? What would standing up feel like after five years? Would walking be a thing again? Going out for a coffee … not in a wheelchair? Making up to Jim for all the things he'd had to do for her? Of course he never complained, but she could see that some of the light in his eyes had gone out over the years … he had gotten to be an old man, but he was only forty-eight …

In thirty households across the region, a similar scene was being played out. Letters from a variety of GPs, all with the same text, all with the same reply slip, all met with the same mix of curiosity, hope, anxiety, or fear; sufferers and their partners or carers wrestling with even the suggestion that it might be possible to improve their situation.

Some had taken a bit more note of the Barcelona conference reports in the newspapers and specialist publications for people with MS. Apparently a miraculous cure in mice that had something very like MS. The work done at their university, a quite handsome young doctor somewhat reluctantly photographed with one of the senior professors and a representative from the MS society. Could this letter be something to do with all of that? Were they being chosen to test a miracle cure? What was the catch ... there's always a catch, isn't there? Nothing good ever happens to folk like us, does it? I suppose we should find out a bit more? Shouldn't we? What do you think? I guess things can't get much worse, can they?

The letters from their own GPs were a requirement of the new ethics system for clinical studies in the UK. When Ray was drafting the protocol for the study, he wasn't allowed to apply to contact patients directly. The first step of the process always had to be with the GP who knew which patients in his practice might fit the criteria to be included in the study. The GP also held their names and addresses which could not be accessed by the hospital or university doctors until the individuals gave permission to be contacted.

In preparing his submission therefore, Ray had had to prepare the text of the letters to come from the GPs, then another more detailed letter from the research team which would be sent to those people who had expressed willingness to be contacted. Along with that letter went a very detailed patient information sheet which described the background to the study, who was doing the study and why, what would be involved for the patient and stressing their rights to decline to take part or to withdraw from the study at any time without giving any reason and without any detriment to their regular treatment from their usual medical team, including their GP and any hospital services they might use. Finally, that pack would contain a patient consent sheet which they would sign if they wished to participate and would be countersigned by one of the study team. In addition, the patients would be given the name of an independent doctor, not involved in the study, whom they could contact if they wanted independent advice about any aspect of the study. The system was designed to prevent patients being exploited and to ensure that their personal data was handled in a secure manner.

In Ray's limited experience, and in that of many other investigators, patients often found all of this information given to them, even before they chose to take part in a study, rather daunting. He was sure that a lot of them skimmed over much of the paperwork in the same way that many of us would skim the small print of an insurance policy. However, in this case, it was very important that the patients should understand exactly what they were getting into, particularly since the treatment had never before been tested in humans, and so the effects and side effects were essentially unknown. In this sense Ray's study differed from most drug trials, for example, where early phase studies were done with normal volunteers to ensure that side effects were understood as far as possible before patients were exposed to the drug. Luckily, because the number of patients required for this study was small, then it would be possible to spend as much time as necessary with each volunteer to explain the detail of the study.

Over the next couple of weeks, there was an anxious wait for Ray and his colleagues until responses came back from the GPs. After the three week cut-off, twenty eight positive responses had come in, that is people who were willing to be contacted. Of course, at this stage, all Ray knew about each person was their name, age and address, and that the GP deemed them to have sufficiently severe progressive MS to qualify for the study.

Once all responses were back, packs were sent out to all twenty-eight patients containing the explanatory documents and consent sheets. They were advised that they had up to one week to consider the information and to take whatever advice they might wish before deciding whether to volunteer. The patient information stressed that the treatment would be randomised, so that only half of those taking part would receive the active treatment, and that neither the doctors assessing them nor the patients themselves would know which they had received until the trial period was complete. Ray and his colleagues had spent a great deal of time on the precise wording of the information sheet, particularly as ethics committees tended, correctly in Ray's opinion, to be very fussy about this in order to ensure that patients did not feel coerced into taking part in any study.

Now there was nothing to do but wait for the replies. One in particular was going to be of great interest to Ray, as the information had gone out to one Eric Strother … he was still alive.

CHAPTER 18

The weekend after the information packs had gone out was going to be a long one. Ray decided that a motorbike trip might be a good way to pass the Saturday, at least.

On the Friday afternoon, after his clinic and coffee in the canteen near the animal house where the Peploe's study was still going on but rather eclipsed by the prion study, he made his pitch to Fiona.

"How do you feel about motorbikes?"

"No strong feelings, except that some people seem to ride them like maniacs and you often get to read about them in the local papers on a Monday," she smiled.

"OK, I wondered if you might want to join me for a very sedate ride up to Perthshire tomorrow. The weather forecast is good and I promise that the pilot will be a non-maniac. Helmets will be provided of course and the package includes lunch and sightseeing ..."

"Well, if you put it like that, how can a person refuse?"

"I'll pick you up at eight – only if the sun is shining"

The following day, Ray arrived at Fiona's flat at two minutes to eight. She was already sitting on the doorstep in the sunshine, wearing a climbing jacket and trousers that would serve as protective gear for the bike. Ray handed her the promised helmet and she climbed aboard.

True to his word, he drove fast but steadily. Fiona had never been on a motorbike of this size and power before, but, once she realised that she wasn't going to slide off the back, she actually got to enjoy it quite quickly. It was a whole different experience from a car, that's for sure.

Ray headed up to and beyond Perth, and then got on to one of his favourite stretches of the A9 towards Dunkeld. This part of the road, when the weather was good, reminded him of parts of New England, particularly New Hampshire and Vermont, where he had shared some great Harley-Davidson rides with Liz. However, he did have to admit that the bike he was riding today was significantly more comfortable and easier to steer than the Harley. He also now had the benefit of headsets in the helmets which let him talk to Fiona as they went along. The Hog he'd used in the US was so noisy that, even if he'd had the headsets, they probably wouldn't have been able to hear each other.

"How about some lunch in Dunkeld? They do great stovies at one of the riverside hotels."

"Haute cuisine, eh? You do know how to spoil a girl."

"No, seriously, you'll love it … I hope. It used to be belong to a folk singer, and they still have music a lot of the time."

"OK, sounds good."

They parked across the road by the side of the river Tay and wandered into the hotel. From the outside, it looked in need of some stonework and paint repairs, but inside, the staff were welcoming and, as Ray had promised, there was a music session going on. Around the big square table in the middle of the room were a couple of fiddlers, a flute player and a young lad with a guitar. Fiona noticed that there were quite a few instruments hanging around the walls and Ray caught her eye scanning them.

"Yeah, that's one of the great things about this place for a guy on a motorbike. You don't need to lug your guitar with you, you can just grab one off the wall and play for as long as you like."

"So, are you going to join in then?"

"No, today's strictly a listening day."

They ordered their stovies which again, as promised by Ray, turned out to be really good; somehow being on a motorbike seemed to work up more of an appetite than sitting in a car. Fiona had a shandy, as did Ray, though she was pleased to note that his was about ninety per cent lemonade.

They chatted about all sorts of things, though to his relief, Barcelona didn't come up. He discovered that Fiona had been married once, briefly, that she was a keen climber (her ex-husband had been too, and had gone off in search of other peaks, was how she put it), and that she had spent some time in South America, before ending up in her current job where she had been for about four years. She was easy to talk to and they managed to pass almost an hour without a mention of work. Suddenly Ray fell quiet, and Fiona sensed that something was not right.

"What's the matter?" she said.

"Oh, just that Allan Taylor song, it always gets me." Fiona then noticed that the young guitarist had begun to sing. "It's called 'Roll on the Day', and it's probably a better description of COPD than you get from any of the text books …" said Ray, falling quiet again.

As the dawn comes creeping, roll on the day,
Another night not sleeping, roll on the day,
Roll on the morning, roll on the day,
I hear the old man softly praying, roll on the day
Praying for another day, roll on the day,
But when it comes, it wastes away, roll on the day
Roll on the morning, roll on the day,
I hear the old man softly praying, roll on the day
Every night you fight for breath, roll on the day,
Hurts so bad, you wish for death, roll on the day
Roll on the morning, roll on the day,
I hear the old man softly praying, roll on the day

"He wrote it for a man called Henry Johnson, but it's about my dad and all the rest of them, too. Oh, my dad would tell you it's all self-inflicted, his own fault for smoking thirty a day, but no matter what, it's a shitty hand that some people get dealt, and there's nothing that we can do for them."

"I'm sorry, Ray." She took his hand gently.

He went on. "To see us out there in Barcelona, patting each other on the back, telling each other what a great job we're doing for humanity … but the reality is we're only scratching the surface, and there's so many folk that we can do little or nothing for …"

"I know that, Ray. I saw a lot of pretty grim stuff in some of the more remote parts of South America, and I guess that's a picnic compared to Africa and other places. But you can't beat yourself up too much. You're on the verge of something fantastic. OK, it's not for COPD, but maybe their time will come too. I know it might not be quick enough for your dad, but who's to say? I mean, where were we a year ago with the MS story?"

"Of course, you're right. Anyway I shouldn't spoil a sunny day …"

With that, the fiddlers and flute player burst into a lively version of 'Stan Chapman's Jig', accompanied by the young guitarist who had now gone into jazz/swing mode. He was using chords he must have learned from the playing of Peerie Willie, the late, great Shetland guitarist who had developed this style. As ever, Ray's spirits lifted almost immediately.

"Amazing thing, music, isn't it?" he said.

"Mainly for those who really feel it," smiled Fiona.

After the tune finished, they thanked the youngsters for their playing, left some money at the bar to give the musicians a drink, and headed back into the sun. They sat down by the riverbank for a while and the chat eventually did swing back to work.

"You know, one of the things I'm really excited about with this trial is that one of the patients who expressed an interest is the young guy that set me off on this MS research thing in the first place. To be honest, I thought he would have been dead by now, but maybe I should have known better. His wife cares for him better than any professional nurse, even though I suspect it's just about killing her. I'll be interested to see him again if he does decide to go ahead. The only thing that makes me slightly uneasy about the whole study is Carter."

"Why is that?" Fiona looked puzzled.

"I can't really put my finger on it. I always just have the feeling with him that somehow it's not about the patients or the advancement of medicine, but more about the advancement of him and maybe even about money … Having said that, we wouldn't be where we are today without him, as CJ might have said."

"What?" said Fiona.

"Never mind, *Reggie Perrin* reference. Probably not your thing, but I like these old TV programmes now and again." Fiona looked none the wiser.

"Anyway, we should probably get home," said Ray, pulling on his leathers again.

The ride back was bit tricky with the sun lower in the sky, but, probably sooner than he would have liked, they were back at Fiona's steps.

"You're welcome to come up, if you want." It was part statement, part question.

"Thanks Fiona, but I think I'll get off. I'm going to see the old man, maybe stay the night with him tonight. Another time though?"

"Sure, that would be good. You're always welcome. Hope you find him not so bad. See you Monday." she said, as she kissed him lightly on the cheek and skipped off up the stairs.

'You fool,' he said quietly to himself. 'You should have gone in.' But to be honest, since being with Liz again in Barcelona, he was not sure where his emotions lay. And he had really planned to see his dad tonight and tomorrow, even before Allan Taylor's song had reminded him how important that was.

He headed off via his flat to pick up an overnight bag.

Chapter 19

Monday found Ray at his desk, awaiting the post, although he knew it was a bit early yet for replies to the study. His old man had been, much as ever, pleased to see him but desperately breathless, and they'd both had a pretty disturbed night. Ray thought that they should be looking at some overnight care for him, but his dad wouldn't hear of it yet. "There's others as needs it more than me," was all he would say.

Although the replies to the study invitations would come by regular post, Ray thought he better look through his e-mail first. Since the Barcelona conference, and the paper which had come out in *Nature*, his inbox had become an altogether more international affair, with messages of congratulation from various colleagues, loads of queries from other clinicians and scientists, and inevitably desperate questions from various sufferers of MS around the world. To begin with, he had tried to reply individually to these, but the volume of requests was such that he had to put out an automated response advising people that clinical trials were ongoing, and that, if/when benefits in humans could be demonstrated, the treatment would become available to people through their own doctors.

He also looked at his diary, as he realised that he would need to schedule blocks of time for recruitment/induction interviews with patients and thereafter for all the follow-up visits that the study would involve over the next year. As expected, it was immediately apparent that there would be no holidays to be had, as it was important to have continuity of examination protocols. He would therefore have to see all the patients himself at monthly intervals, which would basically fill up his week, once added to his existing clinical duties and the admittedly small amount of time that he had to devote to the Peploe's study. To be honest, it didn't really look as though that was going to come up with anything positive, or if it did, it would only be a minor effect, but of course the study still had to be completed and the full analysis done.

At about 11.30, he heard the pigeon holes in the corridor where the mail was delivered being filled and stepped out to see if there had been any response. Somewhat to his surprise, sixteen envelopes were in his section. He took them into the office and began systematically recording which study numbers had responded and what each response said. There were fifteen positives, people who wanted to further discuss and probably take part, and one negative. Not bad for the first day, thought Ray. The negative response came with a short note attached:

Dear Dr Shepherd,
Thank you for sending the information about this study. We are pleased to hear that more work is going on to find a treatment for MS and wish you well with the study. However, after considering your offer carefully, Susan has had so many disappointments in the past that she feels she couldn't risk it again. She has made her peace with God and accepted the inevitable, that she will be with Him soon. She is at peace with her condition. We hope that God will bless your study and that you will find success in due course. Our prayers will be with you and your team.
With blessings
Charles and Susan McGregor

Ray had mixed feelings about that one. He wasn't religious himself in the conventional sense though he did feel that he was quite a spiritual person. If that really was Susan's position, then who was he to question it? Although having seen the response of the mice in the study, he couldn't help feeling that they might be denying themselves a great opportunity.

He immediately drafted a note for Susan's GP, just to keep her in the picture and to thank her for sending out the initial query, and included the note in the reply to the GP, for information. He then deleted all of Susan's information from the study database, as was required in the case of non-participants.

Most of the other replies had simply completed the forms which included a question on when a visit from the study doctor would be convenient. However, one other one had a short letter enclosed, also from a Susan.

Dear Dr Shepherd

Thank you for your letter. Eric would be delighted to be considered for the study. We wondered initially if you were the same Doctor Shepherd that came to see us a while back when Eric had an infection, but then we saw your picture in the paper and Dr Ahmed confirmed to us that you had gone on to great things – no surprise to us of course! We look forward to seeing you soon. You'll find Eric much as you last saw him, though he's a bit weaker still and his breathing and swallowing are not so good now,

Best wishes

Eric and Susan Strother

Ray's heart lifted to know that Eric was still alive, although swallowing and breathing difficulties were ominous signs. It sounded as though if something wasn't done, Eric would soon be dead.

Over the next three days, more replies came in until the final count was available. Of the twenty-eight sent out, twenty-six had agreed to be considered for the study and two had declined. One of these was Susan McGregor who had made her peace with God and accepted her fate. The other, who also included a covering letter, said that she had considered the offer very carefully but realised that she might be randomised to receive the placebo or dummy treatment. She felt that she didn't have the strength to undergo all the necessary examinations and scans, particularly if she was allocated the placebo, and therefore had to decline. Ray wondered if all the others who had replied would have read the information so carefully and would realise that was a possibility. That was something he would have to discuss with them in the first visit.

He began to schedule in the visits according to people's preferences. In reality, most of them had expressed no particular preference for the time of the visit, because, as Ray thought grimly, they weren't going anywhere. One or two of them did have days out at respite centres or similar, but most were largely bed or wheelchair bound and rarely, if ever, left home. They were the people with the most severe stages of the progressive form of the disease.

At the beginning of the following week, Ray began his round

of home visits to brief people on the study, and where appropriate, to carry out a standard physical examination, including an assessment of function using a couple of standardised scales, and to book people in for their baseline MRI scans. He recorded all the data on an interactive tablet computer, which also allowed him to schedule scans into slots that had been pre-arranged with Paul and set aside for the study.

Visit number four took him up the familiar path to the well-tended house where Eric and Susan lived. It seemed eons since he was last here and the weather wasn't quite so good today. However, he did feel that he was coming as the bearer of some good tidings, he hoped, so his mood was a bit more upbeat that when he last left the house.

Susan answered his ring and seemed genuinely pleased to see him. He thought she looked even more tired than when he last saw her, though maybe that was just the duller day.

"Dr Shepherd. How great to see you. Eric's been looking forward to this, you know. We were so excited to read about your study in the papers and then when we got the letter. Come through. Would you like some tea?"

"No thanks, but some water would be good," said Ray. He'd already found that his throat dried up a bit when going through his long discussion with patients and their relatives or carers, partly due to all the speaking, partly emotion, and partly because most of them kept their rooms incredibly warm – being immobile, he guessed they felt the cold a lot.

"Hello, Mr Strother, how are you?"

"Please call me Eric," he said, weakly. Ray thought that he had shrunk even more since he last saw him. "I'm hoping you've got a cure for me. I'm not getting any stronger, you know."

Susan brought the water through, together with some tea for herself in an ordinary cup and some for Eric in a specially adapted cup.

"Do you mind if I stay?" she said. "Eric doesn't."

"No, absolutely. That would be great. I'd prefer to talk to you both anyway, if you're happy with that. I know we sent you some information, but if you don't mind, I'm going to take you through all of it again, just to make sure you know what you're signing up for, if you do decide to go ahead."

Over the next twenty minutes or so, Ray went patiently through all the background, the design of the study, what would be involved for Eric, etc. Then he went over the three most important points again.

"There're three things I really want to stress before you make your final decision. One is that this is a randomised study, so you might be allocated to a dummy treatment and neither you nor I will know if that's what you've had until the study is finished. The second is that there are no guarantees that this treatment will work. We know that it has worked in mice, but no human studies have been done so far."

"So it's like I'm the guinea pig … mouse … guinea pig … get it doc?" Eric laughed weakly.

"Well I'm glad you've still got your sense of humour, Eric. The third thing is that, for the same reason, we don't know what side effects it might have. The agent that we're injecting is like the thing that causes new variant CJD, human mad cow disease, so it could make things worse."

"Listen, doc, Susan and I have discussed all that," said Eric. "I realise I might not get the active treatment, but if it does work, and if I'm in the dummy arm of the trial, is there a chance I'll get it at the end? "

"For sure, Eric. The trial will be monitored by an independent committee, and if they see that the treatment is safe and effective, then they have the power to stop the trial early and give active treatment to everyone who has had the dummy."

"As far as effects and side effects are concerned …" said Eric, "… look at me. I'm one step from the knacker's, so I'll go for the Brian Cox option."

Ray looked puzzled.

"Come on, doc," said Eric. "Keep up … Professor Brian Cox, astrophysicist, television's star scientist, previously drummer in D-ream, main hit 'Things Can Only Get Better'.

"I see," said Ray, still not quite sure that he was on the same wavelength.

"You need to spend more time watching TV and less dreaming up cures for folk like me …" laughed Eric.

"I guess I do. Can I get you to sign the consent form then and I'll countersign to confirm that we've had this discussion?"

"My signature is a proxy. Susan will do it for me and I'll make the mark of Zorro beside it, if that's OK?"

"Fine," said Ray. "Now that's done, I need to ask you some baseline questions and do a full examination. All of this will then be repeated every month. I'll also get you booked in for an MRI."

"Oh joy," said Eric. "I hate that thing. You know the first time I had it done, when I was first diagnosed, was on a Saturday morning. Being in the tube with all the clattering and whirring was bad enough, but the worst thing was that they put on Radio Two through the headphones and it was slightly too loud – just enough to be painful. I had to suffer it for about half an hour."

"Don't worry," said Ray. "The scanners have moved on a bit since then … and so has the DJ, I think."

Once all the paperwork and the examination were done, Ray packed up the study file.

"I'll arrange for you to get the injection in a few days, and I'll see you again in a month."

"Great, doc. Thanks for getting me into the study – much appreciated, even if it doesn't work."

"Not me to thank, Eric. It was your GP who put you forward. Data protection wouldn't let me contact you directly."

"Big Brother nearly gets in the way of helping people again," said Eric, but Ray declined to take the bait.

"See you in a month, cheerio. Remember, once the study starts, if you've any worries or concerns, please contact us, even if it's not time for your monthly review. We'll also keep your GP and Dr Ahmed in the picture."

CHAPTER 20

The scene at Eric's house more or less repeated itself at a whole range of places over the next couple of weeks. Ray was made aware, even more than before, of how this illness was no respecter of social class or income. He found himself in small council flats where there was barely room to move around the patient to complete the examination, through to large comfortable mansions in the posh parts of town. He spoke to people who had been (it was always 'had been') lawyer, shop assistant, bus driver, teacher, dance instructor, musician, farmer and bank clerk, among others. Often he saw the look of desperation and fear in the eyes of people, more often the carers or partners of the patients. It was as if most of them hardly dared to think that any improvement could be possible, and dreaded both the unknown effects and side effects of this treatment. Most accepted that they might not receive the active ingredient. Many were anxious about the mechanics of the study. Would the doctors always visit to do the assessments? How would they get to the hospital for the scans? What if they were allocated to the dummy treatment? Would there be a chance to get the active thing later, if it worked of course?

Although Ray had basically to go through the standard spiel with everyone, it was never quite the same twice, and the clinician in him enjoyed the challenge of making sure that people understood what was being said to them and exactly what the trial might mean, good and bad. He knew that in clinical medicine, most of the difficulties that led to complaints and dissatisfied patients were due to breakdowns in communication between clinicians, patients and their loved ones, rather than to actual clinical errors. In a clinical trial such as this, it was almost more important to get this explanatory phase right, since he also knew, as a researcher, that the worst thing was to get the patient into the trial only to drop out after a few weeks, when their data would then become useless and the whole process would be further delayed. So he took his time. It didn't always go as planned though.

On day seven, he set off to one of those addresses in the posh part of town. As he swung through the gates and between some well-tended shrubs, a large red sandstone house with bay windows and some mock Grecian pillars either side of the door came into view. He had recognised the name on this reply slip as Lady Grenville-Smythe. Her husband was something in the City of London and Ray had heard his name mentioned in connection with various company takeovers and so on. Although he had noted her date of birth, it was still a shock to him when the door was opened by a fresh-faced athletic youngish man, early forties at most, wearing a light blue shirt, chinos and desert boots.

"Hello, you must be Dr Shepherd. I'm Colin Grenville-Smythe. Pleased to meet you."

Ray wasn't quite sure how he was supposed to address a lord of the realm, an institution he didn't really believe in anyway, so he adopted his usual stance and didn't add anything in the way of a salutation.

"Yes. I've come about the trial. Your wife returned the paperwork and this visit is to explain things a bit more to help her with her decision about whether to take part."

"Splendid. You'd better come through. Will you take tea? Samantha is in the conservatory, this way."

"No tea, thanks, though a glass of water would be nice."

Grenville-Smythe pressed an old-fashioned button on the wall and shortly thereafter a young maid appeared and the order for water and tea was dispatched.

"Darling, this is Dr Shepherd from the university. He's come about the study."

"We're very excited about it, you know," he whispered to Ray, as they went through.

Samantha was propped up in a chair with a view across the lawn to the herbaceous border against the far wall. A croquet pitch was set out on the lawn. Some bird feeders close to the window were stocked with a mixture of fat balls, peanuts and nyjer seed and there were a few small birds helping themselves. The conservatory looked to be a place where she spent a lot of time.

She was tall, Ray guessed almost six feet, late thirties, and had the cheekbone structure of an aristocrat. She had long blonde hair which surrounded her otherwise fragile-looking face. Her skin somehow seemed almost transparent. Ray guessed that when she was younger, she would have cut an athletic figure on the lacrosse or hockey field (more likely lacrosse), and he could see her in full hacking gear, riding her horse along a lane in the Cotswolds, or skiing at some expensive resort in the alps or the US. Not now though. The familiar picture of wasted muscles, odd posture of her legs and possibly a urine bag by the side of her chair gave the game away.

"You see how it is, Dr Shepherd," she began. "Time was when the birds would be in the cage and we'd be looking in at them. Now it's the other way. These finches and great tits can fly off whenever they want, and I often get the feeling that they're looking in at me wondering why I'm not joining them. Of course, Colin's been wonderful. We've tried everything, you know, been for every quack therapy around, but nothing has had any lasting effect. We're hoping that your treatment will be different."

"Well, thanks first of all for returning the reply slip for more information. My job today is to take you through the details of the study, and once you have all the information, if you decide you still want to go ahead, to carry out some of the baseline assessments." As he spoke, he realised that the conservatory would be totally unsuitable for examination purposes, but he decided to leave that issue until later. Just then the maid arrived with water for him, in a crystal glass, of course, and tea for the lord and lady, Samantha's in her specially adapted cup.

Once the maid had left, he began his now familiar routine of explaining the background and mechanics of the study. He had reached the point about randomisation when Lord Grenville-Smythe intervened.

"Yes, thank you, Dr Shepherd. We have read the paperwork which I have to say was very clear and concise. We understand that the trial has been designed in a particular way, but you can see the situation that Samantha is in. We have to ensure that she gets the active treatment. Time is of the essence." The Old Etonian was clearly a man used to getting his own way.

Ray was equally firm in his explanation. "Unfortunately, there is no way to guarantee that. As I explained, the allocation has to be random and both the patient and doctor are blinded to the allocation until the trial is complete. We do have an independent trials monitoring committee who will monitor all the data as the trial goes along and they will know who has had active treatment and who has had the placebo. If the active treatment proves to be effective, they have the power to stop the trial at an earlier stage and all patients who had previously had the placebo will be offered the active treatment then."

"Look here, old chap," said Colin, reverting somewhat to type, "you can see the situation we're in here. Samantha was a reserve for the Olympic dressage team only a few years ago and now she's trapped in here and barely mobile. To be honest, it's putting a great strain on both of us, even though we have excellent nurses and so on."

Ray saw Samantha nod weakly as tears welled up in her eyes.

Colin carried on. "Money's no object for us. Dammit, we've been all over the world trying out every new treatment that comes out. Of course none of them have worked, but yours seems to have more to it than most. We'd be happy to pay for the treatment outside of the trial. I'm sure we could probably even fund some other people less financially fortunate than ourselves to have treatments too. Wouldn't that be a good idea?"

Ray had to tread carefully here. They were obviously a very loving couple. Ray's natural instinct was not to have much sympathy for the wealthy; years of indoctrination from his dad about the injustice of inequality had assured that. But he could see that in some ways their wealth, while it could partly minimise physical discomfort for Samantha, probably accentuated their feelings of impotence in the face of this illness. No matter what she had done in the past, she couldn't buy her way out of what she was becoming, nor could Colin do that for her.

"I understand your distress," said Ray. "I think all of us would feel the same in your situation. However, as things stand, this is not officially a 'treatment' yet. Until we have done this trial, and maybe others, we don't actually know whether it will work or not, whether it might be safe or have terrible side effects and so on. Until that work is done, I wouldn't be allowed to prescribe the treatment for you, so the only way to access it is through the study. Within the study, if we didn't have random allocation of active treatment and placebo and so-called blinding of the doctors and patients as to which they have received, then we would be open to possible biases that might give us false results from the study. It's not a question of money, and although your offer of funding a number of treatments is very kind, I hope you'll see that's not possible at this stage."

With that, the slight welling of tears turned into a full-blown flood, and Samantha began to shake uncontrollably. Colin rushed over to hug her, and Ray instinctively moved nearer them too. Although much of medical students' teaching these days was about maintaining professional distances, Ray always found proximity to be a good thing.

Eventually, Samantha calmed a little and flicked her head up to look out at the birds again.

"I hear what you're saying, Dr Shepherd, and at one level it makes sense. I suppose I should go into the trial. There's a fifty-fifty chance I'll get the active treatment at the beginning and, if not, I might get it later, if it seems to work for others. But you know, I don't think I've got the strength to get through it with that amount of uncertainty hanging over me, and over Colin. I keep telling him he should move on, you know. There're plenty of young fillies out there who would bite his hand off if he so much as looked their way. But, contrary to what you might read about bankers, they're not all unprincipled bastards. If you knew what he's put up with and what he's done for me over the past few years …" Her voice tailed off.

"I'm sorry that I can't do this any other way," said Ray. "There's no need to make an absolutely final decision right now. I suggest that you take a bit more time to think about it and maybe let me know your final decision in the next forty-eight hours or so. If you do decide to go ahead, it's no problem at all for me to come back and do the baseline assessments etc. We are hoping that this trial will be complete within fifteen months or so, and it may be that the treatment will become prescribable then, so even if you decide not to go ahead at the moment, you should keep in touch with your own doctor for any developments."

"Thank you, Dr Shepherd. We'll take your advice and let you know. Colin, would you see Dr Shepherd out?"

As they left the conservatory, Ray noticed that she was staring at a goldfinch on the nyjer seed again.

"Yes, thank you, Dr Shepherd," said Colin as they reached the front door again. "You see the position we're in. I suppose you see it all the time, but when it's one's own, well, one just wants to do what's best. She won't go for it, you know. Are you a married man yourself?"

"No, single, at the moment, anyway. Samantha is very lucky to have you ..." he said, in the absence of anything more sensible to say.

"Luck's one thing she doesn't have," and with that, the lord turned back into his grand, sad, house.

CHAPTER 21

By the time Ray had completed his twenty-six home visits, twenty-four people had signed up to be randomised. Lady Samantha had contacted him a couple of days after his visit to confirm that she was not going to take part. The other refusal could not have been more different.

Mr Leonard Glass, 25/2 Dingwall Court.

Ray had driven past the large grey tower block often enough, but realised that, until now, he had never really looked carefully at it. It sure was grim. As he made his way into the grubby main door, two wasted looking youngsters wearing the uniform of baggy trousers and baseball cap huddled in the corner of the hallway. Ray reckoned that they had probably just been shooting up, and, while he saw them, he wasn't sure if they had registered his presence at all.

Praying that the lift was working, he made his way toward it and pressed the 'up' button. As the door opened, he wondered if taking the lift was such a good idea after all. There was a pile of rubbish lying in the right-hand corner and the whole thing smelt like the worst public toilet imaginable. Dingwall Court was one of those tower blocks built in the optimism of the sixties, no doubt launched with some sort of public information film describing the wonderful life the residents were going to have in their little palaces in the sky, served by the fast efficient elevator and with views across the city to the open countryside. Life would be a beach compared with the old, discredited city tenements. Sadly, the reality turned out to be somewhat different. A combination of economic and social decline together with the ravages of drugs and the crime that went with them had turned the dream into a nightmare, where the lifts probably only worked one day in three and older residents who had moved in during those heady days were now trapped in the small apartments, afraid of the pit bulls and their owners that roamed the precinct.

Anyway, it was either the smelly lift or a twenty-five floor hike, so he took the risk on the technology. Eventually, the old thing juddered to a halt on the twenty-fifth floor and he made his way to the door of flat two. A quick check of the doorbell suggested it was not working, so he knocked as loudly as he could. In a moment he heard two deadbolts going and the door opened a little, restrained by a chain. A boy of about twelve or so peeked through the gap.

"Hello, I'm Dr Shepherd. I've come to see Mr Glass."

"That's me dad. Just a minute." With that, the door closed again while the boy loosened the chain and then reopened to reveal a thin lad in grey jeans and a blue pullover. "I'm Sammy. Me dad's in the bedroom," he said, indicating that Ray should follow him.

"Is your mum in?" said Ray.

"Me mum went about a year ago with me sister. It's only me and him now. I don't think he's going to be pleased to see you, but you'd better go through."

Ray headed on into the bedroom, where a thin, stubbly man with slightly matted hair lay on top of the bed. There was a small bedside cabinet with an ashtray full of several fat cigarettes. Ray recognised the smell instantly.

"Hello, Mr Glass. I'm Dr Shepherd. I've come about the study. You know, you sent us a letter the other week. I've come to explain a bit more about it."

"Don't know what I was thinking about. You're wasting your time. By the way, you can call me Lenny, most folk do."

"Bad day, then?" queried Ray.

"Bad day, bad week, bad year, bad fuckin' life …that's me … Do you mind if I have one of my smokes? Dr Richards, she knows about it, doesn't fully approve, I think, but doesn't stop me either. It's good stuff, I get it direct from the Hamster and Sammy rolls them for me. I don't let him smoke them, though," he added quickly.

"The Hamster?" said Ray.

"The local nutter who runs the business. Nasty bit of work. Doesn't hassle me though, on account of me being a cripple … and I always pay up."

"I hadn't heard of him. They do say that hash is good for MS though. I guess we'll be prescribing it one day. How long have you had MS?" said Ray, hoping to prolong the conversation a bit.

"Ten years, about. I was a scaffie, you know. One day I fell off the back of the truck. I'd had a half of shandy at lunchtime so they said I was drunk and sacked me on the spot. By the time your lot figured out I had this, I was too late for compensation, disability and so on. The wife was here then, so she kept things going. She buggered off last year though, took the daughter with her, but Sammy wanted to stay with me. Can't say I blame her really. I mean she wasn't getting much here, if you get my drift – his face almost broke into a crooked smile. She comes by once a month or so. Always very civil, but she's got a new man now. Good luck to her."

"What about Sammy, how do you manage him?" said Ray.

"Other way round … he manages me. He's a good lad but I'm just a waste of space now. He does things for me that 12 year olds shouldn't have to, but that's the only way we get by."

"Do you have any help?" said Ray.

"The MS nurses come in a couple of times a week, but they don't have long. Old Mrs Singh across the hall is good to us too – drops in food from time to time and so on. But she's eighty-two, so I'm not sure how long that can go on."

"Do you want me to tell you a bit more about the study?" said Ray

"Nah, son. Don't worry. The day I sent the form back I was a bit high you know – maybe too many of these," he said, nodding towards the joints. "It's not for me. What if it had some horrible side effect, sent me bonkers or something? They might take Sammy away … it's touch and go anyway… they don't like him missing school. No, if I can just get through another couple of years until Sammy can be on his own, that'll do me."

"Is there anything else that I can do for you at the moment?" Ray realised that there was no point in trying to push the study any further.

"No. Good luck with it though. I hope some other bugger might benefit from it. Could you just tell the lad he's doing a good job when you're going out? Dr Richards always does that and he likes to hear it."

"No problem, Lenny. You take care."

CHAPTER 22

Ray moved some of the chairs around in his newly reconfigured office. Two large lockable cabinets had been brought in to store the patient folders from the study. Everything had to be meticulously filed and indexed, with copies of many of the documents also held at the hospital research and development office. Just as the animal studies were closely regulated by the Government inspectors, human studies were controlled by the MHRA, the Medicine and Healthcare Regulatory Authority. Their inspectors could turn up at any time and ask to review any of the paperwork, interview the staff involved in the trial and so on. If they felt that standards were not being maintained, they could advise changes, and in more extreme cases they could stop the study or even close down the whole research group.

Having all this stuff in the room certainly made it cosier, and when his colleagues arrived with their coffee cups and buns, they had to squeeze into a small corner.

"Thanks for coming, everyone. Can I first introduce Emilie Sanchez? She is the new research nurse who's going to be working on the study. She actually started last week but this has been her first chance to meet folks."

Emilie had previously worked in the neurology ward and had a lot of clinical experience. She was a small woman, immaculately dressed but giving the air of great practicality. She now had a young baby so this job, working part time, suited her perfectly. Her husband, whom she had met in her home country of Brazil, was an accountant and between them they could juggle the childcare pretty well. During the previous week, Ray had had several sessions with Emilie, familiarising her with the trial, getting all her paperwork in order; for example signing confidentiality agreements which bound her to secrecy about patient data and about the progress of the trial, all pretty standard stuff, but essential before she could begin to work on it.

The others smiled and shook hands. Around the table were

Andy Turner, Paul Schmidt, Ray, and Sarah Simpson, who although she was not directly involved in this study, unless terrible things happened and post-mortems became necessary, nevertheless wanted to keep appraised of what was going on. Carter was not present, he was off in London, examining for the Royal College.

"I thought we should meet today as I've now completed all the pre-treatment clinical assessments and Paul has almost completed all the scans. No analysis of them is being done at this stage; they're being stored and will be analysed when the study is complete. We've ended up with twenty-four patients to randomise. I think Andy would have liked twenty-six (Andy nodded), but two of the ones I visited decided not to take part. The rest all seem committed though and if we can get twenty completers that should be enough. We're going to start the injections later this week – Emilie will be doing that, and the anonymised vials are all prepared. As you know, we're planning to bring the patients into hospital for the injections. We'll actually infuse the stuff through a drip over thirty minutes, and we plan to keep them in for twenty-four hours afterwards, just in case they have allergic reactions or anything else. As most of you know, previous studies where foreign proteins had been injected for other purposes have occasionally caused severe allergic reactions or anaphylaxis, which could be fatal if we weren't around to administer adrenaline and resuscitate if necessary. We're going to use three isolation rooms in the Infection Unit so we'll get them all done over eight to ten days. Once the trial is running, they'll be given a mobile contact number through which they'll be able to access either Emilie or me any time of the day or night, in case they have any queries. Paul's block-booked research sessions at the MRI suite for the two-monthly scans for the whole of the year, so I think we're well set up."

"That sounds good, Ray," Sarah was the first to speak. "How did you find the patients on your home visits?"

"Clinically, they're mostly fairly similar: all wheelchair bound, most with very little movement in their arms, a few with permanent partial blindness from previous optic neuritis. The interesting thing about visiting them at home, though, is that you get to see their social circumstances. They're very variable. I've been in some fancy places and some pretty poor tower block apartments. The community nursing services seem to be all pretty stretched, so most of them are reliant on family members or paid live-in carers to look after them. They're all pretty excited about the study, although most of them, and particularly the carers, are anxious that they might be disappointed again. I guess they've all been through false hope before. Part of Emilie's role will be to act as a 'friend' to them through the study. She'll also have access to the ward, so it means that if they have to be admitted for whatever reason, they'll see a familiar face around." Ray knew from previous experience that a good research nurse was worth his or her weight in gold in terms of keeping people on board with a study through the inevitable challenges that would come up.

"I think it's going well so far," added Paul. "We've managed to get them through the scans with no real problems. Some of them hadn't had an MRI for years, so they were pleasantly surprised with the new generation scanner."

MRI scanning required the person to be put inside a large magnet, the components of the machine then moving around as the images were collected. The early scanners had been very noisy and clunky, but also very claustrophobic as the person had to lie within a coffin-sized tube for the duration of the scan, which could be half an hour or more. A certain proportion of people couldn't be scanned at all, due to panic at the thought of enclosure. However, the new scanners were less daunting and certainly quieter and smoother. Paul was confident that they would get the patients to come back at two-monthly intervals without too much trouble.

Andy spoke next. "The randomisation is all done, the solutions are ready, and the randomisation key is stored securely, so you shouldn't need to see me for the next year, unless we need to break the code early. If you don't mind, I'll buzz off now as the Professor of Surgery is after me for some data."

They all looked knowingly. "Well, he's not a man to be tangled with. You might need his services one day," laughed Ray, and Andy took his leave.

"How about the mice?" said Sarah, looking at Ray. "Are you getting inundated with e-mail about giving talks abroad and so on?"

"Well, I'm certainly getting a lot of e-mail, but I think the boss will be doing most of the foreign trips. For the next year, I'm going to be tied to the town here and on the end of this phone." Ray put on a look of mock disgust, but actually he was quite happy with that division of labour. Carter got to do the grandstanding, while Ray got to see the patients, hopefully as they improved. "Some of the interviews have been interesting though … the difference between the tabloid hacks and the folk at BBC World Service, for example. The BBC folk seem to be really well informed. I guess a lot of them have scientific training. The tabloid guys, well that's a whole different business … they do have a certain skill with words though and some of the headlines have been great. I particularly liked 'M-iracul-ouse!' and 'Mad Mice take up their Beds and Walk!" I suppose that guy must double as the religious affairs correspondent, if they have one of them in the red tops."

The rest of them then spent the next few minutes trying to come up with their own headlines, but couldn't improve on these ones. Ray sensed that the serious business of the meeting was over, and suggested that they reconvene again in a few weeks when they might have some more to discuss. In the meantime, Emilie would get on with arrangements for each of the admissions while Ray had another batch of e-mails to deal with before going off to the ward to see some of his regular clinical patients. As he headed over there about an hour later there was a spring in his step, although, catching sight of the animal house out of the corner of his eye, he realised that he was missing working with Fiona on this study. He didn't even have authorisation to enter the animal house any more as his involvement in that study was now complete and his keypass had lapsed. He made a mental note to call her soon.

.

CHAPTER 23

Emilie and Ray walked over to the ward, passing by the virology lab to pick up the precious cargo, vial numbers one to three for the study. Ray was excited about seeing the patients coming in today, two women and one man. Could one of them be the first person to have their progressive MS reversed? Time would tell.

The nurses in the Infection Unit greeted Emilie and Ray professionally enough, but with a degree of coolness. He sensed that they didn't like their beds being taken up for this clinical trial at a time when they were particularly busy with the usual eclectic mix of infectious disease patients. Sadly, in recent years, an increasing proportion of their work was with drug addicts who had severe forms of hepatitis, HIV infection or a myriad of other infections, often due to shooting up with dirty equipment into veins that were wrecked from multiple previous shots. Anyway, Ray reminded himself that he would need to be particularly nice to the nurses here, and hoped that after this first round of injections, the patients wouldn't need further inpatient stays during the trial.

"Your patients are in rooms twenty-three, twenty-five and twenty-seven," the ward clerk informed them. "They're all here already, raring to go," she smiled.

Ray and Emilie headed into room twenty-three first. He recognised Amanda Trail and her partner Joseph. Amanda was her mid-thirties, had been born in the south of England, and had met Joseph when she was working in Uganda twelve years before. Joseph was a lay preacher but also trained as an engineer and they had moved to the UK when her period as a volunteer in a small school was over. Joseph had managed to find work as an engineer and gained full British citizenship, without them marrying. Ray wasn't entirely sure how all that worked. However, they had told him during the home visit that her symptoms had begun not long after they came back to the UK; the usual story, mild and intermittent at first but then gradually progressive. They both had a very strong Christian faith which seemed to have sustained them through the usual setbacks and sadnesses, but he could see from both of them that they were desperate for this trial to work.

"Hello, both of you," said Ray. "Can I introduce Emilie, first of all? Emilie is a research nurse who is going to be working with us throughout this trial and she and I will be your main points of contact. Before you go home, we'll give you our mobile numbers that you can call at any time if you have questions or concerns. Anyway, I should have asked you first of all how you're feeling today, Amanda?"

"Ok, thanks, just the usual. I think the patient transport had had all its springs removed, and it took a while to get here as they had a few pickups to make, so I feel a bit battered, but ready to go."

"That's great," said Ray. "What we're going to do, actually Emilie is going to do it, is to set up a drip in your arm and we'll run the solution in over about half an hour. Emilie will stay with you for the first hour, when she'll be checking your blood pressure regularly and keeping a general eye on things. If you feel anything unusual during that time or during the next day while you're here, let the nurses know immediately. As you know, this is a brand new treatment so we don't really know what to expect in the way of side effects. However, because it's a biological solution, you might develop an allergic reaction, so if you feel your skin or eyes getting itchy, or you feel at all wheezy or get any dizziness, then you must let us know. The main times when you might get that kind of effect would be within the first hour, or about twelve to sixteen hours later; that's what we call a delayed reaction. Hopefully, none of that will happen, but we need to be careful. We'll be doing this with everyone in the study."

"That's fine, doc. Do I get to meet any of the other patients in the study?"

"No, we need to keep you separate to avoid any cross-contamination – sorry, that's a terrible word – but you get what I mean." As he said it, Ray was acutely aware of how they'd got here in the first place. He didn't want all the patients in the same cage …

"Message received and understood. When do we get going? Can I see it?"

"You mean the treatment? Sure, that's it," said Ray, as Emilie withdrew the small vial from the plain box with the study name and number and held it up to the light. Joseph and Amanda looked at it with almost reverence, and some incredulity.

"Doesn't look like much," said Amanda.

"Neither did the loaves and fishes …" said Joseph, the first time he had spoken since they entered the room "… but He fed the five thousand with them. It doesn't take much to make a miracle."

"Well, let's see," said Ray. "We'll just have to take this as it comes. Have you any questions for me just now before we get started."

"Only one," said Amanda. "Will you have the second dance with me once I'm on my feet again? Joseph gets the first one, of course."

"OK, that's a deal, but I have to warn you, I'm no Patrick Swayze."

During the next few minutes, Ray made light conversation with both of them while Emilie prepared the infusion, drew up the solution from the vial, injected it into the 100 ml bag on the drip stand and expertly slipped a cannula into a vein in Amanda's forearm.

"OK, here we go," she said to Amanda as she hooked up the drip after taking a baseline blood pressure measurement and writing the result on the patient record sheet. Amanda and Joseph both looked at the little bag of fluid, and then at each other. There was a gleam of hope in both their eyes that Ray suspected had not been there for some time. He left them to it.

An hour later, he popped his head around the door of room twenty-three again.

"How are we going?" he said.

"Fine," said Emilie. "All the measurements have been stable; no sign of any allergic reaction and the infusion is complete. I'll take the drip down, but I'll leave the cannula in for a few hours, just in case we need to give anything else."

"Good idea," said Ray. "We're going to leave the two of you in peace just now; we've got some more treatments to give. But remember, anything unusual and you must let the ward nurses know. They'll be in to check your blood pressure and so on every hour for the next few hours. The ward folks should be round with some food for you in a wee while, too."

"We'll be expecting loaves and fishes!" said Amanda, smiling.

Ray and Emilie set off for room twenty-five and later room twenty-seven, where similar scenarios played out, albeit without the religious references. However, although neither Chris Higgins nor Lisa Ashman nor their respective partners were religious, Ray noted that they also looked at the vials with a sort of wonderment, as though they were trying to divine some magic from the solution hanging up in the little plastic bag.

Emilie proved to be a whizz with the infusions, inserting the cannulas rapidly and more or less painlessly. All the infusions ran smoothly and none of the patients had any form of reaction, at least in the early phase. After the third observation period was complete, Emilie and Ray went back to the office to file the initial data and to have a coffee.

"Thanks very much for today Emilie. I don't know about you, but I feel quite exhausted now – I guess it's more to do with anticipation. It's not as though I've had an exactly hectic day."

"I know what you mean, Ray. I'm quite tired too. I guess that we are giving something totally new and unknown, so there's always going to be an element of worry about what might happen. Anyway, it seems that so far, so good. Luckily there were no allergic reactions."

"No. I don't want to tempt fate, especially since we've got another twenty-one to go and we don't know about late reactions in these folks yet, but I wasn't really expecting much of a problem. Usually an allergy comes along on the second or subsequent exposure to something – you need the first one to sensitize you. Thankfully in this study we don't need to give the stuff again. I suppose we could get reactions though if they have had some other proteins given in the past – I don't think any of them have been for the goat's blood that some people tried a few years ago, but it's that kind of thing that might catch us out. Listen, I don't want to keep you, I know you've a family to get home to. Thanks for today, and I'll see you again tomorrow for more of the same."

"Thanks Ray. I'm glad I took this job you know. I think it's going to be fun," she said, picking up her car keys and bag and heading out of the door.

CHAPTER 24

As Ray had predicted, none of the patients had any problems with allergy to the infusions, and they managed to complete all of the twenty-four treatments without any great incident. A patient transport ambulance broke down one day which meant that patient didn't make it for their injection. Ray had to speak nicely to the ward manager in the Infection Unit to borrow a fourth room the following day and treat the patient. Luckily the ward was having a slightly calmer period, so that went off smoothly. It did mean Emilie working beyond her normal hours though. Ray was pleased and grateful that she was more than happy to do that. It was one of her husband's working at home days, she said, so he could do the child care for a bit longer, she said.

"Thanks, Emilie, tell him I owe him a pint some time."

"Don't say that, he might sign you up for a bit of babysitting instead."

As well as being slick with clinical procedures, Ray was also pleased to find that Emilie was meticulous in her record keeping. Like a lot of doctors, or maybe it was just men, or male doctors, he found it really challenging to fill in forms, particularly paper ones, but of course it had to be done in a trial like this. As well as all the routine stuff, there could be adverse reaction or serious adverse reaction reports which had to be completed according to a certain format and notified to relevant authorities. Fortunately, at least in the early part of the study, he hadn't had to open up that particular can of worms.

Once all patients had received their injections and gone home, there was little for Ray to do on the study until the first round of monthly reviews. He busied himself with other clinical work and got up to speed again on the Peploe's study. Since the clinical trial had begun, Carter had taken him off that study and employed another part-timer to keep an eye on it, hence Ray's loss of privileges for entry to the animal house. However, he thought he would invite Jessica Shaw, the doctor now assigned to it, and Fiona over to his flat for a curry and a chat. He wasn't really sure how much he wanted to know about the study and how much was just an excuse to see Fiona again, but it seemed like a good idea.

The Friday following completion of the injections, he went home immediately his clinic was done, tidied the place and made a chicken curry, one of the few things he was good at … actually that wasn't quite true, he was really quite a good cook but just couldn't be bothered most of the time. Fiona and Jessica arrived together on the dot at 8 p.m.

"Hi Ray, we decided to share a car. Wow, good smell …" said Fiona, as they came in.

"Great to see you, thanks for coming. Sorry about the state of the place – I know you'd have been expecting a bachelor shambles, but as you'll see, I've tidied up, and it's spookily clean!"

"We wouldn't have expected anything less from the great research genius," said Jessica, laughing loudly.

"Shut up or you'll get no supper …"

"You sounded just like my mother there," said Fiona. "It is great to see you too. I guess you've been ensconced in the hospital for the last couple of weeks, leaving Jessica and me to deal with the furry friends on our own."

"Well, as you know, I'm not allowed into your building. In fact, unless I'm mistaken, it was you who signed the order rescinding my access, Ms Graham."

"SOPs are SOPs, as you should know. You're history now. Jessica has to deal with Prof Carter and with Peploe's."

"How are they taking all this?" said Ray.

"Well, they're not exactly happy." said Fiona. "The last couple of meetings with Professor Carter and Dr Lassky have been decidedly frosty, and we haven't seen any sign of Dr Da Cruz since that meeting you were at. The study's going on, but there's nothing dramatic happening."

"Yeah, it's not great for my research," said Jessica, "but I'll get my MD thesis out of it, and after that I'm hoping to go for the BTA."

Ray noted puzzlement on Fiona's face.

"Been To America," he said. "All young UK medical researchers like to spend some time over there. Good for the CV, though maybe a bit less important now than it was twenty years ago … so I'm told, I wasn't in medical research then."

"I hope not, you old codger" laughed Fiona.

"Anyway, let's not talk about work for the rest of tonight. Hope you like chicken curry and Ben Harper."

"I don't think we've tasted him, have we Jessica?"

The rest of the evening was spent talking about everything but medicine. Jessica turned out to be interested in music too, but much more highbrow. Her mother had been a concert pianist and a single mum, so she had spent lots of her youth in the wings at various recitals around the UK and Europe. She had missed quite a bit of conventional schooling, but her mum had arranged tutoring and in the end she had won a scholarship to study medicine at Oxford. 'Clearly a bright cookie,' thought Ray.

"Who's your favourite then?" said Ray.

"Composer? I like loads of stuff. Favourites probably Rachmaninov and Gershwin, and Reg is pretty cool too."

"Reg?"

"Sir Elton, to you, my boy. I'm not totally classic'd out, you know ..."

Before Ray knew it, the clock hit midnight and Fiona stood up.

"Sorry Ray. It's been a great evening, but we're going to have to go. I'm heading off to the Angus Glens first thing – it's quite a long drive, but the forecast is good and we're hoping to do a bit of rock climbing in Glen Doll. I'm the driver tonight, so when I go, Jessica has to go too. It's been fun though. I'll get you both around to my place soon to return the complement."

"That'd be great," said Ray. "I'll look forward to it. A night off the pot noodles."

"I don't believe you've ever eaten a pot noodle in your life."

"Ah, there's lots of stuff you don't know about me. Hope you have a good weekend, both of you. I've got to be around here in case any of the study patients call, but I might dig out some Reg to listen to, now that I know who he is ..."

As they left, both of them gave him a hug. He sensed that Fiona's was maybe a bit more urgent. Or maybe that was wishful thinking ...?

CHAPTER 25

In virtually no time, the scheduled review visits came around. During the first weeks of the trial, there had been a few phone calls from patient and carers reporting coughs and colds, but nothing significant. Ray was slightly disappointed that no one had phoned in a miracle cure yet, though his logical self told him it was too soon to expect anything. Despite that, he felt excited as he headed up the path to Amanda and Joseph's small terraced house.

Joseph opened the door and welcomed him into the house without giving away much emotion. He led him through to a bright room facing out on to the back garden, Amanda lay on a reclining chair, looking out towards the potted plants neatly arranged on the gravel which seemed to Ray to cover most of the plot. There was certainly no grass to be seen. Amanda caught his gaze.

"Low maintenance, you see. No grass to cut. No weeds to pull. Joseph likes that. He's a lazy sod you know ..." said Amanda, as Joseph shuffled slightly uncomfortably in the corner of the room.

"I don't believe that for a minute," smiled Ray. "I had an uncle once who worked hard in his garden, making sure that nothing, plant or weed, got a chance to grow. He did have grass, right enough, which was mowed like a US marine's hair. Anyway, I didn't come to talk *Gardeners' Question Time*. How are you doing?"

"Oh, not bad," said Amanda. "Can't say as I've noticed any great change so far, though just in the last few days I have had quite a lot of shooting sensations down my legs. They don't last long and they're not painful, more of a sort of pins and needles feeling. I'm actually finding them quite uncomfortable at night. Not sure if they mean anything, though I did have similar feelings a few years ago."

"I'm going to take you through all the standard questions now, and then I'll need to do a full examination. By the end of this trial, you're going to know this routine as well as I do, and you'll probably be fed up with it, but we've got to record everything in a standard way for the analysis of the results."

"No problem, doc, especially if the treatment works, it will all have been worthwhile."

Ray worked his way methodically through the standard questionnaires, which dealt with sensation, movement, power, coordination, control of bladder and bowels and so on, and moved on to things such as combing hair, walking, climbing stairs and a whole range of other activities. At the end of the standard questions, there was also a free text box where the patient and their carer could add any further observations.

He moved on to the physical examination which involved an initial inspection of the patient, followed by a methodical examination of the cranial nerves, including sense of smell, eye movements, visual fields, hearing, facial movements and sensation, etc., and movements of the tongue, and then on to examine across the chest and abdomen followed by muscle tone, power, sensation and coordination in each limb. In Amanda's case, she had so little power in her limbs that testing coordination was redundant at this stage. Hopefully if she was on active treatment, and if it had worked, the examination might take longer at subsequent visits. Ray completed both a written account of the findings and shaded in some diagrams of the body to record the areas where she had reduced or absent sensation etc.

"Well, doc, what do you think?" she said.

"To be honest, Amanda, it's too soon to expect anything yet. The fact that you're noting some paraesthesia, I mean the pins and needles feelings that you describe, might just mean that something is happening and that your nerves are beginning to wake up a bit, especially if you've not felt anything like that for some time, but we'll have to wait and see. I'll be scheduling in another MRI scan for you in a month and we'll do all this again. In the meantime, you must let us know if there's anything worrying you as time goes by, or if you have any general queries. You'll always get either Emilie or me on the phone, any time of the day or night. So far it doesn't seem that you've had any adverse effects. What about you, Joseph, how do you feel about it all?"

"I've had the feeling that Amanda is a bit more agitated occasionally. I guess that's just excitement about being in the study, or maybe the pins and needles are making her a bit grouchy, but otherwise I've not noticed any great change so far and no major side effects that I can think of ..."

"Ok," said Ray. "I'll see you again in a month. I have to get on round the rest of the folks now."

"How's it going with them?" said Amanda, then correcting herself, "Sorry, I guess I'm not supposed to ask that ..."

"I think it's going to be a bit early for everyone yet," said Ray, "but you're right, officially I can't really tell you how the others in the study are getting on."

"OK, thanks doc. Joseph, will you take Dr Shepherd out? See you next month."

As Ray headed back to his car, he had mixed emotions. No obvious miracle cure there, but it was only a month, and there had been no major side effects either, which was good ... or maybe just a sign that she had received the dummy treatment. However, she had mentioned pins and needles, and that could be a sign of recovery. Of course that was a purely subjective thing that could only be reported by the patient, so if the mice had felt these during the early phase of their recovery, there would have been no way of knowing ... patience, Ray, patience.

He decided to carry straight on to his next patient who only lived five blocks away.

This time, he found himself in front of an old style pre-war bungalow. The garden here had obviously once been well tended, but now weeds were coming up through the gravel, the grass was cut but the edges had not been trimmed so long wisps of grass mingled with the shrubs and bedding plants that filled the borders. A small blue car sat at the side of the house with weeds growing up between the wheels, beside the collection of waste and recycling bins that seemed to be mandatory for everyone now.

He rang the doorbell and a small lady answered. She had grey hair pulled back into a bun, and was wearing a thick tweed skirt and a slightly faded flowery apron above grey slippers.

"Hello, Dr Shepherd. Please come in. Sandy's through in the back room today."

"Thanks, Mrs Main."

Sandy was in his mid-forties, tall and thin with wispy red hair. He had been a bank clerk until five years ago when his illness had forced him to give up work. He had been married, but his wife had left him about eight years previously and he had gone back to live with his ageing parents. His father had died about one year ago, so now there were only the two of them in the house. As with the other people in the study, Sandy was fairly severely disabled by his MS, unable to walk, requiring an indwelling bladder catheter, He still had some movement in his arms and was able to feed himself. He moved around the house in an electric wheelchair, but he wasn't able to get out now. His dad had been able to drive but since he died, there had been no way for him to travel away from the house, except on the occasional trip organised by the MS society. Today he was in the kitchen/dining area at the back of the house. The room was tidy and clean, the furniture a bit dated but all looking quite smart. Ray sensed that Mrs Main was still able to keep on top of the housework but couldn't really manage the garden, which would probably have been her husband's pride and joy at one time.

"Well, Sandy, how are you today?"

"OK, I think, Dr Shepherd. Can't say as I've noticed any great changes since the injection, but I suppose it's a bit soon. I did get a bit of a pain in my lower belly the other day, as though my bladder was filling up. Haven't felt anything like that for a while ... but maybe it was just imagination. I suppose we're all looking for the slightest thing ..."

"That's fine Sandy, I'll take a note. As you know, there are lots of uncertainties about this study. We don't know whether the treatment will work, or if it does how quickly we can expect to see some results. We also don't know about side effects, so it's important to report everything, no matter how small, if you can. The plan today is to go through all the standard questions with you and to do the full examination again. Next month, you'll get all that again plus another MRI scan. It might be sensitive enough to pick up whether these sensations you're having are due to changes in the nerves."

Once again, Ray ran methodically and meticulously through the detailed questionnaire and physical examination. Again there was nothing new to find.

"What about you, Mrs Main. Have you noticed any change?"

"The only thing is he started taking sugar in his tea. He hasn't done that since he was a wee boy. I had to dig out an old box of sugar lumps from the back of cupboard."

"I hope they weren't ones you'd kept since I was a wee boy," joked Sandy.

His mother raised her eyebrows and shrugged. "See what I've to put up with, Doctor Shepherd. Let's hope this treatment makes him less cheeky!"

As Ray left the house, he thought about the dynamics of that situation. To some extent, Sandy's mum had begun to treat him like a child again. She made most of his meals, helped him to the toilet, did all his shopping for him and so on. 'Supposing this treatment does work and he begins to improve,' thought Ray, 'I wonder how that dynamic will change again? Will she be pleased or will there be a bit of resentment that he doesn't need her again?'

All of these questions would be answered over the next few months.

CHAPTER 26

The same pattern repeated itself in most of Ray's visits over the next couple of weeks. Most people reported no change in the symptoms or very minor sensations that they felt could be down to imagination. Ray began to feel a little despondent although his rational self told him that it really was too soon to expect much and, on the plus side, no one had reported any significant side effects. As Ray knew, this next period would reflect the reality of most clinical trials: a long period of meticulous, but tedious, data collection during which the outcome of the study would remain a mystery. It was good during this phase to also have a clinical job to do, as the problems that threw up were unpredictable and required him to work in more of a response mode.

He had a regular research meeting with Carter scheduled for every second Monday, though these were frequently cancelled as Carter was out of the country. On the few occasions when they did happen, he noted that the collection of artefacts in Carter's office was growing as he was invited to speak at yet more international events.

The first round of MRI scans was largely equivocal. They were reported by Paul Schmidt and the data were stored but Ray, as the clinical investigator, was not given access to them in case it should bias his clinical examinations. In any case, it actually made it easier for him when the patients began to ask about the results of the scans. He could honestly report that he had no access to the scan results and could give them no information.

During the next few weeks, Emilie fielded calls from several of the patients and went out on home visits to deal with specific issues. Some reported coughs and colds, urinary infections, chest infections and the other common minor ailments that afflicted people with MS as much or more than anyone else. She recorded detailed notes of all these visits in the patients' trial records and in their regular case notes, but none of the complaints seemed out of the ordinary, or likely to be considered related to the treatment that would require to be formally recorded as an adverse or serious adverse reaction.

Ray and Emilie met regularly to debrief on all of these visits and a general catch-up on any other observations. He enjoyed these meetings. They gradually built up trust in each other's judgement and it was important to maintain their momentum during this phase of the trial.

About fifteen weeks into the study, they sat down in their shared office on a Thursday to discuss progress. Ray made the coffee and brought out caramel wafer biscuits.

"Caramel wafers, eh? You must be feeling a bit low," said Emilie.

"Maybe you're getting to know me too well," laughed Ray. "Not low exactly, I guess I had just hoped that we'd be seeing more at this stage. Some of the people are getting pins and needles and other vague feelings that might be important, but there's nothing much else so far. It would be great to know if the MRI scans match up to that, but of course we're not allowed to know that at this stage."

"Yep, that's more or less what I've been hearing too. The only other thing I've heard from some of them is that they seem to be getting some mood changes, mainly bad temper that's a bit out of character. I suppose the patients must be even more frustrated than we are ... it's a bit like getting a lifeline thrown and then finding it's not attached to anything."

Ray nodded. "I keep going over with them that we don't know what to expect, if anything. But I suppose if I was in their situation, I'd be just as desperate to see something happening. Quite a lot of them think they've had the dummy treatment, but again of course there's no way of knowing at this stage. There's nothing for us to do but press on."

"Have you heard any more about the mice? Is the vitamin D study showing anything?"

"Well," said Ray, "I met Jessica the other day. Apparently, it looks like there might be some effect though it is not dramatic. I think some of the other work coming out at the moment is suggesting that vitamin D might be important in preventing MS, but less good at treating it. I suppose if that were the case, Peploe's might turn out to be happy bunnies after all, as they might be able to make a case for mass supplementation of the population as a preventive measure. That would be good for their sales, especially if it turns out that vitamin D is also important in preventing heart disease. There's some data from Scotland and elsewhere that suggests that might be important too."

"I always thought the Scots covered up too much, and of course they never go outdoors ..." laughed Emilie.

"Except for the smokers, since the ban came in. Wouldn't it be ironic if standing outside the pub for your cigarette actually boosted your vitamin D levels? The public health doctors would have trouble handling the PR on that one. The cigarette companies would probably bring back that old poster of Ronald Reagan sitting on his horse in the great outdoors smoking a fag! Anyway, I think our job over the next while is going to be keeping all the people on board with the study. I guess there's a risk that if they're not seeing any benefit, they might decide that the hassle of the two-monthly scans and the repeated physicals is not worth the bother."

"I'm not sensing that at all at the moment, Ray. I think you've made a great job of managing expectations, and the fact that they are managed as individuals probably makes it easier to control that. I've seen problems before where patients are managed as a group. I suppose the classic is patients with kidney failure on dialysis. I was involved with one study where one of the patients died, not of anything directly related to the study but of an incidental heart attack, but the effect on morale of the group was pretty devastating and we had a lot of trouble getting them through the rest of study; in fact three dropped out as a result of that death."

"I'm afraid if we lose three from our study that will be a disaster," said Ray. "We're already at pretty much the minimum sample size, and I'd hate to have to start over ..."

"Come on ... you've haven't touched that caramel wafer yet. Get it down you and it'll all seem much more optimistic..."

"Where's the evidence for that?" laughed Ray.

"n of 1 trial. Always works for me ..." said Emilie, as she picked up her jacket and headed for the door.

Chapter 27

The breakthrough came at the five-month visits.

It was a bright day, the schools were on holiday and so the roads were quiet as Ray headed into the riverside apartment block to see Lisa Ashman. She was the third patient to have received the injection, but the first on his schedule for the five-monthly visits.

Lisa had been an electronics engineer and had worked with a renewable energy company until her illness made that unmanageable. She lived in a smart riverside flat with her partner Lucy who was a lawyer with an environmental protection organisation. Lisa had suffered from MS for about twelve years and over the past three years it had become rapidly progressive. As well as Lucy, her mum called in regularly to help out and was usually with her for the visits. Being a working day apart from schools, Ray was slightly surprised when Lucy answered the door today.

"Dr Shepherd. Please come in. I don't think I've seen you since the day Lisa had the injection. Come through, she's in the living room."

"Thanks, I wasn't expecting to see you, nice though it is," he said.

"I had to be here for this," said Lucy, as she opened the living room door.

Lisa was sitting in a chair by the fireplace. She had the widest smile Ray thought he had ever seen.

"It's working!" she said, bursting into tears. Lucy moved over to hug her. "It's working! Nothing ever worked before!"

Ray decided to sit down and give Lisa a few minutes to compose herself, although he too was inevitably caught up in the emotion.

"OK, Lisa, sounds promising. Now, once you feel like it, you must take me slowly through what's been happening since I saw you last."

"Thanks, doc. Sorry about that, but you've no idea …" More tears. "You remember last time that I said I'd been having some pins and needles in my arms and legs. A few days after that, I thought I could tense the muscles in my forearms and calves a bit. I couldn't make them move anything much at first, but there was definitely something there that had been missing for years. Within about three more days, I thought that I could pull my foot up and down a bit, but I was scared to say anything to anybody, even Lucy. The pins and needles got worse and worse, but I put up with that because there was definitely a bit of movement there. We were having some friends round two weeks ago for a meal, and Lucy dug out a pair of red party shoes that I hadn't worn for years. Halfway through the evening, I said to Lucy 'My feet are killing me'. She said, 'What did you say? Be quiet everyone!' I said, 'My feet are killing me'. Don't you see, I hadn't been able to feel my feet for years? Of course they were sore because they're a bit swollen with the MS and the shoes didn't really fit. But I've got the feeling back, and I can move my toes and my ankles … look!"

Sure enough, she had slight but definite movement of her toes and ankles. Ray then began the routine of the questionnaire and examination again, as he had done on four previous occasions with Lisa after the injection. This time, the whole pattern of answers had changed. She had much more in the way of sensation and had certainly regained some limited power in muscles that had been previously redundant. On the routine physical examination, once again the number of positive responses increased. On movements such as flexing and extending toes and ankles, where there had previously been nothing, she could now move a little against gravity, though not yet against any resistance, which would be the next step up in the grading system for power that Ray was using. The diagrams of sensory loss also changed significantly. The areas of shading where sensation was completely absent diminished. Some areas that had been completely numb could now detect a pin prick, though not yet light touch. Some could distinguish hot and cold, all suggesting that different parts of the nervous system were beginning to recover. Ray knew he was seeing something that had never before been seen in severe progressive MS, but struggled to maintain his cool professional exterior.

"Well, that's all good," he said, as he completed the physical examination.

"Good, it's a bloody miracle," said Lisa. "Every day it's getting better. I don't really know what else to say. I had given up, you know. If I'd had a ticket for Switzerland, I'd have been off there a few months ago. I know that some people think assisted suicide is wrong, but you know you get to that stage. But now …" She dissolved into tears again.

"What do you think, Lucy?"

"I agree; miraculous is the only word. Every day she seems to be getting better. Mind you, she's not the quiet character she had become. It's more like the old days again, nipping my ear about this and that. It's great …" Lucy also dissolved again …

"OK," said Ray. "You'll be due another scan next month and of course I'll be back to see you then too for another examination. In the meantime, I'm going to get Emilie to visit you. Now that you have some movement and some feeling, because they're not complete or normal yet, you might be at more risk of injuring yourself, burning your skin and so on, without noticing. So I want Emilie to go over all of these sorts of activities of daily living with you to make sure that you're safe. Now that things are beginning to improve, we don't want you inadvertently making them worse again. It might be good if Lucy and your mum could also be there when she comes, just so that everyone understands how to prevent problems. Would that be OK?"

"That would be fine. Emilie is so nice and helpful. What do you think will happen now? Am I going to go back to normal? Have you seen this with other people yet?"

"It's too early to tell what will happen. In the original mouse experiments, they did go completely back to normal, but I don't want you getting your hopes too high. Your nerves and muscles have been out of action for quite a long time, so I don't know what capability they have to go back to normal. As for the others in the trial, I'm afraid I can't discuss them with you because of the trial design."

"Yes, I know, doc. I'm sorry, it wasn't fair to ask that. I'm just so excited, you see."

"Never have guessed it," smiled Ray, packing away the file and his examination equipment. "See you in a month."

As he walked down the riverside path from the flat, Ray thought his heart was going to burst. He had just about managed to stay cool and detached in the flat, but this was it. There was no question that her nervous system was recovering. Miracle might not be a word that scientists use, but this was as close as you might get to one in clinical medicine. Could he really be the first to have seen MS truly reverse itself? He had two more visits that day, but thought he better have a quiet coffee first and compose himself before moving on.

Next for the day was Chris Higgins, one of the other 'first day treatments'. Chris lived with his wife in a small country cottage, about three miles out of town. On the previous four visits, Chris had nothing much to report apart from some abdominal discomfort that he hadn't previously experienced, but again he and Ray weren't sure what the significance of that might be. As Ray pulled up in the car, Chris was sitting outside in his wheelchair. Apart from visits to the scanner and the admission for the injection, this was the first time Ray had seen Chris outside his house. Could this be a sign of something happening here too?

Ray jumped out of the car, then reminded himself that he had to be dispassionate and professional on these visits, so deliberately slowed his walk as he went forward to see Chris.

"It's nice to see you outside. Not a bad day. How are you doing?"

"Oh, much and such." said Chris. "Not sure if I've very much to report. If this treatment is going to work, it might be going to take a long time for me. Those funny feelings in the tummy that I mentioned last time seemed to have stopped again, and I don't think there's much more to say, unless you can find anything on examination."

"OK, Chris, not to worry. As I've said many times, you're probably fed up hearing it; we've no idea when this treatment might kick in. I'll have to do the full questionnaire and examination as usual. We can do the questions outside, but we'll need to go in for the examination, I think."

"That's fine. Kath is just up the road with the dog, but she should be back by the time you've done the questions and we can move the circus inside. You might get a cup of tea or something then too. How's the whole thing going anyway?"

"Oh, you know, just collecting all the information at the moment; too soon to tell about the treatment." Ray then pulled out Chris's study file and began to work his way through the questionnaire routine. As he expected from Chris's initial reaction, there was really nothing new to report in the way of symptoms or activities. Chris didn't seem to be any worse, but nor was there any sign of improvement. Just as they finished the questions, a large black Labrador bounded into the garden and up to Chris, almost knocking him over.

"Hey there Major, calm down," said Chris. "I wish I had a fraction of his movement. He gets a bit excited when he sees folk for the first time, but he calms down pretty quickly. Here's Kath, she'll help us get inside for the exam bit."

"Hi, Dr Shepherd. I thought that some time in the sun would be good for Chris today. I've heard that vitamin D might be good for him. It doesn't seem as though the injection is doing anything, at least not yet."

"No, we've just been talking about that. Obviously I'll need to examine him, but on the basis of the questionnaire there's no change so far. Still, it's early days, and you're certainly no worse," he said, turning back to Chris.

Once the examination was completed and the cup of tea duly taken, Ray headed back to the car. A number of possibilities were running through his mind. Could Chris be a slow responder? Had he had the dummy treatment? Did men react differently from women? Were there different kinds of MS? On balance it seemed most likely that he might have had the dummy treatment, but of course all this speculation was based on only two people, so it was really a bit daft to be thinking through these possibilities at all. However, even the most dispassionate researcher generally couldn't help speculating at each stage of the process. In fact, without that constantly questioning mind, you probably shouldn't be a researcher at all.

One more visit was planned for the day. 'Best of three', thought Ray and then immediately chided himself for such a flippant thought. It was back now to Amanda Trail's little terraced house.

"Come in, come in, Dr Shepherd!" Joseph was beaming from ear to ear, the second time today that Ray had seen that reaction. As usual, Amanda was on the reclining chair, but there was something different about her demeanour. She looked up as Ray entered the room.

"I hope you've got your dancing shoes looked out. I think you're going to be needing them after all. Not quite yet, you've got some time for rehearsal, I think. Joseph will be happy to show you the steps … The Lord moves in mysterious ways, but this must be about the most mysterious of all."

"I take it you've noticed some improvement?"

"I can hardly believe it, Dr Shepherd. It began just after your last visit. Remember I mentioned those pins and needles? Well they got more and more annoying, but I could put up with it because I felt that my nerves were waking up again. Then one night Joseph was snuggling up to me in bed – he does that you know – and I had to ask him to move his knee because I felt it pressing into the back of my thigh. Although he'd done the same thing for years, I hadn't actually felt him there at all in the past couple of years anyway. Since then, I've started to get some movement back in my legs. It's not much yet, but it's definitely there. None of the other treatments that I've tried have had anything like that effect. Do you really think it's going to go on improving?"

"I don't know, Amanda, but the studies that we did in the mice did show progressive improvement once it began. So I think we can hope …"

As he said that, Joseph almost seemed to do a little dance across the room to give Amanda a hug. "You know, Dr Shepherd, I never thought I'd be so grateful to be accused of having knobbly knees!" he laughed.

"Anyway, Amanda, I need to go through the usual rigmarole of the questionnaire and the examination, so if you don't mind, we'll get started."

As with Lisa, Ray found that he was ticking a lot of new boxes on the questionnaire compared to the previous four months, and the examination confirmed that there was definite return of both sensation and muscle power in Amanda's arms and legs. 'Two out of three, both female,' he thought to himself as he went along.

Once the examination was completed, he explained to Amanda and Joseph that he would be asking Emilie to visit them for advice on gentle mobilisation while avoiding injury. He was sure that they would take everything on board. Just as he was about to get up and leave, Amanda spoke again.

"Dr Shepherd, would you mind joining us in a short prayer? I've no idea if you're a religious man or not, but it would mean a lot to Joseph and me."

"I'd be delighted," said Ray, although the truth was that he was not a religious man, at least not in the sense of organised religion. He did regard himself as quite spiritual though, whatever that meant.

Joseph began: "Dear Lord, we thank You for the improvement that You have brought to Amanda. We thank You for the skill and dedication of our doctors and nurses, especially Dr Shepherd, and we pray that You will bless their work. We especially pray for all other sufferers of chronic illnesses, that they may be given the same hope that we have found in the past few weeks, and we pray that where the illness cannot be cured, You will comfort and support them and their loved ones to the end of their earthly lives and beyond, Amen."

Amanda echoed the Amen, and then turned again to Ray. "Thank you for being a part of that."

"My privilege," said Ray. "I have to go now, but I'll see you again in a month when your scan will be repeated and Emilie will be in touch before then. Take care."

Back at the office, he was disappointed to find that Emilie had already gone for the day. Sharing his excitement with someone was going to have to wait until tomorrow. He went home, poured a large dram and put on an old Judy Collins album. He wasn't religious, but 'Amazing Grace' did seem to take on an added dimension as he drifted off to sleep on the sofa.

CHAPTER 28

Emilie arrived at the office at nine o'clock as usual. Ray had already been there for a couple of hours. He wasn't entirely sure what he'd done during that time, apart from looking out the files for the day's visits and looking at some online journals. He wasn't really concentrating though.

"You look a bit pleased with yourself," said Emilie, sensing immediately that something was going on.

"I think it's started, Emilie. I saw three people yesterday and two of them have very definite return of function, both sensation and motor functions. You should have seen their faces, they were so excited."

"What about the other one?"

"Oh, he's really not changed at all. Interestingly the two that had improved were both women and the one man I saw seemed completely unchanged. Maybe he had the placebo of course, or maybe there's something about being female. It's too soon to tell. I'd like you to arrange to see the two women as soon as possible, with their carers if that can be arranged. Although they're making some improvement, I think they might be at more risk now of injuring themselves as they begin to move more with incomplete sensation, so you need to take them through all the necessary precautions and so on."

"Of course, I'll be excited to see them. Do you really think this could be something big?"

"Well at the moment it seems to be 'Of Mice and Women', but there's no doubt that something's going on. Of course we need to keep this to ourselves at the moment. I've also asked the patients not to broadcast anything about yet. We don't want expectations getting ahead of themselves. But it sure is exciting."

"What's next then?" said Emilie.

"Well, I've got a bunch more patients to see this week, and then a meeting with Carter in the middle of next week. It'll be a few weeks until their next scans, but I expect there will be some changes to be seen then, although we won't be told, of course."

"Fair enough. I'll get on to it straight away. I've also got to see one of the other men. His wife thinks he's being a bit over-emotional, not quite his usual self, so I'll pop out to see him. I don't think you're due to see him until early next week."

"Which one's that?"

"I think he's your pet patient, Mr Strother."

"OK. Tell him I'm asking for him and I'll see him next week."

Ray gathered up the files for the day's visits and set off. The day passed quickly and by the end of it the 'score' was 4 improving and two unchanged. One of the two improvers was a man, so maybe there wasn't a gender bias. As the week moved on, the same patterns repeated again and again. Households where nothing had changed but people remained hopeful, others where there were smiles, laughter and tears. Of course it was an emotional roller coaster for the patients and their loved ones, but almost as much for Ray.

By Friday evening, he felt that he needed to do something to take his mind off it, so he slipped on his running gear and set out along the canal towpath. He was pushing himself as hard as he could, mainly to try and make his brain stop for a bit and let the pain in his muscles take over. He almost didn't see the slim female figure coming towards him, until she stopped and shouted out: "Whoa! Are the bats from hell after you, or are you just trying to avoid me?"

It took a second for his eyes to focus, then gradually the familiar shape of Fiona materialised in front of him.

"Fiona. Sorry, I wasn't trying to avoid you. In fact I could hardly see anything at all apart from red mist."

"Who's made you that angry?"

"Oh, it's not anger. It's just … well … I guess you could say it's been a tough week, up and down a bit."

"Up sounds good?"

"Yeah, I can't really say anything … about the study you know." He felt bad, but rules were rules.

"I know, just in the same way I can't let you into the animal house. Don't worry, I guess I'll know soon enough. I had hoped you might call at some point, but I guess you've been busy."

Ray's heart sank again. "I know. I feel terrible. I guess I've just got so wrapped up in this thing that I've forgotten to do any living outside of it."

"Don't worry, when you're ready, I'll be ready too. How's your dad?"

"Oh much the same … well actually a bit worse I think, but he won't hear of having anything else done at the moment."

"Ah … the stubborn gene …!"

"OK, guilty as charged. Let's aim to do something at the end of next week. I can ask Emilie to be on call for the study patients for an evening. I'm sure she won't mind and it will give her a bit more overtime … cinema next Friday then?"

"Sounds good. Now I suggest you complete your run a bit more slowly. I don't want you keeling over on top of the swans. I'm heading the other way at a more sedate pace. Mind you, I'm going to kick boxing later, so watch out …"

Ray ran more gently for the last couple of miles, happy that he had done the exercise but happier still at the chance meeting. For just a short period of time he did forget about the study.

CHAPTER 29

Monday afternoon found him walking along the familiar path to the Strothers' door. He had spoken with Emilie about her visit at the end of the previous week. From what she had said, it seemed likely that Eric was one of the active therapy group. He had definitely regained some power in his arms and legs and he seemed to be feeling his bladder a bit more than before. He was obviously pleased and had told Emilie that it was all positive, but Susan had told her privately that she thought he was much more labile than before, sometimes very elated and other times quite depressed. Emilie thought that it was quite understandable, given the momentous possibilities that Eric could see opening up, and had sought to reassure Susan about that, as well as letting her know that she would forewarn Ray before his visit. On first impression, as Susan opened the door, it seemed that reassurance had worked.

"Dr Shepherd, how great to see you! Come in."

Ray sensed immediately that there was something lighter in her mood. As if to confirm that thought she went on: "You're not going to believe this."

The most immediate change in the room was that the bed had been pushed to the corner of the room, and Eric was sitting up in a chair by the fireside, a huge grin on his face.

"Hiya doc … well, what do you think … an upright citizen again…"

"Emilie told me that you had noticed some improvement …"

"More than some … it's getting better every day … it's a miracle, you know … don't know if anyone else has told you that yet, but I can't tell you … Of course I'm not ready for the rugby field yet, but who knows? Look at that …"

As he spoke, he waggled his right big toe which was sticking out under the cover that Susan had draped across his knees. The movement wasn't complete and the toe still looked weak, but the fact that he could move it against gravity certainly showed that it was improving.

140

"And that …"

He now raised his left index finger, not a large movement, but again a definite one.

"Ok, Ok," said Ray. "Don't tire yourself out all at once. I've got to go through the full rigmarole, as usual, you know: all the usual questions and a full physical."

"Bring it on …" laughed Eric.

As before, throughout the whole questionnaire procedure there were a lot more positive responses than at previous visits, and on examination, there was again the pattern of returning power and sensation. Ray spent about an hour meticulously completing and documenting all of the responses. Finally he came to the open-ended questions at the end.

"Is there anything else you want to add, Eric?"

"Not really, I think you've got the picture. I'm just looking forward to getting down the pub on my own two feet. I'll be buying you know, so you'd best keep that evening free, when it comes."

"Susan, is there anything else you want to say?"

She hesitated, almost imperceptibly. "No, it's all great. We've never seen anything like this before with anything that Eric has tried. How quickly do you think the improvement will go on? No, I know you can't answer that … I guess we just have to wait and see … There is just one other thing," she said taking Eric's hand. He rolled his eyes as if he knew what was coming.

"I think Eric's been a bit more unpredictable, maybe a bit more bad-tempered to be honest, over the past couple of weeks." He grimaced. "Emilie said that was probably just to do with the changes that are happening after such a long time of being immobile."

"I didn't know you discussed that with her," said Eric. "When was that? Were you talking behind my back?"

"No, love, I just mentioned it as she was on the way out the door."

Ray intervened. "Emilie's right. I think it's inevitable that you will feel up and down a bit. I imagine that over time, you've got used to doing most everything, Susan. As Eric improves, I would guess that he's going to want to do more. Sometimes he'll manage and sometimes it'll be difficult and frustrating for him, so he's bound to feel annoyed with himself, and maybe with you and the world. Of course this is new ground for all of us. We've never seen people with

141

severe MS begin to make any sort of recovery of this type. I think the most important thing is that you are able to talk these issues through with each other, and with us, Emilie and me. That's why we are always available on the phone and can visit at short notice if need be. We're all going to have some adjusting to do, but hopefully it's all going to be working towards a good outcome."

Eric was the first to speak.

"Of course, you're right, doc. Sorry if I was a bit short. I know you've been worried, Susan, and we just need to take things as they come. I'll try not to be snappy."

Susan leaned over and kissed him on the cheek. Tears welled up in her eyes, but she held it together.

"You know, Dr Shepherd, we are so happy." Her face lit up like Ray had never seen before.

"OK. I'll schedule in another visit in a month, and you'll be having another scan in due course too. I'm also going to get Emilie to come back and see you to go over a lot of practical stuff about how to avoid injuring yourself as you begin to do more, assuming that the current rate of improvement continues. I'd like you both to be there for that."

"Where else would I be?" smiled Susan.

As Ray walked down the path, he reflected on all that had happened since his first, and life changing, visit to Eric and Susan. He had felt so frustrated that he had nothing to offer them then, that Eric's life was just going to waste away, and in many ways, Susan's life too. Now everything had changed and Eric potentially had a future. However, as he improved, and the others in the study too, a whole range of new challenges was going to come up. How would the patients cope physically? How would they cope psychologically? All of them had been severely disabled for a long time. They had mostly become dependent on carers, often family members, whose main role in life was to support them. How would the patients cope when they no longer needed that? How would the carers cope when their raison d'etre vanished? How would the patients find the world, which had moved on since they were last in work or out and about in society? Clearly, managing these people and fully re-integrating them into society was more than simply a 'take up thy bed and walk' task. Ray made a mental note to discuss this with Carter at their next meeting.

CHAPTER 30

"He's in good form today," said Barbara, as Ray checked with the secretaries whether Carter was expecting him. "I think he got a good reception in the States."

Carter had been off to North Carolina, where a major grouping of academic institutions and commercial companies had formed around Research Triangle Park, based in the Raleigh-Durham area. Ray had visited that area some years before, when he was working in the States. His abiding memories of Raleigh were the overpowering smell of tobacco from the old processing factories, an industry which was now in decline, and the fact that the town centre seemed to shut down on Sundays, even many of the eating places, very unusual for the USA where it's usually possible to gorge twenty-four hours a day.

"Come in, come in, Ray. Have a seat. Coffee?"

'Wow, he has had a good time,' thought Ray.

"How are things going?" said Carter, settling back after Barbara had brought the coffees and winked at Ray as she laid them out.

"Well," said Ray, "There's no question that we are now seeing a group of clinical responders. It seems to have begun between the previous visits and these ones, although of course a few had mentioned some return of paraesthesia before that, but I wasn't sure then whether that was just wishful thinking. However a group of them, ten that I've seen so far, now undoubtedly have a return of sensation and some return of power in peripheral muscle groups. Mostly just movement with gravity eliminated, or movement against gravity at most, but they are all reporting that they feel progressive change. I've brought a couple of the trial folders just as examples."

Ray laid two large blue arch files on the table and opened the first one. These contained the entire trial record for each patient from recruitment and consent documents on to the questionnaires and physical assessment forms completed at each visit, etc. Electronic copies of all these documents existed too, but for medico-legal purposes signed and dated copies of records had to be kept and it was probably quicker to use the paper documents to show Carter some examples.

Ray produced a couple of outlines of the human body relating to one of the patients, one completed on entry to the trial, and one completed the previous day at the five-month visit.

"This is pretty typical," he said, pointing out the dramatic reduction in the shaded areas which indicated loss of light touch sensation. He followed this up with some charts of muscle groups and the power recordings from these, which were graded on a scale from zero (no power) to five (normal). In these patients, power recordings had moved from zero to grade one or two, indicating movement against gravity in the best-case scenarios.

"None of them is yet at a stage for measuring coordination, but I don't think there's any doubt that function is returning. I've still a couple more to see, but it looks like about half of them are responding. The others are unchanged or slightly deteriorating and I assume they've had the placebo, although we don't know that, of course. They are due repeat MRI scans in another month, but again, according to the protocol, we don't get to see the results of the scans until the observation period is complete. The trial monitoring committee is getting all of this information and the scan reports and they are unblinded, so I guess if this improvement goes on, they might take a decision at some stage to stop the trial, but I would imagine it's too soon for that yet.

"Certainly," said Carter. "However, this does all look splendid so far. A lot of these patients will have significant muscle wasting from long periods of inactivity, so even when the nerves are fully functioning, it may take them some time to regain full power. They will also probably be at increased risk of injuring themselves as they begin to mobilise again, especially if their sensation is still impaired."

"Yes," said Ray, "I've asked Emilie, the research nurse, to see each of them with their carers or partners to go over all of that and make sure that they try to avoid any injuries as much as possible. The other thing that I've realised is that rehabilitating them after such a long period of immobility and dependence is going to have its own challenges, not just for the patients but for their carers, who in the best-case scenario will become redundant in that role. We are going to have to put a rehabilitation programme in place for them."

"Agreed, but not while the trial is running. Let's not run before we can walk, if you'll pardon the pun," said Carter, smiling.

"There is one other thing," said Ray. "Some of them seem to be having some mood swings and behavioural changes. It's only happening among the ones who have noticed some physical improvements. I assume it's to be expected, given the dramatic nature of what's happening to them, although I realise that we haven't involved a psychologist or psychiatrist at all. Do you think we should have done that?"

"No, no, certainly not at this stage; it's only to be expected that they'll have some psychological adjustments to make, so I don't think we should concern ourselves too much with that. Just keep an eye …"

"Thanks, Professor Carter. That was more or less what I thought too."

"Now, Ray, I had some very useful meetings while I was in the States. Most importantly I spoke with people from Nefelsen Pharma. They have a wide portfolio but are interested in biologic therapies and they have the capability to prepare the prions in large quantities. They've developed a process for building the proteins without extraction from biologic specimens and can demonstrate that they have identical properties. They are very keen to enter into an exclusive licensing deal with us. Their normal practice would be to draw up agreements with our institution and with us as individuals. They are talking about substantial sums, assuming the trial is positive. We have the potential to make the institution rich, and I think it is appropriate that we also take a share for ourselves. There's no need for you to do anything at this stage. I'll have confidentiality agreements drawn up and I'll speak to our research and innovation director to keep them on board. I think our modest investment in this study is going to provide a substantial return."

Carter looked decidedly pleased with himself, but Ray was less than enthusiastic. It hadn't occurred to him that he would have to get involved in this sort of negotiation and the dual prospects of the treatment being under the control of a drug company whose main driver was profit, and of him benefitting financially from it, were equally alien to him. Of course, he could always donate his share to a research charity, he supposed. Obviously this would need more thought on his part.

"Well, thank you, Professor Carter. That's not really an area I had thought about at all, I have to confess."

"Don't worry. I'll deal with all of that at this stage. You just concentrate on keeping the trial running smoothly."

With that, Carter pulled out another sheaf of papers from his briefcase and Ray sensed that the meeting was over. He moved towards the door, paused and turned to speak again, but Carter was deep in his next correspondence or whatever, so Ray decided to leave it.

He walked back to the office with a vague feeling that a slight shadow had come over the sun. Emilie met him at the door and sensed something too.

"Penny for them?"

"What?"

"Your thoughts. Looks like someone just died or something. Did the meeting not go well?"

"No, no, quite the opposite; he was delighted. 'You've all done very well' as some old TV sitcom character used to say ..." joked Ray.

"Emilie laughed too. "Young Mr Grace ... *Are you Being Served?* I've seen the re-runs," she said by way of explanation, heading off for another home visit.

CHAPTER 31

During the next few days, Ray completed all the month five visits. Twelve patients appeared to be improving, the other twelve had noticed no change or were worse, and anxious with it. Ray did his best to reassure them, though still without, at this stage, informing them that there were some responders. To be honest, he was amazed that the news hadn't leaked across yet. Surely it was only a matter of time until one of the patients yielded to temptation to sell their story to the tabloids or similar, although he had spent a great deal of time with them stressing the importance of confidentiality, and so far his influence had held.

The five-month MRI scans even passed off without any of the 'responders' meeting any of the 'non-responders'. In the midst of that process, Ray met Paul Schmidt in the corridor.

"Well, Ray, I guess you must be pleased. Of course my lips are sealed and I don't know the randomisation any more than you do, but some of these scans have changed dramatically. It's like the mice all over again. How's the boss feeling about it?"

"Oh, you know him. Wheeling and dealing, but yes, I think he's optimistic. He asked me the other day if I thought we'd need to go right to the end of the exposure period. I think he's anxious to get a result, as the footballers say."

"Well, for what it's worth I haven't seen a normal scan yet. And I would guess you won't have had a normal neuro exam yet either, so it's a bit soon to be getting the bubbly out."

"Agreed," said Ray. "I'll try to keep a lid on them all."

While all of this was going on, Ray found his own emotions about as stretched as the patients. His night out with Fiona to the cinema had gone well. They had enjoyed the film, a slightly crazy spy thriller that mainly seemed an opportunity to showcase several European and American cities, and they had even shared a short kiss at the end of the evening, but that was as far as it went. Ray felt that he was behaving like a young teenager again, although he didn't feel awkward in Fiona's company as he had done when he met girls at school. However, he really just didn't feel ready for any more commitment at this stage and his sense was that Fiona felt the same. Still, she did have a soothing influence on him and she genuinely seemed to enjoy his company without anything more. For him, life seemed complicated enough at the moment. Little did he realise just how much more complicated it was going to become …

The problem began at the six-month visits and at the scene of the first triumph of the study.

***

Ray was optimistic as he headed down to Lisa Ashman's riverside apartment again. He had resigned himself somewhat to Carter's financial ambitions for the treatment, even although he was still uneasy about the commercial company involvement. However, he was aware that for the treatment to be delivered on a wide scale and internationally for a relatively common disease, the manufacturing and distribution capabilities of a multinational company would be essential. The potential income to the university could help to bring research in the faculty to new levels. For himself, if there was to be income generated, he would have it paid directly into a charitable fund to support research in neurological and chest disease, taking no personal income from it at all. That way, he could justify the arrangements to himself. He hadn't personally seen any of the patients since the five-month visits, but he had heard from Emilie who had done some home visits that the improvements were continuing among those to whom he was now referring as responders.

The scale of that improvement became obvious when he went into Lisa's sitting room, having been let into the house by her mum. She was standing with Lucy by her side. He could see that Lucy was steadying her, but apparently not bearing much, if any, weight. They were both smiling.

"What do you think?" said Lucy. "Me and my shadow, strolling down the avenue …"

"Be careful who you're calling the shadow," said Lisa. "My former self might have been a shadow, but I'm now a non-shadow of my former self … if that's an expression …" They both dissolved into laughter, and Lucy lowered Lisa carefully into a chair by the fireplace.

"So as you can see, improvement just goes on and on …" said Lisa. "I've been taking care to follow Emilie's instructions so I can now stand and I've even managed to take a couple of very small steps. You've no idea how good it feels to stand up. I've had such a long time of chairs, beds and wheelchairs that I was beginning to think like a small person. My hands are much better too … see" she said, waving her hands around. "They've even been good enough for some sex, and that has been a long time …." Again they both laughed, though Ray sensed that Lucy was slightly embarrassed by Lisa's mother's presence. She, however, seemed completely delighted for them and obviously felt no embarrassment herself.

"Well, that's all good," said Ray. "Let's just run through all the usual stuff again."

As before, he spent the next hour or so recording all of the questionnaire and physical parameters. Everything had improved considerably. Sensation was much more complete, power had improved to movement against gravity and some resistance for most muscle groups which had originally been completely paralysed, while it had returned to normal for groups where it had been only partially reduced when the trial began.

"There's only one thing," began Lucy, when Ray had completed the examination and note taking. "I've noticed that Lisa gets some incredible mood swings. One minute she can be quite cheery and the next she's biting my head off or bursting into tears for no reason. She was never like that before this illness, so it's very out of character for her."

"What do you feel, Lisa?"

"Well, it's hard to explain, but I just suddenly get incredibly angry or sad. There's nothing obvious to trigger it off. You remember when the Incredible Hulk used to turn green and swell up – I think he was called Dr David Banner when he was a normal person, but then something would set him off and he'd turn into the Hulk – it's a bit like that. I can't explain it, but I guess it's maybe something to do with the shock of improving so much so soon."

"Yes," added Lucy. "We're not complaining about it, but it's just that … well sometimes it scares me a bit, to see her like that. It's like she's someone else."

"OK, thanks for letting me know," said Ray. "I expect it will pass as you continue to get better and to get more back into normal life, but remember, if you're worried at any time, just call the study number and you'll get either me or Emilie for advice or a visit if you need it. I'll see you again in a month. Maybe we'll get a short walk in the grounds next time?"

"That would get the neighbours talking," laughed Lisa. "Lisa the Lesbian seen walking out with eligible man ... whatever next?"

Ray smiled as he packed up the case folder, having written down the gist of the consultation. Again he made a mental note to discuss this with Carter.

During the next few visits, the same scenario played out several times. Physical improvements were immense. All of the responders now reported that sensation was improving and that power seemed to be returning at an increased rate. Some of them were having problems with pretty severe pins and needles in their arms and legs, enough to keep them awake at night, but they all reckoned it was a small price to pay, and some of them actually enjoyed sensing that their nervous systems were recovering. Their carers were also delighted with the improvement although Ray could sense that some of them were getting anxious about what the future might hold for them. However, he decided not to bring it up at this stage. It was still possible that it could all go wrong, that these improvements could just be signs of a temporary remission and that the patients might lose function again. Also none of them yet was close to having entirely normal function, although week on week they all felt that they were getting better.

There was only one thing raising some concern. Of the next few responders that he saw, six were apparently having quite sudden mood swings, similar to the ones that Lisa had described so well as her Incredible Hulk moments. Mostly it was the carers who brought this up, and some of the patients denied it completely.

"Oh, he's just imagining it. He's got so used to having a turnip for a partner that he doesn't like it when I have an opinion on something ..."

Others, however, were concerned about it themselves.

"I don't know why it happens. It's like you were a little kid again when you threw your toys out of the pram. It generally doesn't last long, but it does scare me at the time."

Ray tried to be reassuring with all of them, although he too wondered why this was happening. Still, he thought, coming back from the nearly dead was never going to be entirely straightforward. Most of the patients and carers were happy to accept this sort of reassurance and put it to the back of their minds, at least for the moment.

CHAPTER 32

"It's all going splendidly," said Carter at the six-month review meeting. "I think there can be little doubt now that these people are going to go on to complete recovery, just as the mice did. Looking at your data, they could even be fully restored by nine months. It is possible that the trial monitoring committee will be willing to stop the trial early."

Ray thought that was an interesting choice of words. It suggested that Carter might try to influence the committee which was, after all, supposed to be completely independent. Maybe he was being too sensitive though.

"There's only one thing that worries me," said Ray. Carter raised a quizzical eyebrow. "A number of the responders are reporting quite severe mood swings. They seem to get angry for no apparent reason, and, for all except one, who was prone to that sort of thing before she got MS, it's quite out of character. I hope it's not some sort of side effect of the treatment."

"Oh, I think that's most unlikely," said Carter. "It's quite possible that they will react in different ways to the recovery of function. It might be that their carers are unconsciously provoking them by treating them as if they were still total invalids, while they are beginning to feel more like real people again."

"I suppose that's possible," said Ray, "although most of them seem to say that these episodes come out of the blue with nothing particular to provoke them. Anyway, I've noted it in the case files."

Carter tensed and sat forward in his chair. "I don't think there's any need to do that at this stage."

"But surely we have to record all the events that are reported in the trial. I mean, I've not yet called them adverse reactions or gone through any kind of reporting mechanism as such, but I think we do need to have the record."

"No," repeated Carter. "I don't want that sort of negative information recorded in the case files. I know that you've not been involved in this up to now, but I have reached a fairly critical stage of negotiations with Nefelsen Pharma, and I don't need to tell you there's a lot at stake. At some point, they might want to review some case files and I don't want any impediments to the deal appearing there, especially as it is likely to turn out to be nothing. I would be grateful if you could remove references to this issue at the moment, at least until the seven-month assessments, when you can reconsider whether they might be of importance. That's my final decision" he said, leaning forward and staring directly at Ray.

"OK, let's review it at the seven-month period," agreed Ray.

"Excellent!" smiled Carter, and leaned back contentedly in his chair.

The meeting finished with a review of next steps. Carter was about to head off on one his world trips again, including a visit to North Carolina, so they agreed that the next meeting would take place after the seven-month visits.

As Ray left the office, the enormity of what had just happened began to sink in. Was he just being over-sensitive, or was Carter actually asking him to amend the study case files of individual patients? That would be ethically improper and probably illegal, or at the very least severe research misconduct. On the other hand, although he didn't much like Carter and had misgivings about his style, he couldn't believe that a man who had reached his position could possibly be suggesting any kind of serious misconduct. Maybe Ray was just overreacting? Of course mood swings would be likely as people experienced such a dramatic change in their circumstances, even though it was for the better. As he had already considered, and discussed with Emilie, the carers and partners would also likely be in a hypersensitive state at this stage of the process, and maybe they were exaggerating the importance of small changes in behaviour.

But he couldn't go changing the case records. He would like to have someone to discuss this with, but it wasn't really appropriate to discuss it with Emilie, and in any case he didn't want to add any extra stress to her. Unfortunately, there was no equivalent of Dr Oldham, the animal inspector, for human studies. Ray was sure Oldham would know what to do in these circumstances. All of a sudden, he began to feel very exposed and unsure of himself. By the time he reached the office, he had made a decision.

"How did the meeting go? Was he pleased?" said Emilie, cheerily.

"Yeah, he was pretty pleased," Ray said, somewhat vaguely.

"You look a bit distracted. Something wrong?"

"No, no. He's going to be away for the next few weeks, so we've to carry on and meet again after the seven-month reviews. Listen, I know you'll be keeping in close touch with all the patients over the next wee while. I want you to let me know about any of these behavioural issues that they've mentioned. Don't go asking any leading questions, only do something if they report spontaneously or to some sort of open-ended question about whether anything is bothering them. If they do mention mood changes, tantrums or similar, can you record the specific circumstances, as much detail as you can without letting them think that you're overly interested in it?"

"Do you think it's a problem?" Emilie looked concerned.

"I don't know, but we need as much info as we can get. I've got to go over to the ward just now, I'll see you later."

Actually, he could have gone to the ward any time, but he wanted space to clear his head. He had no intention of altering the case files for all the reasons he'd already rehearsed to himself. Carter was going to be away for the next few weeks, so he had time to wait for the seven month review visits, and if Emilie was also collecting information as the trial went along they would be well informed when decisions had to be made. Hopefully Carter would prove right and all of this would blow over as the patients continued to improve and more psychological adjustments were made, but the whole thing about research was to observe, collect and interpret data and Ray was determined that they would do that, whatever Carter thought.

CHAPTER 33

It didn't take too long for some more reports to come through. Three days after his meeting with Carter, Emilie called him to say that she'd been asked to visit Theresa McCann. She was one of the responders who had had the most rapid recovery of function and both she and her partner Mickey had been delighted so far. However, Mickey had now called Emilie to ask if she could visit.

"I'm not sure what the problem is, nurse," he had said on the phone. "She seemed to be doing so well. She can walk now and she even made a coffee and a slice of toast for us the other day. She hasn't been able to do anything in the kitchen for years. But she keeps bursting into tears, and when I woke up in the middle of last night she had got up and was sitting in a chair, staring out of the window at the streetlights. I tried to talk to her, but it was like she couldn't hear me for a while. Eventually she just said that had been feeling a bit warm and got up to get some cool air. When we woke up this morning, she said she couldn't remember anything about it at all. She thought she had slept through."

Emilie went straight to the house and rang the doorbell. Theresa answered the door.

"Hello, Emilie, I wasn't expecting to see you today. Isn't it a nice day? I was just saying to Mickey that he could maybe take me in the car down to the beach for a while. We haven't been down there for ages, and it's years since I was able to walk on the sand, but I think I could manage a few steps today. Isn't that amazing? Anyway, you should come in and we'll get Mickey to make some tea. Mickey, look who's here! We weren't expecting her today, were we?"

Mickey looked a bit sheepish. "Actually I called her. I was a bit worried about that episode last night and I thought someone should look you over."

"Oh Mickey, that was nothing. I don't even remember it. Apparently," she said, turning to Emilie "I got out of bed during the night. I don't remember anything at all ... I guess I was just

155

sleepwalking. I don't think he needed to bother you with that. I'm sorry if you've had a wasted trip."

Mickey intervened: "Well, it wasn't just that, love. You know you've been having these crying episodes. It's not like you. I've been worried."

"Listen, Mickey. Nothing's 'like me' at the moment. Remember I've lain in that bed or sat in a wheelchair for the past five years. Sometimes I can't believe that I'm up and walking again, and all the rest of it. I get the odd panicky moment when I think it could all slip back again and that gets on top of me. You just need to give me some time and space."

Emilie interrupted: "You're probably right, Theresa. But because this is a new treatment, it's important that we just check everything out and Mickey was right to call me. I don't think we need to get Dr Shepherd involved, but if you could just let me check you over and take a couple of routine blood tests we can all rest happier. I have to say you do look amazing …"

"Oh well, I suppose flattery will get you anywhere, including into my precious blood." Theresa laughed and sat down in a chair by the window.

Emilie went over some mental state examination questions, some general functional questions and a very basic version of the examination that Ray would normally do. All seemed to be fine.

"That's all perfectly in order. I'll just take the blood and let you two get off to the beach now. Remember, if either of you have any concerns, you should let me or Dr Shepherd know. We're quite happy to come out for anything, and you'll not be wasting our time. It's very important to us to know how everyone in the trial is reacting to the treatment. Promise me you'll do that."

Theresa held up her hand in a mock courtroom pose. "We solemnly promise to tell the truth …" Mickey seemed to visibly relax as Theresa made light of it all. Maybe he had been reading too much into it.

After two weeks, Emilie had been out to four similar incidents with different patients. Ray decided that they should go through the circumstances one by one and make detailed notes, although for the moment he filed them separately from the patients study files. The last one they came to gave him a start.

"The last visit I made was yesterday," said Emilie, "I went to see Eric and Susan Strother …" She hesitated.

"And?"

"Well, I thought the atmosphere in the house was a bit weird. He's making amazing progress. He's up and walking about now. He can use his hands pretty well. The catheter's out. He seemed to be in expansive mood, talking about re-starting his rugby, getting back to work, all of that. He'd even been out for a pint with a mate. It's almost too good to be true ..."

"And is it? You said the atmosphere was weird."

"It was. I don't really know how to put this, but I thought that Susan seemed to be a bit afraid of him. Every time I tried to ask her a question, she seemed to look at him before she answered and then she just gave kind of bland answers. She didn't seem to be as pleased as I would have thought, given his obvious improvement."

"And is he having the mood swings? Did either of them say?"

"They both said that he got 'a bit tetchy' from time to time... probably just frustration, according to Eric."

"And according to Susan?"

"She wouldn't really add anything. She more or less went along with what he said. She maybe didn't want to upset the applecart but, like I say, I thought there was maybe a bit more to it than that, like she wasn't willing to contradict him."

"Well, I'll be seeing them in a couple of weeks for the seven-month visits, so I'll check it out then. In the meantime let me know if there are any other developments."

CHAPTER 34

That night, Ray went home early. He made himself a carbonara and washed it down with a small bottle of Peroni. He thought he would read some journals for a while, but he couldn't really settle. The events of the past few days kept replaying themselves. Emilie seemed to be gathering more evidence that something was happening to the mental state of some, actually most, of the patients. However, when she went to see them, they mostly made light of it and explained it all away as part of the adjustment process. Was it really important? Should he be recording it? Was Carter right that such events were not of any great import and not worthy of recording? And so on and so on … Eventually, he drifted off to sleep. Somewhere in his dreams a phone rang, and rang … and rang.

He jerked back into consciousness and picked up the phone from the table by his settee.

"Hello, is that Ray Shepherd?"

"Yes."

"This is Florence Smythe."

"Sorry?"

"Flo, your dad's neighbour, son. He's been taken bad. We've called for the ambulance and they're on their way. One of the lads from the building who's a nurse is with him now. He's going to have to go to the hospital. I think you should get here as soon as you can."

Ray was now fully alert. "Sure, I'm on my way. I'll go direct to the hospital. Thanks for letting me know."

"You're welcome, son. Drive carefully …"

Ray thought for a moment about taking the motorbike, but decided it might be a bit dangerous when he was as tired and stressed as he felt at the moment, so he opted for the car. As he drove up the motorway, he began to curse himself for not having been up to see his dad for the last couple of weekends. There really was no excuse for that. Of course he had been tied up with trial stuff, but he could have got a day away. Was he just lazy? Did he not care? Was there an element that he couldn't face up to illness in his own family when he was already stressed out dealing with patients? What kind of an attitude was that? How was his old man going to be? Ray knew that any acute event for his dad now could be the final one. Was this it? The drive passed by with these and other thoughts spinning around in his head.

His dad was lying on a trolley in the A&E department. He looked exhausted, not a good colour, and was blowing quite hard. He was hooked up to an ECG monitor, an oxygen mask and had a drip in his arm. He was still wearing a pair of tracksuit bottoms and a Harvard tee shirt that Ray had brought him from Boston some years before. But he was alive …

"Sorry to make such a stir, son," he said between gasps. "It just came on a bit worse tonight. I've been on the steroids and antibiotics for the past couple of days but they didn't seem to work this time. I didn't mean them to drag you all this way in the middle of the night though."

"That's no problem, Dad. I should have been at the weekend."

"Don't worry, son. There's nothing more that you could do. I think I've just about run out of lungs now. They're going to keep me in this time, so I'm just waiting for them to find a bed. They told me that might take a few hours. It started around tea time, just couldn't get me breath. Flo was good though, she came through and got the young boy from the building to look me over … he stayed with me until the ambulance came. I don't think I could have managed this one at home."

"No, Dad. You're in the right place. I'll have a word with the registrar and see what their plans are. I'll wait until you get into the ward and things are settling down too. Is there anything you need from home?"

"No, Flo helped me pack a bag a while back. I've kept it ready. I knew this was coming sooner or later. I've got all me papers sorted out at home. They're in the black box in the kitchen cupboard. There's not much, but there'll be enough to get me fried when the time comes…"

"Dad …"

"Come on, Ray. I'm not daft and we've talked about this a bit before. To be honest, I'm getting a bit tired of the whole thing. So if the Big Guy, or whoever decides these things, says it's time, then it's time. I've no regrets, no big ones anyway. Anyway, how's your work going? Can you let me in on the secret yet? I'm not going to tell anyone, not in this life anyway …"

"Well, it is top secret, but it looks bloody good is all I can say."

"Great, bloody great …" His dad's hand closed weakly on his and he dozed off again, exhausted by the effort of this short conversation.

As it turned out, it only took about an hour to find a bed in the chest ward for his dad; maybe Ray's presence had something to do with that, he wasn't sure, but whatever the reason, it was good to see him settled on the ward. He seemed to have shrunk even since the last time Ray had seen him and his assessment that it wouldn't be long was probably right. Ray decided to stay overnight in the ward day room and travel back in the morning, assuming things had stabilised.

The consultant arrived early, about 7 a.m., and confirmed what Ray had thought. His dad was moving into ventilatory failure, possibly the end-stage of his lung disease. They were going to give him a try with a machine to assist his breathing but, according to his dad's express wish, if that did not work he would not be admitted for full intensive care and artificial ventilation. Ray agreed that was sensible. People with very advanced lung disease of his dad's type rarely survived that type of treatment with any quality of life and he was sure that his dad would not want it. Although it was serious though, the consultant did not think there was any imminent danger of him dying, and so Ray decided to head back to work for the rest of that day at least. In some strange way, the acute problem with his dad had slightly defused some of his stress over the way the trial was going and let him think more logically about it.

"You're a bit better this morning, Dad. I'm going to head back down to work, but I'll be back up if there's any problem. They've got my number. You take care."

"No worries, son. I'll not be going anywhere in a hurry. You drive carefully …"

On the drive back, he considered all the options and concluded that his current approach to the study was the right one. He would continue to collect data and do the seven-month assessments. If there was evidence of persisting behavioural disturbance then, he would demand that Carter allow him to record it in the case files and, if necessary, report it as a potential adverse reaction to treatment. Whatever the consequences for any commercial deal that Carter might be cooking up, that was the correct and ethical thing to do.

He wondered about calling Liz. She would understand the issues and could give an independent view. But it wasn't really fair. He'd spent a lot of time leaning on her in the past, and that dependency had cost them their relationship. Their more recent time in Barcelona had been great, and for a few hours as they lay together they had both considered whether they had split up too easily. But although the sex had been good, the whole episode had felt more like some sort of closure. Maybe best left like that.

CHAPTER 35

When he got back to the office, he explained to Emilie what had happened overnight with his dad.

"God, Ray, you must be exhausted. Are you sure you should even be here? I can take the calls you know. Why don't you get home and get some rest?"

"I've got a few things I have to do this morning. But I might go home this afternoon and get a couple of hour's kip. I'm going back to see my dad tonight, though if he's doing OK I'll try to get home later so I can get some sleep. I've got an extra clinic to do tomorrow since Carter is away."

"That's fine. Leave the study phone with me today. I've got your mobile so if anything major happens I can keep you posted. There's not been anything in the past twenty-four hours that I've heard about, so maybe it's beginning to settle down."

"Let's hope so."

That night, Ray found his dad sitting up in bed. He was hooked up to the BiPAP machine. This was a kind of ventilator, but one step back from the type of thing used in the intensive care unit. It basically assisted the patient's own breathing, helping to make sure that they got enough oxygen in and carbon dioxide out, but also in the process giving his breathing muscles a bit of a rest.

"You're looking a better colour. Don't try to speak, you won't be able to do it comfortably with that mask on. Some signs will do fine. Are you feeling a bit better?"

His dad put both thumbs up.

"Did you get some sleep?" Thumbs up.

"Did you manage to eat much?" Thumbs down.

This was one of the problems for people with bad lung disease such as COPD. They found it difficult to eat at all, as they got breathless while they tried to chew. If they did manage to swallow much they would feel full very quickly due to the pressure of their diaphragm on their stomach, so they usually couldn't eat big meals. Finally, in a cruel twist of fate, research had shown that their requirements for intake of energy in the form of calories actually rose if they had COPD, in much the same way that a normal person's energy requirements would go up if they were at high altitude. So their bodies needed more energy but they were physically only able to take in less. People had tried all sorts of ways around this, including feeding small high energy meals often, putting a tube in the stomach and giving nasogastric feeds in liquid form, and others, but in general many patients with COPD gradually wasted away, in exactly the way that Ray's dad was doing now.

Anyway, at least he was getting some fluid in the form of an infusion and Ray could see from the end of bed chart that his oxygen levels looked much healthier, so he did seem to be improving. Ray stayed for while and read some of the paper to his dad, picking out the parts he thought he'd be interested in but avoiding things that might make him agitated or laugh since he didn't want to kick off more severe coughing fits.

After a couple of hours, he said he'd head off again but would be back tomorrow.

His dad pulled the mask to one side for a brief few seconds

"Thanks, son, I've enjoyed tonight." With that, he pulled the mask on again and closed his eyes. Ray thought he looked more contented than he had seen him for a while.

It took about five days for his dad to be weaned off the breathing assist machine. Ray didn't manage to see him every day, but by day six, he was clearly better and they were thinking about letting him home again. Ray sensed that although he had improved, he had lost a bit of ground overall. He decided to speak to the consultant about it.

"Thanks again for all you've done for him. He's obviously much better than when he came in, but he seems to lose a bit of strength every time he gets an exacerbation."

"I realise that. We have an assisted discharge programme now, so when he goes home he'll have a lot of help. We're also putting in a telecare system so that he can alert us if he has an acute problem, although I understand he has good neighbours too. I think he'll manage OK for a bit yet."

Ray nodded. "Unfortunately, I have to be close to the hospital for my clinical work and for this trial I'm involved with. I'll try to get to see him more."

"I know how difficult it is for you. I understand you're working on MS. I did read about the mouse studies – I guess we all did – an amazing piece of work. Incidentally, your dad says you're doing more work in that area but it's all hush hush – his lips are sealed …"

"I think we were lucky with the mice," said Ray blushing a little, "and yes we are doing more but I can't really say anything about it at the moment. It's pretty full on though …"

"Well good luck with that. We'll do our best for your dad in the meantime, and if there's anything you need at any time just give me a call. He's a great patient, you know, mainly because he's got definite ideas about how he wants to be treated and he's not slow to let us know if he thinks something's not right. He is a true gentleman though, and proud as punch of you, incidentally, although I don't know whether he'd ever tell you that."

"Thanks, I am very grateful for all you've done, the whole of your team actually. There's a great feeling to the ward here."

With that, Ray went back to see his dad briefly.

"So you're getting home again. Sounds as though you'll have good support, but if there's anything up you must let me know. I'd rather that than panic phone calls in the middle of the night."

"I know, son. I'll try to keep things together but I will let you know if things are not right. You take care too."

As he drove home, Ray knew that the next few weeks were going to be challenging for his dad, but also for him. The seven-month visits were due to start soon and he might have to confront Carter if things were not going smoothly.

CHAPTER 36

The seven-month visits came round almost quicker than he had expected, although he was glad to be getting going with the formal assessments. Emilie had fielded a few more calls and visits over the past couple of weeks, with the same issues coming up again and again. She hadn't been called back to the Strothers' though.

As Ray went around, a pattern began to emerge. The non-responders, those who had likely had the dummy treatment, were declining slowly but surely. A number of them were having increasing episodes of urinary and chest infections and were losing more muscle strength.

Chris Higgins was typical. Every time that Ray visited, there was no sign of improvement. In fact, looking across the serial charts in the notes, there was a slow but sure progressive loss of sensation and a further decrease in muscle power. During the past two or three visits, Chris had been in bed when he arrived. Ray felt that Kath was always on the brink of asking him how the other patients were doing but that she held back, perhaps out of respect for the trial, or perhaps because she didn't want to hear that no one had responded and that hope was gone. Ray went through the usual routine, documented everything carefully and made the usual noises about not knowing what to expect from the trial, the potentially long incubation period for prions and so on, but he knew that they were both losing hope. Ray left with mixed feelings, knowing that he might have a potential treatment to offer them, but not just yet.

The responders, on the other hand, were going literally from strength to strength. In most of them, power had returned virtually to normal, as had sensation. Some of them still showed some difficulties with coordination. Among the usual clinical tests for this were asking the patient to touch the tip of their nose with the tip of each index finger, to run their heels up and down their shins, and to walk in a straight line. Given that none of them could walk at all at the beginning of the trial, to see them complain about not quite following the straight line exactly was almost comical.

However, as well as the physical improvements, most of them seemed to have some complaint of mood changes. In two or three cases this mainly took the form of episodes of acute and extreme depression. They would cry, lose motivation, stare out of the window for a while, or describe feelings of worthlessness. These attacks, for there was no other word to describe them, seemed to come on very suddenly for no apparent reason and could last anything from a few minutes to five hours in extreme cases. Once the attack was over, the patients would return to normal emotions until the next attack happened. Amanda Trail was one of those affected.

"It's really weird, Dr Shepherd," said Joseph, after he had completed the routine examination. "Amanda can be sitting in the chair, doing nothing, and suddenly she'll burst into tears. It's really hard to get through to her, and it lasts for anything up to a couple of hours. I don't know what to do about it."

"And you know the strangest thing?" added Amanda. "Sometimes when I get these attacks I feel profoundly that the Lord has left me, that He doesn't exist. I try to call out to Him, and nothing comes back. How can that be? I know that He has brought me to where I am today. Through you, He has brought me this miracle treatment. He has made me walk again and brought the feeling back to my limbs. And yet, from time to time, He seems to desert me completely. During those times, I'm terrified …"

Other patients reported sudden loss of temper. On his return visit to Lisa and Lucy, once they had completed the formalities and rewound the jokes about Lisa walking out with him, they both admitted that Lisa's sudden and violent temper tantrums, as they called them, were still a major problem.

"You know I broke a vase the other day … just threw it on the floor because it had a flower on it that I didn't like the look of. It reminded me of a particularly unhelpful nurse that I once had in the early days of the illness when I was in for a lumbar puncture. I thought she was staring out at me again from that vase so I smashed her on the kitchen floor. How crazy is that?"

Lucy added: "It does seem when she has these episodes that I can't get through to her at all. They never last long and compared to all that's happened before they're a minor thing, but we thought you should know about them …"

"Yes, thanks," said Ray. "I'm not sure what to advise. It would be a good idea, if you can, to make a note of any events immediately preceding each attack, just in case there's some precipitating factor that you haven't identified yet. Do you get any warning that it's going to happen?"

"Now that you mention it, Dr Shepherd, I often feel a lot of energy just before the attack comes on. It's almost as though it has to find somewhere to go, and it comes out as bad temper. Like I said before, it's that Incredible Hulk thing. I know that sounds mad, but it's a bit of a mad world just now. Everything else is good though, better than good."

Ray's greatest anxiety began, however, when he went to see Eric and Susan Strother.

They were expecting him, but there was still a short delay before the door was answered. For the first time since he had met them, Eric answered. He was beaming from ear to ear and even at first glance was obviously gaining muscle bulk.

"Hiya, doc. How are you doing? Great to see you! Come in, come in …"

Ray made his way through to the living room. The bed was gone now, replaced by new carpet and two large armchairs. Some more pictures had been laid out on the mantelpiece and there was a vase of fresh flowers on the sideboard that had served as the tray for the catheter equipment when Ray first visited.

"What do you think, doc? Looks more like a real house now, eh? The hospital took their bed back last week so I guess there's no going back. Would you like a cup of tea? Susan, have you not got that kettle boiled yet?"

"Just coming!" shouted a familiar voice from the kitchen.

Susan came through carrying a tray with some cups, a pot of tea and a plate of biscuits. As she came in to the light, Ray could see that she was wearing quite a lot of make-up, more than he had ever seen before. As she came closer to hand him the cup and saucer, he noticed a slight discoloration around her right eye, and maybe even a hint of some swelling.

"Sorry about the state of my eye. I dropped a stretcher when I was hanging out washing the other day and it caught me full in the face. Didn't I, dear?"

"Yep. They do say that most accidents happen in the home. I

suppose that includes the back green," said Eric.

"Sorry to hear that," said Ray. "It looks pretty sore."

"Oh it's nothing really," replied Eric. "Anyway, do you want to see what I can do now? I think I'll be ready for an arm wrestle with you soon. I would say I'm about ninety-nine per cent of normal now, but I suppose you'll want to go through all the tests again …"

"Of course," said Ray. "That's what I'm here for, but it sounds like all good news."

Ray spent the next hour on the usual routine. Eric's estimate of ninety-nine per cent return to normal wasn't far off the mark. In fact a lot of ordinary folk would probably have felt one hundred per cent at Eric's level of function, but of course he had been a keen athlete, so probably carried even higher expectations. At the end of the systematic examination, Ray asked the usual question.

"Is there anything else that either of you want to report at the moment?"

"I don't think so," said Eric. "Is there, dear?"

"No, nothing," said Susan, studiously avoiding eye contact with either of them.

"Earlier in the study, you were having some mood swings. Is that still a problem?" Ray was determined to follow this up.

"Not at all. I'm absolutely fine, thanks to you and the worms."

"Worms?" queried Ray.

"These things you put in my head … Prions is it? I prefer to think of them as worms. Worms are good things you know … ask any gardener."

"I suppose you're right, Eric," said Ray. "I guess worms get a bad press a lot of the time."

"Just like men, eh Susan?" added Eric. "Well if that's all for today, I'll let you get on your way. I suppose you want us to keep mum about the trial for a bit longer, although I have to say the neighbours are talking a bit now. 'Cripple goes down the pub under his own steam' … that sort of thing …"

"Yes, we'd prefer not to have publicity yet, although if everyone improves as fast as you, I guess we'll be making it public soon," said Ray.

"I'll see you to the door," said Susan.

"No need for that, dear. I'm quite capable now …" said Eric, hastily.

As Ray walked down the path, his mind was in overdrive again. Eric was obviously transformed physically and seemed in excellent spirits. However, at the very least, the dynamic between him and Susan had changed dramatically. It was as though she'd been relegated. And what about the clothes pole story? Was that really what had happened? However, Ray had to admit to himself that there was nothing concrete to record in this case note apart from dramatic and sustained improvement.

CHAPTER 37

The next meeting with Carter came around just as Ray was finishing off the seven-month visits.

"Well, Ray, I hope you've more good news to report," he beamed as Ray came into the room carrying some of the patient study files.

"There's certainly no doubt that half of them are improving and the other half are unchanged. Most of the improvers are nearly up to normal sensation and power now. Some still have slight coordination issues, but I think that will come as their muscle strength builds up. The non-responders, who I assume had placebo, are slowly deteriorating as you would expect. One or two of them are going to struggle to reach the end of the trial, I think."

"Yes, yes. I think we might to have a quiet word with the trial monitoring committee. They haven't met formally for over six weeks now, not since before our last meeting," said Carter. "I assume you've corrected those case files as we discussed?"

"Actually I haven't made any changes to the case files. Indeed we've collected a bit more information about the mood swings and attacks of aggression that a number of the patients and carers are reporting. I think that we have to include that information. In fact I think that one of the patients I saw recently, who's among the most advanced in his physical recovery, might be beating his wife."

"Really, did he tell you that?"

"No."

"Did she tell you that?"

"No ..."

"What did they tell you?"

"Well, actually nothing. Earlier in the trial they said that he was having mood swings but he says that's all stopped now and she backed him up, although I think she was afraid to speak ..."

Carter rose deliberately from his chair, walked over to close the door, and sat down again, leaning towards Ray in a menacing manner.

"Listen to me, Dr Shepherd. I said I wanted these trivial reports of mood swings removed from the case files and that's what I expect to happen. I am not sure how your mind is working on this, so let me spell it out for you. I took you on to this research team when you said you were interested in helping people with MS. Well, the progress we have made so far is more than we could ever have imagined back then and you are due some credit for that. However, we are now on the brink of a breakthrough that will revolutionise the lives of patients all over the world. To make that happen, we need to have a major pharma company on board. I spoke with Nefelsen's chairman and CEO last week in Raleigh, and they are going to visit in a few weeks' time. I am going to have to show them some case files. The deal we are about to do with them will mean that, as well as the academic acclaim we will get for this work, our institution will be rich, as will we. I have already invested a large amount of my time and departmental resource in this project and I will not see the successful outcome jeopardised because you want to document some minor mood swings and, worse still, some totally unfounded speculation about wife beating, in the case files ..."

"I didn't say we should record anything about that incident as it is unproven, but some of the other things are matters of fact ..." countered Ray.

"I don't agree and I don't think you're listening, Dr Shepherd. I made your career in medical research and I can just as easily destroy it. There are plenty of bright young things who would give their eye teeth for the post you have at the moment. So ... I would suggest that we bring this meeting to a close now; that you go off and amend the records accordingly, and we meet again in ten days to plan the pitch to the Nefelsen people when they come. Is that clear?"

Ray said nothing, but gathered the folders and made to leave the room. Turning the door handle was awkward with the large folders under his arm, but Carter made no effort to help, having gone back to his main desk and already being engrossed in something on his laptop.

By the time Ray reached his office, he was shaking. He wasn't sure why, was it fear or anger or a combination of both?

Emilie looked concerned as he came through the door.

"You look like you've seen a ghost. I take it the meeting went badly. Can I get you something, tea or coffee?"

"Coffee would be good, thanks, Emilie and then could you shut the door? I need to talk this through with you."

Once Emilie had produced the coffee, they sat down and Ray relayed the events that had just taken place.

"I didn't want to involve you in this Emilie and I'm sorry that I have done, but I'm kind of at my wit's end and I don't know who else to speak to. You've seen the patients. You know this isn't an entirely trivial thing. Altering the case files is at the very least research misconduct, and I think is probably illegal, too. He's demanding that I break the law. On the other hand, who am I to argue against him? Just about everyone in the world knows who he is, and if they don't they will soon, and he's right, he could swat me like a fly and nobody would notice much after a few weeks. I really just don't know what to do. I've got seven days before we meet again. One thing is for sure, I'm not going to change these records, that would be just wrong."

Emilie sat for long time. "This is terrible, Ray. Did he really say that you were due *some* credit? I would say that this whole breakthrough is more to do with you than him. He just swans around the world glad-handing people. He wouldn't know any of the patients in this study if he fell over them in the street."

"That might be true, Emilie, but he is still the international face of the study and he's right that there is a lot at stake. On the other hand, I think if we were upfront with the Nefelsen people, they might well accept that this is a significant side effect but compared to the benefit the patients have gained, it's not a deal breaker. Carter doesn't see it that way though. I wish there was someone, an expert, I could talk this through with."

"There is," said Emilie, her face brightening up. "Aren't you a member of some sort of medical insurance or indemnity thing? Don't they have lawyers and people like that who could advise you? Surely you could speak to one of them?"

"Emilie, you're brilliant. That never even crossed my mind. I pay hefty subscriptions to the Medical Defence Society. I always thought of them as more to do with my clinical work, but this is a clinical trial. I'll call them today …"

"I have to go out and see a couple of patients today, so you'll have the office to yourself. I suppose I should keep collecting any information that we think might be relevant?"

"Of course … and thanks, Emilie, you're a star."

As soon as she'd gone, Ray fished out his Medical Defence Society membership card and called them. After negotiating his way through one of the dreaded push-button menus, he found himself speaking to a young adviser, whose name he didn't quite catch at the first introduction.

"How can we help you, Dr Shepherd?"

"Well, this might be a slightly unusual request, but I'm involved in medical research, actually a clinical trial, at the moment, and I'm coming under pressure from my boss, who is a senior clinical academic, to make alterations to the patients' trial records, removing references to symptoms that I think are important but that he doesn't wish to have recorded at this time."

"Can I stop you right there, Dr Shepherd? This sounds potentially serious but is an area of specialty practice. You need to talk to my colleague, Dr Singh. If you'd like to hold, I'll try to put you through to him now."

"Thank you very much," said Ray. The effort of getting even this first bit of the story out had exhausted him and he was shaking, but at least he felt he was on the right track now.

Shortly, a very cultured Asian voice said: "Good morning, Dr Shepherd. My name is Dr Singh. I am one of the specialist medical advisers with the society. How can I be of help to you?"

Ray briefly recounted the events to date in the trial and his meeting today with Carter.

"You did the right thing in contacting us, Dr Shepherd. Now I would like to take you through events in much more detail …"

Ray spent the next thirty to forty minutes telling the whole story from the beginning. Dr Singh stopped him quite frequently to clarify dates and times of certain events and for Ray to read verbatim sections from the case files, without disclosing any personal details of the patients. Ray sensed that he was making detailed notes. Eventually Dr Singh said: "Thank you, Dr Shepherd, for that first outline."

Ray was taken aback; he thought he had catalogued every single event. Dr Singh continued: "This is indeed a serious business and will require to be handled carefully. On first impressions, there are a number of areas in which Professor Carter is culpable. He has demanded that you alter a clinical case record which is illegal; he is intending to divulge confidential information to a potential commercial partner before the trial is completed, which is at best bad practice and at worst misconduct; and he is using his position as an internationally recognised academic to bully a junior colleague which may infringe employment law. However, we need to collect more concrete evidence as at present it would simply be your word against his. I would therefore like to visit you within the next forty-eight hours to discuss how we take this forward. Time is of the essence here."

"What is likely to happen?" asked Ray.

"Well, first we must collect more information, evidence if you like, and then you will be required to report it to the authorities, both the university as a research misconduct issue and the General Medical Council as a medical malpractice issue. In the meantime, before my visit, I would like you to document all that you have just told me together with all other data that you think might be relevant. In due course we may need to see extracts from case files etc. as evidence. In terms of our meeting, how would 9 a.m. in two days' time suit? You should set aside the entire morning if possible and it might be best to meet outside your place of work, perhaps our regional office – you'll have the address on your membership card."

"Thank you, Dr Singh. You've been most helpful."

"One other thing, Dr Shepherd. I can tell you from experience that this will be a very stressful process for you. You should be prepared for that …"

With that, he was gone. Ray wondered how you prepared for this sort of thing. There was no quick guide. However, he knew that the most important thing was to stick to his principles.

CHAPTER 38

In the flesh, Dr Singh proved to be much as Ray had imagined him from the telephone conversation: small, handsome and dapper, in a very smart suit, blue shirt and silk tie. He appeared of indeterminate age, although Ray knew from some checking that he had done during the past day that he was in his late forties and was both a qualified doctor and a barrister. He carried a metallic laptop/briefcase which he opened to reveal, again as Ray had expected, detailed notes from their telephone discussion.

After the usual handshakes, introductions and production of coffee for Ray and a glass of water for Dr Singh, they got down to business. First Ray handed him the document that he had prepared, setting out all the details of events to date so far as he could recall them. Dr Singh asked for an up-to-date copy of his CV, which fortunately he had had the foresight to bring, and also briefly questioned him on any previous convictions, complaints about his clinical practice, etc. Ray was pleased to be able to confirm that there were none. Dr Singh then produced his first bombshell of the day.

"Well, Dr Shepherd, that all seems to be in order. I'll go through your statement later and combine it with anything else that seems relevant from our telephone discussion. I'll then produce a final draft, dated document, that I will require you to sign with a witness and we'll keep that on file. However, as I said to you the other day, at the moment we have only your word against that of Professor Carter, who could, of course, deny that the conversation ever took place. What I suggest therefore is that we record your next meeting with him, in case he should repeat these threats, which I think in the circumstances is very likely."

"Record it, how do we do that?" said Ray.

"We ask you to wear a concealed recording device; a wire, if you like."

"I can't believe we're having this conversation," said Ray. "You mean a wire, like in the Bond movies or something?"

175

"I think you'll find the technology now is rather better than in the old Bond movies." Dr Singh smiled. "With modern digital technology we can get video and audio of very good quality that would be admissible in a court or GMC proceeding. In fact, I have brought some suitable equipment with me."

He reached into the briefcase again and brought out a miniature camera and recorder that could easily be concealed in the collar of a garment.

"We can lend you this for the meeting," he said in a matter-of-fact sort of way. "Once you have some video or audio evidence of Professor Carter repeating these threats, then we can support you as you submit it to the relevant authorities. Of course I don't know what the implications will be for your study."

"Well, I've been thinking about that," said Ray. "I think we just carry on with the trial as planned. Once I've told Professor Carter that I am going to report this to the authorities, I suspect it will take Nefelsen Pharma out of the picture, at least for a while, but if we complete the trial and confirm that the treatment is successful, albeit with some side effects in terms of mood swings, which seem to be the only issue we've found so far, then they or other companies might want to come back on board. I don't think that outing Professor Carter, if he repeats his threats, would necessarily take the research down, in fact the opposite should be the case."

"I agree, Dr Shepherd, but as I said on the phone, these things can take twists and turns and no matter what, it will probably not be quite as simple as you outline. However, you have done the right thing and the important issue to keep in mind is that you continue to act in a morally and ethically defensible way throughout. Now, let me show you how this piece of kit works …"

An hour later, Ray was fully trained in the art of espionage, as he saw it, and was back out on the street. As he left the MDS offices, he found himself looking at people in the street in a new light. He wondered if they might be filming as they went … His eyes also strayed up to the ubiquitous CCTV cameras. Of course he knew from the newspapers that Britain was probably the most surveyed population in the world and that many people's movements would be on CCTV footage somewhere. However, until now he hadn't really thought too much about it.

★★★

The next few days were difficult for Ray. The whole thing had now moved into territory that made him very uncomfortable. Reports coming back from Emilie indicated that the responders continued to improve but were also suffering quite dramatic mood swings. Ray carried on collecting data and recording as much as he could, but every quiet minute, he would find himself replaying his conversation with Carter, speculating on how the next meeting would go, wondering how it would feel to take the first moves on the whistle-blowing process. Telling the tale to Dr Singh had not been so stressful, indeed had been a bit of a relief, but that was probably because he felt that Dr Singh was on his side. Replaying it to a potentially more hostile audience was going to be a much more difficult experience. He began to realise that he needed to confide in someone, but who? He decided to take a risk.

"Thanks for coming," he said, handing over a coffee in a quiet corner of the small coffee house where he was sure they couldn't be overheard.

"I was intrigued, sounded all very cloak and dagger. What can I do for you?" Paul Schmidt leaned forward in his chair and cocked his head slightly to one side.

"Sorry for all the drama," said Ray, "but what I am about to tell you is extremely confidential. In fact I'm not sure that I should be dragging you into this, but I had to tell someone otherwise I was going to explode. You need to know that there is a potential problem with the MS trial."

Over the next fifteen minutes Ray recounted all the events: the clinical data that he was collecting; the conversations with the patients and carers; the discussions with Carter; his advice from the Medical Defence Society; and his meeting with Dr Singh. "... I'm afraid that you are going to be dragged into this at some stage as one of the principal researchers ..."

A long pause ensued when he had finished. Paul took a big breath and leaned back in his chair. "Wow, that is a story. I don't really know what to say ..."

"I don't think you need to say or do anything right now. I'll be having this meeting with Carter soon. Maybe it will all blow over; he'll see the sense of recording the data properly and taking the consequences on the chin. However, I have to say I don't think that's likely. If he holds his ground and repeats his threats, I don't think there is any alternative for me other than to report him to the relevant authorities. Once I've done that, I guess all hell will break loose and they'll probably want statements from us and so on. I also don't know what will happen to the trial, although my instinct is that if the treatment proves to be as successful as it looks so far, then we won't have trouble finding funding partners, maybe even Nefelsen, if everything else is handled correctly.

"I guess that's right," said Paul. "Certainly, and without giving anything away since I don't know the allocation codes either, there are some people whose scans are improved beyond all recognition, and others who haven't changed or have worsened, so I am seeing a pattern of responders and non-responders in the radiology, just as you are with the clinical findings. If the behaviour disturbance becomes an even more major issue clinically, I suppose we might be able to see something on the functional MRI images, but I'm not aware that I've seen anything like that so far, although to be honest I've not been looking specifically for something that might be very subtle."

Ray stayed quiet …

"But there's no doubt that you're doing the right thing," continued Paul. "If you're looking for support from me, then you'll have it. There's no way that I would want to be associated with anything that was less than rigorous science. You poor guy, I can't really imagine how it must feel for you. After all he's only my colleague, even though I'm sure he wouldn't see the relationship as quite that egalitarian, but he is your boss, and it is something to have to take him on. But as long as you are doing what is right, then you shouldn't have to worry."

"Funny, that's more or less what Dr Singh said too, although it doesn't help too much at four in the morning when I'm still awake. Anyway, thanks for listening and for your support. As I said, I just had to tell someone or I was going to explode. I'll keep you posted and in the meantime I guess that we just 'Keep Calm and Carry On' …"

"Surely you're not reading these posters too!" Paul laughed for the first time in the meeting. He punched Ray playfully on the shoulder and headed off to pay for the coffees. The least he could do, he thought.

CHAPTER 39

After the meeting with Paul, Ray felt a little lighter. Over the next few days he found that he was able to focus better on the work in hand, and less on the what-ifs. Emilie too noticed that he seemed to be a bit happier... not quite his usual self, but better. However, he still couldn't totally free himself from the background worry and from the thought that more bad things were going to happen. As it turned out he didn't have long to wait.

The phone rang just after eleven in the evening. Ray was listening to an old 'British Blues Invasion' album and trying, unsuccessfully, to read a five-week old edition of the *British Medical Journal*. Normally he was quite good at keeping up with the main journals, at least reading anything of relevance to his specialty, but lately he had slipped behind and the pile of unread print journals on his floor was growing ominously. Nowadays, of course, people mainly used the internet and online resources, but Ray always found that while the internet was good for checking and finding specific things, paper journals were still better for browsing. Sometimes the lateral thoughts that came from that process were among the most useful ones.

"Ray, it's Billy Hood here, A&E." Billy was a contemporary of Ray's from medical school; he had gone off to train as an emergency medicine specialist. They hadn't been close pals, but they had been on a couple of hillwalking trips when they were students, although in terms of his climbing, Billy had moved on to greater things. When he wasn't being an A&E doctor, he was most likely to be off in the jungle or in the Karakoram, climbing serious peaks.

"Hello Billy, it's late for you to be calling. What's up?"

"The strangest thing ... I've got an unconscious patient here, a young woman called Trail. It seems she's taken an overdose. There's a bloke with her, says he's her partner, Joseph I think his name is. He says she's got severe MS but has had some miracle treatment that has made her walk again. Well, she seems to have walked down to the chemist and bought enough over-the-counter stuff to flatten a mule. She's taken a mix of things, including paracetamol, so we're just getting on with the blood levels, the gastric lavage and so on. Joseph was most insistent that we call you; he was going to do it, but I wasn't sure that he'd make any sense; in fact I wasn't sure that he wasn't just some nutter who might have tried to do her in. Does all this mean anything to you?"

"I'm afraid so. She is a patient of mine and all that Joseph has told you is true. I'll come down straight away and can fill you in then. As far as treatment is concerned, she's not taking any medication at the moment, and you should just treat her in the standard way. How's it looking anyway?"

"Oh, she's sick, but I think she'll be OK. Joseph got to her pretty quickly so there should be plenty of time to give her the NAC and so on. Give me a shout when you get here. It's a bit of a zoo as usual, but we might even stand you a coffee, in return for more inside info on whatever you're up to."

Ray gave a wry smile. 'If only he knew the half of it,' he thought to himself as he fished out some smarter looking clothes and prepared to head down to the emergency department.

As he entered the waiting room, he saw the usual morass of anxious old people whose relatives had some acute problem; tattooed neds whose mates were probably drunk, drugged or injured from fighting and some of whom would like to carry on the fight in the waiting room; tearful young women whose pals had flaked out on drink or drugs or who had been molested in some nightclub or other; and other people there for miscellaneous reasons. Joseph was moving towards him from the corner of the room where Ray guessed he had been trying to make himself as inconspicuous as possible.

"Dr Shepherd, I'm so glad you're here. I just came home and found her on the settee. She seemed to have taken a lot of pills and she was moaning but not making any sense. I'd only been gone for a couple of hours. I shouldn't have left her, you know. She's been a bit low for the last few days, but today I thought she was brighter and she said she wanted to go out for walk on her own. I thought that was a good thing. I never thought …" He couldn't continue.

"Listen, Joseph, you've done all the right things. If you don't mind I'll go through to see her now and talk to you after that. From what Dr Hood said on the phone, I think she's going to be okay, partly due to your quick thinking, but I'll be able to tell you more once I've seen her …"

"I was with her, you know, but they asked me to come back here while they did some treatment – a gastric something …?"

"Yeah, that would be routine. I'll be back in a little while."

It wasn't surprising that Joseph had been asked to leave while the 'gastric something' went on. Ray had seen and done enough gastric lavages when he was a more junior doctor to know what to expect, although he also knew that this treatment had largely gone out of fashion now and was only very rarely performed. As he reached the treatment room, the scene was familiar, but it was still a shock to him to see someone that he knew on the treatment table.

Amanda was lying on her side, the table tilted to keep her head down. Her hair was matted and wet in places. A tube had been placed in her windpipe through which oxygen was being administered. Another large tube had been pushed through her mouth and down into her stomach and a saline solution was being flushed in and out of her stomach using a large filling funnel. The material retrieved from her stomach was being examined for evidence of pills or other material. Billy and a nurse were holding the funnel, wearing blue plastic aprons and gloves.

"Oh, hi Ray. Come in. We don't often do this these days, but I wasn't entirely sure what she'd taken so we thought we'd wash out her stomach and leave some charcoal at the end." Activated charcoal was often used to try to prevent further absorption of toxins from the stomach of overdose patients. Conscious patients could be asked to drink it, but in those with reduced consciousness it had to be put in via a tube. "We'll get some paracetamol levels shortly and decide on the NAC then."

Paracetamol, taken in overdose, could cause severe, potentially fatal liver damage. However, its effect took a while to come on and could be blocked if an antidote called n-acetyl cysteine or NAC, was given in the right window of time after the overdose. The dose of NAC was determined by checking a blood paracetamol level which had to be taken more than four hours after the overdose had been swallowed to allow time for absorption. As Joseph had found Amanda quite quickly after the overdose, there was plenty of time for this to be done. However, the fact that she was unconscious indicated that she must have taken other poisons as well. Billy

181

hoped that they might be able to identify these from the stomach washings or from a series of other blood screening tests that he had taken. Once they knew what they were dealing with, they would be able to deliver any other specific treatment. In the meantime, it was a case of monitoring her carefully; making sure that she was breathing adequately and that she didn't vomit and inhale stomach contents into her lungs; and keeping an eye on other parameters such as blood pressure and heart rate.

"Once we've finished here, I'll get her through to high dependency and we'll get the NAC going if needed. Now what about this miracle cure for her MS?"

"I'll tell you about that in a minute. I think you promised a coffee …?"

"OK, let me get finished up here and I'll meet you in the docs' room …"

Five minutes later, over a cup of coffee, Ray told Billy a little about the trial. Of course, he explained they were blinded to which treatment, active or placebo, that Amanda might have had. In theory, they could ask for the trial code to be broken now since Amanda had another acute medical problem. However, Billy didn't think that was necessary as it would not alter her current treatment in any way. It did seem most likely that she had had the active treatment.

"Any reason why she might have done this?" asked Billy. "I'd have thought she'd be on the top of the world right now. Any previous?"

"Well she did have some episodes of mild depression years ago, but that was put down to her early diagnosis of MS. So far as we know, there's no previous history of overdose. They are a very religious couple, not that that guarantees lifelong happiness and an absence of mental health issues."

"Certainly not," said Billy. "We have our share of God squadders through here, as you know."

"I suppose coming back from the near dead might not be without its own stresses though," said Ray, not wishing to commit himself any more at this stage.

"I guess so," said Billy. "We've seen it in some mountaineers who've survived near-death experiences and then go on to feel guilty at their good fortune. I know, before you say it, us climbers are all one piton short of a via ferrata anyway."

"Each to their own … I'd better get back to talk to Joseph. He's a really nice guy you know, and they're devoted to each other. He'll be devastated at this."

"Well, I think she'll do OK. Of course it's always a worry while she's unconscious but I think she'll come through that and we've got her early enough that the paracetamol shouldn't be too much of a problem."

"Is it OK if I use your interview room to talk to Joseph? It's a bit of a madhouse in the waiting room."

"You mean you don't like our happy families out there? You can see why we need full-time boys in blue to keep a lid on things. You're welcome to the interview room and you can tell him to come through to the high dependency unit once you've finished. We'll tidy her up a bit and he can sit with her then. I'll let you know when she comes round in case you want to talk to her then. Of course she'll have to see the duty shrink once she's awake." A psychiatric review was routine for all suicide attempts.

Ray headed back to the waiting room and ushered Joseph through to the calm of the interview room. He was stunned, but keen to talk.

"I can't really believe this, Dr Shepherd. I shouldn't have left her. The last few days have been pretty tough, but today she seemed better."

Ray nodded and leaned closer to Joseph as he carried on.

"I would have thought she'd be great you know. We prayed and prayed for a miracle and then you came along and gave us it. You know she can walk normally now and do pretty much everything else. But she's been having these episodes of crying and crying. She says that she can't make contact with God. He's been there for her, for us, all the time of her illness. No matter how bad things were, she could always lean on Him. But now she has times when she's says He's not there. She thinks He left her because she got this cure and so many others out there are so poorly. She had started to read all of the aid organisation websites. I thought it was to look at things we might do when she got the all-clear from you, but I think she was actually just storing up tales of people in a worse state than herself. Today, though, I thought she was brighter and calmer and it would be OK for me to be out for a while. Maybe she was calmer because she had made her mind up to do this."

"I don't think we'll know that for sure until she comes round. I've had a good chat with Dr Hood and I've seen Amanda in the treatment room. She still hasn't woken up, but she's had her stomach washed out to get rid of any other poisons and they'll be taking her through to the high dependency unit soon so that they can keep a close eye on her. You'll be able to get through to sit with her soon. I would suggest that you talk to her, even if you're not sure that she can hear you. Don't go on about the overdose just now, except to let her know that you know it happened and you are sure she's going to improve. Otherwise concentrate on normal stuff. That might help to bring her round more quickly. Dr Hood is confident that she'll come through this OK. When you see her at first she'll probably have a tube in to keep her breathing normal and to stop anything going down the wrong way into her lungs. She'll need that until she wakes up a bit more. She'll also have a drip in to treat the effects of paracetamol that we know she has taken. That antidote should work just fine, thanks to your quick thinking in getting her here for treatment. You said that God had always been there for her, but she did have previous episodes of depression, didn't she?"

"Yes. I think when the MS was first diagnosed she needed some treatment for depression, more than once. But as it got worse, her faith seemed to get stronger and to carry her through like I said … until this …"

Ray rested his hand on Joseph's. "In a way that's reassuring because it probably means that this is just a recurrence of the depression, brought on by all the stress of recovering as she has. As part of the routine, Dr Hood will be asking a psychiatrist to see her, and he or she will be able to help. Emilie and I will also be around for as much help as you need. Could you let me know when she's waking up? Dr Hood has also promised to contact me. I'd be quite keen to talk to Amanda if she's willing once she is on the mend … but only if she's willing of course. Tell her there is nothing to be embarrassed about with this – it's just another part of the illness that we will be able to help her through. I'll take you through to the HDU now and you can sit with her."

"God bless you, Doctor."

Ray again marvelled at the strength of Joseph's faith. He also wished he could believe that this was just another part of the illness … but what if it was due to the treatment? He would have to document all of this for the record. What would Carter say now?

CHAPTER 40

Two days before the meeting with Carter, both Billy Hood and Joseph contacted Ray to say that Amanda was now fully awake. Joseph said, as Ray had anticipated, that she was full of remorse, embarrassed about all the trouble she had caused but apparently stronger in her faith again. She had seen a very helpful psychiatrist who had promised to keep in touch with her over the next few days and weeks and she hoped to be getting home soon. She would be happy to see Ray again, although she wondered if Emilie could maybe visit first – she might find it easier to talk to her. Ray agreed that he would ask Emilie to see her in the hospital that day and at home over the next couple of days. Assuming all was going well, he would see her in three days' time, but could call sooner if there were any problems. He would ask Emilie to collect the necessary clinical details to add to those he had already documented in Amanda's trial file. This would be one he would take to the meeting with Carter.

The day before the meeting, he decided to visit his dad who had made it home again with an 'enhanced care package', according to the management-speak of the day. Although Ray hated this kind of jargon, he had to admit it was a great service. His dad was getting regular visits by care workers twice a day and a respiratory specialist nurse once a day. He also had some home monitoring equipment in place and access to an emergency telephone helpline.

Ray managed to get away from work at about 4 p.m. and headed up the motorway on his motorbike – he felt he needed the release of that, although couldn't entirely get rid of the feeling of the condemned man eating his last breakfast. He knew in himself that part of the reason for this visit was entirely selfish, a hope that seeing his old man would take his mind off the impending meeting for a while at least.

As he opened the door, he heard quite a cheery shout from his dad. His voice sounded stronger than it had been for some time, and as usual the old man didn't miss a trick.

"Hi, son. What's up? Midweek visit usually means trouble at mill ..."

"No," Ray lied through his teeth. "Just come to see how you're doing ..."

"OK, if that's how it is, no need to tell me right now. Actually I'm pretty good. What do you think of all this stuff? See that on the sideboard – hotline to the Kremlin, you know."

There had been a few changes in the room. The oxygen was there as before but the room was now fitted with some movement detectors, a carbon monoxide alarm as well as a smoke alarm, and a small console on the sideboard that included a finger probe for measuring blood oxygen saturation and heart rate, a blood pressure cuff and a set of scales and a call button to reach an emergency call centre by telephone should his dad feel more unwell. Ray knew that these telemedicine devices also asked the patient a series of questions each day about their breathing, cough, phlegm and so on, and raised an alert if things seemed to be worsening.

"Jesus, Dad, it'll soon be like the Starship Enterprise in here. How's all this monitoring working out?"

"It's good so far, son. No sign of Lieutenant Uhura, but I'm not fit for that sort of thing these days anyway. Actually the girls, and one young man, who come in are all great. They hope that this stuff can predict when I'm getting bad and they can up my treatment without having to take me off to the hospital ... we'll see. Anyway, if you're not going to tell me what's up with you, you could at least do something useful and get the kettle on ..."

Ray was glad of the diversion, making them some food and a cup of tea. Nothing fancy, but he managed to rustle up some mince and potatoes with carrots and a couple of dairy custard desserts from the fridge. As usual, his dad wasn't able to eat very much, but he did make a better fist of it than when Ray had last seen him.

Just as they finished eating, the door opened and in came a young woman in a hospital nurse uniform. She looked momentarily surprised.

"Oh, hello, Mr Shepherd. I didn't realise you had a visitor. Just in for the usual call."

"No problem nurse. He's not really a visitor, he's just my son, Ray. He's a doc, you know, but at the moment he's doing research ... Top secret trial, you know ... have to kill you if we told you more ..."

"Oh shut up, Dad." Ray turned and held out his hand. "Hi, I'm Ray. I just came up for a quick visit … quiet night tonight, you know …"

"More like something's up," said his dad "But he won't tell me …"

"I'm Vicky, one of the respiratory nurses. We're just checking on your dad daily until he gets more used to the telemonitoring kit. He's pretty good already, you know, so we're hoping that he can go on to the full service soon."

"It's great," said Ray. "He certainly seems a lot better than he's been for bit. I'll leave you to do your stuff while I get the dishes done. I've got to head back to the hospital later tonight. Thanks again …"

When Vicky had gone, Ray spent another hour or so with his dad. He did seem genuinely better, more confident and a bit more relaxed than before. Eventually Ray stood up to go.

"I'd better be off, Dad; big meeting with the boss tomorrow. There are one or two problems with the study but I'm sure it will all work out. I'll be able to let you know more soon …"

"That's fine son. Thanks for coming. I enjoyed the mince and the chat. Whatever it is, I'm sure you'll do the right thing …"

As Ray climbed back on the bike, those words came round again …'do the right thing'.

CHAPTER 41

Ray woke at 4 a.m. in the old familiar cold sweat. The ride back had been uneventful and to his surprise he had fallen asleep with no problem. He was glad to have seen his dad looking so much more content and well supported at home. We might not be able to cure everything, he thought, but we do run a pretty good, caring health service in this country. However, when he woke, things were not feeling quite so rosy. He'd been having that dream again about moving through a large building looking for the exit. The harder he tried, the more difficult it was to find. He had dragged himself through small corridors where there was no room to stand up, had climbed up narrow stairwells to find himself in dead-end turrets and so on. It was while he was trapped in one of these that he woke and realised the big day had come. He immediately felt the chest tightness and the pounding in his ears ... next thing would be the sickness. He remembered how Liz had often held him during these episodes, how gradually they had become less threatening, and how eventually he had been able to control them by himself by thinking through a ritual series of events. The most important thing was to try to put away any thoughts of the three serious depressive episodes that he'd had when he was younger. During the worst of them, his confidence to make any kind of decision had completely evaporated and he'd developed extreme lethargy, difficult to explain to someone who'd never experienced it. It was as though the severe anxiety and multiple phobias that he suffered when the depression was bad used all his available energy. The lowest point, still etched in his memory, was the day when he became afraid to eat; just raising a fork or spoon to his mouth made him incredibly tense, although he retained enough insight to realise that if he didn't eat he would die. These episodes had all needed antidepressant therapy and he had responded slowly but surely. Gradually he had developed a strategy of using a routine series of thoughts which allowed him to find a place in his mind where he could stay calm and think logically. This morning it took about ten minutes, but he got there in the end.

Since there was to be no hope of more sleep, he decided to get up and shower. He then turned on the twenty-four hour news channel which seemed to be giving the usual diet of suicide bombings, financial crashes and earthquakes, along with the occasional dog that had won the latest agility test or something similar. However, he thought it might be a good chance to try out the wire again, so he dressed in his day clothes and put on the wire. A miniature camera/microphone in his collar led to a wire that extended down his chest into a mini recorder that was held in a sort of money belt arrangement inside his trouser belt. The equipment was all very small, slim and silent and could be controlled from a special watch that had a wireless connection to the kit. After getting it set up, he sat down and recorded about three minutes of the news bulletin. He was then able to play that back through his TV set. The quality of sound and picture was amazing, given the tiny size of the camera, so long as he pointed it in the right direction. He realised this would involve quite a bit of direct staring at Carter, but given the nature of their last interchange when things got tough, he didn't think that would be too much of a problem. By the time he had done all that, had a slice of toast and a coffee, or half a slice and a few mouthfuls to be precise, he was ready to head into his own office, gather the selected notes and rehearse some of what he might say to Carter.

Nine o'clock found him again outside Carter's office, the notes lying on the chair beside him. He could hear some classical music playing inside. Carter knew he was there as the secretary had phoned through his arrival, but nevertheless it was about five minutes before he was called in. He resisted the temptation to fiddle with his collar, or with the very slight bump in his waistband which would have been invisible to anything but the closest inspection. Eventually the door opened.

"Come in, Dr Shepherd. Have a seat. Ah, I'm glad to see you've brought some case folders. I trust everything is in order."

Ray sat down slowly and laid the folders on the desk by his right hand. Carter sat opposite, facing him directly. So far, so good.

Ray fiddled briefly with his watch, apparently checking the time, then realising that Carter probably thought he was drawing attention to having been kept waiting, but at least he had taken the opportunity to turn on the camcorder.

"I've brought some of the case folders, as you asked. I'm afraid there's been another development though."

"Oh?" Carter leaned forward, interested but almost like a crouching tiger, Ray thought.

"I'm afraid one of the patients attempted suicide the other day. She took an overdose of pills including some tranquillisers and paracetamol."

"And how is she?"

"She's regained consciousness now and is probably going home as we speak. She was in for few days after a gastric lavage and n-acetyl cysteine. She's been seen by the psychiatrist."

"And ...?"

"She thinks that she will be OK. She's keeping a close liaison but has let the patient home with her partner and doesn't think that any medication will be needed."

"Which one was it?"

"Amanda Trail. She lives with her partner, Joseph."

"I remember," said Carter. "Doesn't she have a previous history of psychiatric problems?"

Ray was slightly surprised that Carter was so well informed. "She did have some episodes of milder depression after her original MS diagnosis. She had a bit of cognitive behavioural therapy and two courses of antidepressants then and seemed to have a good response. No previous history of suicide or parasuicide attempts. She and her partner are very religious. During the past few weeks she's been reporting episodes where she feels that she's lost touch with God. It had been particularly bad the last few days before the attempt. On the day she took the pills, she seemed to be better and Joseph had left her on her own for a while. She went out to the chemist and got some over-the-counter stuff which she then took. She's one of the ones who has made a virtually complete physical recovery, but has clearly been having mood swings. I've noted all the circumstances in her case record ..." He paused, waiting for a response from Carter.

"Good," he said. "I think it's important to record this event in the light of the previous significant psychiatric history. I don't think there's anything here to link this to the trial, other than the fact that we've made her mobile enough to go out and get the means to self-harm. There's no need to link this to any of the other mild things that you mentioned last time. Have there been any other major events?"

"No ..."

"And how are the other patients doing from a physical point of view?"

"Clinically, their examination scores are mostly back to normal tone, power and coordination now."

"Excellent. Do we know anything about the scans?" Ray sensed that Carter would probably have spoken to Paul already so there was nothing to do but admit what he knew.

"Well of course the code is not broken yet, but Paul Schmidt did tell me that some of the trial patients' scans are virtually normal now."

"Splendid," Carter smiled. "So I trust that you've corrected these records as we discussed last time."

Ray was maybe being hypersensitive, but did Carter's choice of indirect words suggest that he knew the conversation might get out somehow? He decided to be direct.

"If you mean 'have I removed references to mood disturbances in other patients' records', the answer is no. Apart from the fact that it would be misconduct to do so, since Amanda Trail has had this episode it's even more important in my view to record these findings. We could be uncovering an important side effect of the therapy here."

Carter tensed and leaned forward, so close that Ray thought he must see the microphone and mini camera in Ray's collar, but thankfully it was very well concealed.

"Listen here. I shouldn't have to spell this out again for you, but it seems I do." Carter was almost growling. "A great deal rests on the results of this trial. This is probably the most important breakthrough in neurology of this century. Our potential sponsors are hugely interested and willing to invest a great deal of money and effort into further trialling and delivering this treatment. However, with all the pressures on big pharma at the moment, any spurious hint that there might be some problem with the treatment is going to make them very wary and possibly pull out of the deal. What we have seen so far is a group of patients who were crippled, entering the terminal phase of their illness. What are they like now? They are walking, running, going out, living normal lives. Perhaps they might be a bit moody from time to time, but they are making a huge adjustment as they return to normal life. One of them has had a parasuicide attempt, but she has a history of psychiatric problems. That needs to be documented, but I want these other records changed, and all references to mood swings and so on expunged." He stopped briefly for breath.

"This is your career we are talking about here, Dr Shepherd. Get these records altered and when the deal goes through with Nefelsen and the results are published, we will be famous. Money will flow to us and to the department and we will be among the most famous medical scientists on the planet, up there with Christiaan Barnard and Alexander Fleming."

"That's all very well Professor Carter, but we can't change what we have observed in the trial. The records must stand as they are. I will not change them."

"You just don't fucking well get it, do you?" Carter was now almost purple, the veins on his forehead standing out. "I can finish your career right now. I can take you off the study. I can easily find any number of people willing to take your place. I can point out your weaknesses as a researcher. People, important people, know me and my reputation. You are nothing without me ..." Momentarily he seemed to calm down a little. "... Because we have gone this far, I am going to give you another forty-eight hours to get these case files corrected and we'll meet again then. If it's not done, then you know the consequences. For now, we're done."

Carter pulled away from Ray and moved back to his desk. The conversation was over.

Ray gathered up the case files and left the room. His heart rate must have been about 200, he thought, and he felt a bit light-headed as he walked back to his office. On the way he took a detour via the toilet to remove the camera, wire and recorder and slipped them into his briefcase. He would need to check the recording, but he couldn't bring himself to do it just yet ... not before a coffee and a rest.

Back in the office, Emilie was waiting. As he went in, she got up to put the kettle on. "How was the meeting?" she said, trying to be as casual as normal.

"Difficult ... I do need a coffee."

"Coming up. You can tell me about it later. Just have a seat for a while. I've got some patients to see anyway. Most of them seem to have pretty much normal function now. Some of them, and their partners, are finding the adjustment quite challenging. I think a lot of them are afraid that they could just a suddenly go back to their old state without any warning. Anyway, they seem to benefit from talking to me about that … maybe it's easier with a neutral. Their partners too often share the same worries, although they don't talk to each other about it."

"Thanks Emilie, you are a star. I'm going to head home a bit early today. I've got a few things to do. I'll see you first thing tomorrow. Any problems, I'll have my mobile."

"Understood," said Emilie, handing him the coffee and heading off to her home visits.

CHAPTER 42

As soon as Ray reached home, he took out the camera, recorder and wire. He felt his pulse rate rising again as he hooked up the recorder to his television and pressed the play button. Carter's huge face occupied the whole of the screen. Now that Ray had time to study it, the level of contempt and anger in that face was even more frightening than it had been at the actual meeting. As well as the words, he could hear Carter's breathing and possibly even his own heartbeat racing in the background, though maybe he just imagined the last bit. The recording quality was superb and the message coming from the screen was unequivocal. This had to be reported. Ray pressed the pause button and picked up his mobile. He was put through to Dr Singh almost immediately.

"Well, Dr Shepherd, do you have good news to report?"

"I'm not sure what you mean by that, Dr Singh. If you mean that Professor Carter has backtracked on his previous threats and that things have all settled down, then I'm afraid not. On the other hand, if you mean have I got some hard evidence to support what I've been saying then the answer is most definitely yes, so far as I am concerned. But of course I need you to look at the recording I've just made and give your expert opinion. I met with Professor Carter today. There had been a development as one of the patients had a parasuicide attempt. As you'll see in the tape, she had a previous history of psychiatric problems so Carter is keen for that to be recorded but for the records of mood disturbance in other patients to be altered. He repeats his demand for that in the tape and also threatens me with dismissal if I don't comply. He's arranged another meeting in forty-eight hours to check that I've done it."

"Sounds like you have the evidence you need. If you could copy the video file to your computer and send me it to me, I'll look at it immediately and come back to you this evening with more advice. We are probably reaching the stage where you should be notifying the GMC and your university authorities, but I'll give you more detail on that later."

"Thanks, Dr Singh. I'll do that right now."

He hung up, removed the USB cable from his television and plugged it into his laptop, then copied the file onto the hard drive and put another copy onto a memory stick which he filed in a fireproof box where he kept valuables such as his passport, insurance policies and pictures of his mum and dad. He wondered as he glanced at them what she would have made of all this if she'd still been around. It would have been so far out of her sphere of experience she probably wouldn't have known what to think, like something from a book or a TV programme. But she'd certainly have worried about Ray, that's what mothers were for. He closed the box and pulled himself back to the present.

With a ping, the video file left his outbox and headed on through cyberspace. Somehow in that moment Ray realised there was no going back. The evidence was out there. If he chickened out and didn't report this now, then he would be just as culpable as Carter. He wished that he could have a face to face with Dr Singh, he thought that would be more reassuring, but clearly time was against that. He began to wonder about the next steps. How was he to approach the GMC? Could you just phone up and say 'Hello, I'm Joe Bloggs, I'd like to speak to the ending of professorial careers department.' What about the university? Better look at the website, research misconduct section ... and so on. Someone else to talk to would be great right now too. He decided that once Dr Singh had got back to him, he'd call Paul to update him and in truth, to unload to him a bit too.

Ray spent the rest of the day and early evening making more notes on the most recent events in the trial as he was sure that Dr Singh would be asking for that in due course. About 8.30 p.m. his mobile rang again.

"Dr Shepherd? This is Dr Singh from the Medical Defence Society. Sorry to ring so late, but it's been one of these days ... I've reviewed the video that you sent and it seems fairly incontrovertible. I would suggest that you make another copy and store it in a safe place if you've not already done so. Tomorrow morning you should call the General Medical Council. Tell them that you wish to lodge a formal complaint against a senior colleague involving medical malpractice and research misconduct. They will advise you of the necessary procedures and will take it from there.

They'll probably require a full written deposition, copies of any corroborating information, such as the video file, and they'll want you to attend a hearing in due course. As I said before, this is not going to be an easy process for you, but you have done the only correct thing possible in the circumstances and we will be there to support you. I would like you to send me copies of anything that you plan to submit to the GMC and other authorities – I can vet them for presentation and style, etc. – that's often quite helpful, but the substance of them is firmly yours. Once you have notification of a hearing, I'll also attend that with you. In the meantime just keep turning up for work and go about your work as normally as possible. It is very important that this trial is completed to the highest possible standards and so long as you are there, that is your responsibility."

"What if Professor Carter decides to remove me from the study?"

"I think you can pre-empt that. Tomorrow, you must report this to your university authority and they will advise you how to proceed. However, I think in the circumstances, it is quite likely that it will be Professor Carter rather than you who is removed from active participation in the study."

"Who can I talk to about this? I have to admit I've already had a conversation with Dr Schmidt, the radiologist involved in the study, to alert him that there is a potential issue. I just felt that I needed to speak to someone and since he was directly involved, I thought it was important that he was forewarned to some extent."

"I think that's OK. It is probably quite important for you to have someone to confide in, although you have to be a little bit careful that you do not compromise his position or create an impression that you are trying in some way to bias any evidence that he might be required to give to the GMC in due course. Certainly there is no problem in telling him that we've had this conversation, that you have collected video evidence, and so on. However, I wouldn't show that recording to anyone other than the necessary authorities at this stage."

"Thank you Dr Singh, you have been very helpful."

"That's what you pay your exorbitant fees for ..." laughed Singh, "Goodnight, and keep in touch with any developments or queries."

Ray laid down the phone and sat quietly for a few minutes. It seemed that after each little event of this saga he needed time to let his mind settle, and probably for his blood pressure to come down a notch or two. He decided to call Paul again.

After a couple of rings, a female voice answered.

"Oh, sorry," said Ray, "I was looking for Paul, it's Ray Shepherd here."

"I'm afraid he's been called out for emergency scans. I think it's some major road traffic accident with a few casualties so I'm not expecting him until pretty late. Is it urgent, can I take a message?"

"No, no. I was just ringing for a chat. It's nothing that can't wait, thanks."

Ray stood up and walked over to the cupboard. He took out a bottle of whisky and pulled the cork – a dram would do him good, he thought … then he pushed the cork back into the bottle. I need a clear head – no drink at all for the next while, he told himself. Instead, he decided to start collecting all the materials he might need for his deposition to the GMC and the university. Three hours later, with a filing system for the necessary papers and a further draft of comments written, he collapsed into bed and, amazingly, fell deeply asleep.

CHAPTER 43

Ray woke with his head buzzing ... no, it wasn't his head, it was the phone. He dragged himself from bed and staggered around the room looking for his mobile. Anyone looking on would have thought that he had drunk the whisky the previous night.

"Morning, Ray ... Paul here ... you were looking for me ..."

"Sorry, Paul, it could have waited ... you've been busy ... up all night?"

"Most of, I suppose, but that's what we get paid for, isn't it?" Echoes of Dr Singh ...

"I just wanted to update you on events. I had a meeting with Carter yesterday ... not good, I'm afraid. I made a recording of the meeting and the MDS have seen it. They've told me to alert the university and the GMC so I'm going to be doing that today. I guess that's when the shit really hits the fan. Carter wants to remove me from the study, but the MDS guy reckons that it might be Carter's involvement that will be suspended. I don't really know how these things work but I suppose you'll be notified as a principal investigator by someone. In the meantime I guess we just keep the study running."

"Thanks for letting me know," said Paul. "I'll keep schtum of course, until I hear something official. How are you anyway? You sound like shit ..."

"Thanks! I was asleep when you rang so that's my excuse. But you're right, I can't think of a day where I wanted to go to work less than today ... but it's got to be done."

"And you'll have my full support when needed. Now I'm off to sleep for a bit. At least with this new regime they give us some time off after a night out of bed. Not like the old days ..."

Ray heard the click as Paul hung up. He made a quick decision to go for a short run, just fifteen minutes or so to clear his head, before facing the music.

An hour later, he arrived in the office to the sound of the kettle boiling. Emilie was already at her desk.

"Hi, Ray. Kettle's on. You look like you've been running."

"Well spotted. I wanted to clear my head for today. I'll get us some coffee and then I want to have a quick chat with you. I'm going to need the office for most of the morning, I'm afraid. I've got to make some quite tricky calls. Would you be able to work elsewhere for a bit? Sorry about that ..."

"No problem, Ray. I've got visits to make anyway. Actually I'm going back to see Amanda and Joseph again today. I've had a couple of long sessions with her. She's doing pretty well now. She seems to have got over that bad spell. It's Joseph who needs more help now. He's afraid to leave her on her own. I guess he blames himself for the overdose, but he really does need to back off a bit, he's not really doing her any favours by trying to wrap her in cotton wool. Anyway, I think I'm getting that through to him a bit now. In fact I'm going to try to take him for lunch without her today to give her a bit of space. No idea how that will go. All part of the varied life of the research nurse ..."

"Thanks Emilie, you've been great through this. Today is crunch day, though. As you know I had a meeting with Carter yesterday. I told him all about Amanda and he accepted that that episode needed to be recorded, but he thought it was all attributable to her previous psych history. He repeated the demand that I change all the other patients' records, removing any mention of mood swings and so on. He told me if it wasn't done, he would take me off the study and bring in someone else who would do as they were told. He said he could finish my research career."

"That's awful. No wonder you looked a bit shell shocked yesterday. What can you do?"

"Well actually I've done it, or at least the first part of it. On the advice of the MDS guy, I recorded the whole meeting yesterday."

"Wow, you've got a tape?"

"Not just an audio recording, I've got a video of the whole thing. The MDS guy has seen it and advised that I have to report Carter to the university authorities and to the GMC today. That's kind of why I need the room to myself for the morning."

"I can hardly believe that. What will happen? To you ... to the study ..."

Ray was acutely aware that Emilie had not asked about what would happen to her, although that must be a concern for her. He tried to reassure her, realising he was also trying to reassure himself.

"Well, the MDS guy thinks that the university might suspend Carter. The study hasn't actually been compromised in any way yet, so there's no reason why it can't go on to completion. In fact Dr Singh–he's the MDS guy, really sharp but really helpful too–thinks that it's imperative that the study is completed and he thinks that I'll be able to keep my role in it. But, of course, I suppose I'll know a lot more about that in the next few hours and certainly by tomorrow, when the next meeting with Carter is scheduled. From your point of view, there shouldn't be any change in the day-to-day stuff."

"You poor guy, you must feel got at from all sides at the moment. Anyway, I'll do as you say, just keep things ticking along. You must have some assessments coming up soon?"

"Yes, I do. I've been thinking about that too. Some of the folks who didn't respond and so probably got the placebo are getting pretty desperate now. We'll have to think about whether they should be offered active treatment before it's too late for them, although that's really a decision for the trial monitoring committee. As soon as the next assessments are through though, we'll have to think about breaking the code and running a formal analysis, including the scan data. It's just been difficult to think about that with all this other stuff going on at the moment."

"OK, I'll leave you to get on. Only one other thing to mention, to add to your concerns I'm afraid. I saw Eric Strother and Susan yesterday. There's something very odd going on there. Physically he looks great and he seemed on top of the world. But Susan seemed to have shrunk somehow. She didn't say very much, he seemed to speak for her all the time and I got the feeling that she was a bit afraid of him. I know that sounds crazy, but that's how it was."

"You might be right. We're going to have to keep an eye on them too. I'll try to get out to see them once this thing is resolved. His next review is due in a couple of weeks so I'll definitely see him then if not before."

Emilie finished her coffee, put some things in her bag, gathered up some case files and put on her jacket. As she walked past his desk, she let her hand rest briefly on his shoulder.

"You take care … see you later." She closed the door behind her.

Ray took a deep breath and considered his options for the morning. 'I should tackle the university first and then the GMC,' he thought, running through his opening line a few times in his head before picking up the phone.

"Good morning, my name is Dr Ray Shepherd from the Faculty of Medicine. I would like to speak to Mr Shandwick, please."

Richard Shandwick was the 'Secretary to the University', not in the sense of someone who took notes and typed letters, but in fact the most senior administrator in the organisation. Ray had learned from his trawl through procedures that he was the person who had to instigate investigations of research misconduct. That, however, was only one small part of his job description and he was a very busy man, though not one with whom ordinary members of staff came into contact with on many occasions.

"I'm sorry, Mr Shandwick is very busy today. Could I help you?"… the standard response of a good PA.

"Well, I'd really like to speak to him personally. I want to report a matter of research misconduct and medical malpractice involving one of our senior clinical professors."

That was it, another irrevocable step on the journey.

"Hold on, I'll see if he's available now."

After a few bars of Vivaldi, a cultured Irish voice came on the line.

"Dr Shepherd, Shandwick here. I understand you have an issue of potential research misconduct to report. Before you go any further, I should reassure you that the university takes such issues very seriously and that this conversation will be treated as strictly confidential. You should be aware of our policy of safeguarding whistle-blowers … an unfortunate term you'll agree, but we're stuck with it … but also that we regard any malicious allegations as an equally serious matter. We require any allegation to be submitted in writing, but it is always useful to have a brief heads-up on what might be coming. Now, what do you want to report?"

Ray spent the next few minutes outlining briefly the background, before coming to the main thrust.

" … and on the advice of the Medical Defence Society, I took a video recording of my most recent meeting with Professor Carter where he reiterated the demand that the patient records be altered, and threatened to dismiss me and impede my career if I did not do this. The Medical Defence Society barrister saw the video last night and advised me to report this both to the university authorities and to the General Medical Council immediately. I have prepared a written report for you. I can e-mail that to you now, and it is my intention to contact the GMC this morning also. I should say that it is giving me no satisfaction to do this, in fact it is about the most stressful thing I've done in my life to be honest, but I feel I have no alternative."

There was a long pause when Ray stopped speaking, so much so that he thought the line had gone dead.

"Hello …"

"Yes, Dr Shepherd … sorry … this is an extremely serious issue and I can see that it has not been easy for you to contact us about it. You mentioned that Professor Carter has arranged a further meeting with you tomorrow?"

"Yes. That is to check that I have adjusted the case files according to his wishes, in advance of a meeting with Nefelsen Pharmaceuticals which is coming up soon. As I mentioned, they may be willing to make a large financial investment in the future development of this treatment. If I haven't altered the files, then he intends to remove me from the study at that meeting."

"This is most unfortunate, but thank you for letting me know about it. What I suggest is that you send me the documentation immediately. I will involve the senior vice-principal this morning and we will attempt to convene a small group to begin the investigation this afternoon."

"What about my meeting with Professor Carter tomorrow?"

"I will contact you later today to advise on that. I think you can expect that the meeting will not take place, but until I have spoken to other senior colleagues I do not wish to be definitive about that. In the meantime, as you have said, your duty as a doctor is also to contact the General Medical Council. I would appreciate it if you could let me know when you have done that. It would not be appropriate for me to hear the content of any discussion you might have with them, but it would be useful to have confirmation that you have contacted them in terms of the discussions we will need to have with Professor Carter. I will come back to you later in the day with an update. Good morning …"

And with that, it was done, and he was gone. Ray turned to his laptop and quickly e-mailed the document tagged 'highly confidential' to Shandwick's office, then gathered his strength for stage two of the process … the General Medical Council.

CHAPTER 44

"Good morning, General Medical Council, how can I help you?" The voice was clipped and professional, female, of indeterminate age, and probably Home Counties.

"I wish to report a matter of research misconduct associated with medical malpractice."

"Are you a member of the public, a medical professional or a hospital manager?"

"I am a medical professional, and the matter concerns a senior colleague."

"Hold the line, I'll put you through to one of our Investigations Team."

There was a few moments silence, then another female voice came on the line.

"Good morning, my name is Dr Veronica Whitbread. I am a member of the investigation team. Can I take your name please?"

Ray gave his name, his current post and his GMC registration number. A bit like the army he thought: name, rank and serial number. He hoped they wouldn't be reading it off a dog tag on his metaphorical corpse in a few months. There was a momentary pause, during which he assumed that Dr Whitbread was checking his details on the GMC register.

"Thank you, Dr Shepherd. I understand you want to report a colleague in a matter of research misconduct. Perhaps you could give me a few details in the first instance and then I can advise you how we might proceed."

Ray once again explained the background to the case, the involvement of the MDS, the fact that he had video evidence of Carter's demands and the threat to his career, and finally that he had already alerted his university who were taking the matter forward as they spoke.

"Well, Dr Shepherd. This is quite unusual, especially the existence of video evidence, but it seems on the face of it that malpractice may have taken place and it is certainly appropriate that we investigate it. In the first instance, I would like you to provide us with a detailed report within the next forty-eight hours. In due course, I expect that we will have to see the video evidence, but that is not necessary at this point. Once we have reviewed the report and carried out some of our own investigations, and assuming that we consider that medical malpractice may have taken place, we will have to take the matter to our Medical Practitioners Tribunal Service. They will convene a panel at which you will be required to give evidence. Given the circumstances of the clinical trial, there will be some urgency about this and I would anticipate that a preliminary evidence gathering hearing would take place within about two weeks. You will be required to make yourself available for that."

"Thank you, Dr Whitbread. I understand. I'll have the report to you within forty-eight hours and will await further advice from you about the next steps."

With that, the conversation was over and he hung up. He amazed himself that he had managed to sound so cool. In fact, he did have a feeling of detachment, as though it was happening to someone else. He had heard other people who had gone through traumas of various types, such as field combat or involvement in a road traffic accident, describe a similar sort of feeling. He guessed it was something to do with the mind creating a protective buffer to allow him to continue to function.

The report was of course already written, but he had remembered Dr Singh's offer to proofread anything he submitted and felt he should take him up on that. He immediately fired off an e-mail marked urgent/confidential to Dr Singh with the draft report attached. He also sent a text message to Paul: *Uni and GMC now aware. More later …*

Once that was done, he decided to walk down to the corner shop. He didn't really need anything but he wanted to have a conversation with someone about the price of milk, the weather or the football just to remind himself that some sort of normal world was still going on. Halfway down the street, a familiar figure rushed round the corner and almost knocked him over.

"Oh, Ray, I'm sorry. I'm in a bit of a rush … just ran out to get some cakes for a research meeting. We've got Dr Oldham coming for a study review. How are you, everything OK?"

"Oh, yeah … fine. Just out for some supplies too," he stammered. Fiona was gone before he could say anything else. That was probably as well in the circumstances; where would he have started?

He spent a few minutes in the shop, scanning the newspaper headlines and looking at the biscuit shelves. Wagon Wheels … there was a ghost from his childhood … didn't seem as big now as they were then, but surely just as comforting. He picked up a packet, then laid it down again. This is mad, he thought. He settled on a newspaper and some soft mint sweets, just to say he had made a purchase. He put the change in the charity box, muttered thanks to the young lad behind the counter, and headed back to his office. On the way back a text came in from Paul.

OK. Keep me posted. Call anytime … P

It was good to know that Paul was supporting him, although he was conscious of Dr Singh's advice not to compromise Paul as a witness for any later proceedings. He decided to keep most of what was going on to himself for the moment. His mind drifted back to Fiona. It would have been good to tell her more. Sitting down with her and Dr Oldham over a coffee to work out the problems would have been great, but of course this was way out of their sphere of activity. He hoped that Dr Singh and the university bosses would come back to him quickly … he didn't have long to wait.

Within two hours a message came back from Dr Singh: he had read the report and had made one or two minor stylistic changes; a second draft marked up with track changes was attached. Ray could accept or reject these changes as he saw fit – it was his report after all – and should go ahead to submit it. As Dr Singh had indicated, there were only minimal alterations but they did improve the sense and flow of the document. Having carefully re-read it, he accepted all the changes and sent it off by e-mail to the GMC, with a hard copy also sent by post, both marked confidential. By the time all of that was done, it was after one o'clock. Emilie popped her head round the door.

"OK to come in? I just need to pick up some things for the afternoon visits."

"Fine, Emilie. I'm kind of between calls at the moment, fancy a coffee?"

Emilie took her jacket off and sat down. Ray told her all the morning's events; that the report had gone off to the GMC and that he was waiting for a call from the university about the next steps to be taken. For some reason, he didn't mention that he had met Fiona, he wasn't sure why.

"Well, you've done all the right things, Ray. You didn't have any alternative. I know it must be pretty horrible for you … to be honest I feel pretty sick too … but in the circumstances, there was nothing else to be done, and you should know that I, for one, am right behind you."

"Thanks for that, Emilie. You've been great, so has Paul who knows a bit about what's going on. It just seems so different to anything that I expected when I came into research. I mean I knew that Carter could be a difficult character and that people had left his team before, but the impression was always that maybe they weren't quite up to it, to the high level of research he was doing. Now I begin to wonder what really went on with them … although I doubt that it would have been anything like this."

"I wouldn't think so," said Emilie. With that Ray's phone rang. She made a hand signal that she was off, picked up some notes and her jacket, waved briefly to him, and left.

"Dr Shepherd, Shandwick here, University Office. I've been in touch with the Senior Vice-Principal, we have convened a small team to look into the issue you have described, and we will be meeting with Professor Carter later today. I don't want to pre-empt the outcome of that discussion so I will call you later in the afternoon, probably around 5 p.m., to let you know how to proceed in terms of the future conduct of the study."

"Thank you for letting me know, Mr Shandwick. I have contacted the GMC and their investigation team has requested a report which I have submitted. They will contact me in due course about further action, though they have told me that it is likely that a preliminary evidence gathering hearing will be held in the near future. In the meantime, I am continuing to conduct the study and data collection according to the protocol."

"Thank you for that, Dr Shepherd. We'll speak later."

With that, he was gone. Ray slumped back in his seat, suddenly exhausted, yet in some way relieved too. It no longer felt as though he was in this alone.

CHAPTER 45

Ray now had two or three hours to kill while he waited for further advice from Shandwick. He considered going to the ward to see some patients there although he wasn't actually due to do rounds until the following day. On reflection, he thought he might not be in the best frame of mind for making clinical decisions today so decided to stick with the planned timetable. Instead he began an overview of the current clinical position of the study with particular reference to those patients who had probably received placebo treatment. Their files made grim reading. Since the beginning of the study, two had remained more or less stable but the others were all showing continuing and progressive deterioration. Two of them were now having recurrent chest infections associated with some swallowing difficulties. This suggested so-called 'aspiration pneumonia' which meant that liquids and/or food were 'going down the wrong way' into the lungs and causing inflammation and infection. This was often a sign of a pre-terminal phase of the illness and these patients were running out of time. The trial monitoring committee should be convened, but he really had to wait until he knew who was in overall charge before he could suggest this.

Of the patients who he assumed to have had the active treatment, most were now back virtually to normal in terms of their motor function, sensation and coordination. Eight of them had reports of varying degrees of mood disturbance. The most dramatic episode was Amanda's suicide attempt but three others, including Eric Strother and Lisa Ashman had given cause for significant concern. None of them, with the exception of Amanda, had yet had a formal psychiatric assessment and none had had any form of specific treatment, either behavioural therapy or medication. Again this was an issue that should probably be addressed sooner rather than later. It could of course be that it was mainly related to the huge adjustments they were having to make in their own lives and those of their partners, families and friends, but if there was some biological or biochemical basis to it, then it should dealt with. This was another issue to be brought up at a trial review meeting as soon as the chain of command was clearer. Reviewing and writing this up grabbed his attention such that he was startled when his phone rang again.

"Dr Shepherd, Shandwick here."

"Oh, I wasn't expecting you so soon ..." said Ray.

"It is after five o'clock you know. Still, I sometimes lose track of time too. You should know that we had a meeting with Professor Carter this afternoon. He denies the allegations that you have made and says that you have misinterpreted what was said ..."

"That's ..." exclaimed Ray.

"Let me finish, Dr Shepherd ..." Shandwick sounded exasperated although, as Ray thought later, he probably hadn't had the best of days either. "Professor Carter denies the allegations. We have informed him that there is video evidence which suggests misconduct, although we have not yet seen that evidence. We have advised him that in the circumstances, we consider it appropriate that he take gardening leave with immediate effect until the matter is resolved. The Senior Vice-Principal will take statutory responsibility for the study, although operationally, we will expect you to supervise the day-to-day running. You will meet with the Senior VP tomorrow at 10 a.m. at his office to brief him on the current position of the study. In the meantime, there will be no external publicity concerning this matter and we require that you inform the members of the research team only that Professor Carter is stepping down from the study pending further enquiries. We have not at this stage advised Professor Carter that the matter has also been referred to the GMC, although he may well have guessed that it would have been. We expect that the GMC will contact him in due course. We have also advised him that he should have no further contact with you or with any of the study materials until this matter is resolved. Similarly, we would advise you that you should not seek any contact with Professor Carter until the matter is resolved. I will be putting all this in an urgent e-mail to you this evening. Is that all clear?"

"Yes, thank you, Mr Shandwick. I am sorry to have had to bring this matter up, but you will understand my position."

"We will expedite investigation of this as quickly as possible. In the meantime it is your responsibility to continue to deliver this very important study to the highest possible standards. We will notify Nefelsen Pharmaceuticals that Professor Carter has had to take leave for urgent reasons and that negotiations with them will be suspended temporarily until certain matters regarding the trial have been resolved. That way we are not closing the door on future options. Do you have any other questions at present, Dr Shepherd?"

"No, that all sounds clear. Would you like me to send you a copy of the video file which will also be submitted to the GMC?"

"That would be helpful. Thank you."

With that, Shandwick signed off and the phone went dead. Although the room was quiet, inside Ray's head seemed to be thundering. There was so much to think about, so much to be done. 'Gardening leave'… of all the things he considered Carter might be interested in, gardening was not anywhere on that list! He picked up his mobile and dialled.

"Paul, could I come round to your place for a bit … I need to talk this through with you … Oh yeah, some supper would be great, although I doubt if I'll be able to eat much. See you soon."

CHAPTER 46

The Office of the Senior Vice-Principal
Professor Derek Sharpe

Ray knocked on the large, oak-panelled door and heard a soft voice calling him in. He had met Derek Sharpe a few times before, and indeed had received a personal letter of congratulation from him after his Barcelona presentation. Sharpe was a medic and had had a distinguished research career himself many years ago, but for almost twenty years now had been out of clinical practice and research and was really a full-time academic manager and strategist. He was on a whole variety of national and international academic committees, mainly concerned with teaching, rather than the research functions of the university. He stood up as Ray walked in and waved him across to a couple of large armchairs in the corner of his vast office.

"Raymond, good of you to come. Bad business all of this. I'm sure it is all very stressful for you. I don't want to talk about the investigation today, that will be for another time, but, as you know, I will be taking oversight of the study while the investigation proceeds. I've ordered some coffee for us which should be through shortly. In the meantime, I'd like you to update me on the study. Please assume that I know nothing about it and take me through it from the beginning, although I have had a read of the protocol last evening."

Ray did as was requested and started with a quick overview of the preceding animal work, an outline of how the study was designed, and an update on progress to date. He wasn't really surprised when he found Sharpe interrupting from time to time with highly pertinent and incisive questions. He might have the appearance of an avuncular elderly academic, but his mind had clearly lost none of its sharpness, and at times Ray felt as though he was going through a viva for a higher degree. Just as he was winding up his initial summary the coffee arrived. Good china cups and a higher class of biscuit, Ray noted.

"Thank you, Raymond," said Sharpe, pouring the coffees and offering Ray milk, which he accepted, and sugar which he declined. He did however have one of the high-class biscuits, realising that he might not get to this echelon of the university too often. "What are the immediate next steps for the study, in your opinion?"

Ray outlined his immediate plans. He had the next round of assessments to complete beginning within the next couple of days. The trial was now nearing its planned completion. Of course, the response of the patients who he assumed to have had the active treatment was beyond all of his initial expectations and since many of them had returned to apparently normal function, it was a moot point whether it was necessary to wait until the completion date of the study before carrying out the analysis. As well as completing the protocol, there were two other pressing matters, namely what to do about the patients who were deteriorating and were assumed to have had placebo, and whether to instigate formal psychiatric review of all those patients who had described mood disturbances.

Once again, Sharpe proved decisive in both matters.

"I totally agree these are key issues, Raymond. Firstly, with regard to the mood disturbances, I think the most appropriate thing would be to initiate psychiatric review of all the patients who have made physical improvements. That could be regarded as an amendment to the protocol and would need approval by the Ethics Committee, but I can't see them objecting to that in the circumstances. It would probably require additional patient consent, but again I doubt if that will be a major stumbling block. As well as being of clinical importance to those individuals affected, it will provide further useful information to the study as a whole. Could you prepare a substantial amendment application to ethics and get that considered ASAP? I'll have a word with the chair and the secretary to the committee to advise them that it will be coming. As far as the non-responders are concerned, you are right that we probably are at a point where they should be considered for active treatment, especially since that was an explicit feature of their original consent to be randomised. Of course the intention was that that would be done after the study had finished but it does sound as if time is of the essence. However, it is not our place to make that decision; that is for the trial monitoring committee to decide. I understand they haven't met for some time, but I will ask them to convene within two weeks. That should give them time to review your next round of clinical assessments and the most recent scan data."

"I hope that's not too late for some of the patients," said Ray.

"Of course that is a risk, but I doubt that we can expedite things much faster and frankly, if they are that critical, then treating a few days earlier is not likely to make much difference. We should meet again in three days to review progress. You should also feel free to call me at any time if you have concerns about any aspect of this study."

"Thank you Professor Sharpe, that's kind of you …"

"Kindness doesn't come into it. I am now responsible for this study and I have to be informed at all times of the current state of play. I am conscious too that you have been under a lot of pressure and will come under more in the coming weeks. You have done outstanding work so far and it is my job to ensure that we keep you supported and able to deliver the rest of the study. I don't need to tell you how important this study is; probably the most important piece of work ever done at this university. That reminds me, there are of course commercial considerations around this work as you know. My feeling is that at present we should put all of that on the back burner. I have already contacted Nefelsen, informing them of the interim arrangements for managing the study, and of the need to temporarily suspend any negotiations about future developments, but also stressing that we will be happy to engage in further discussion with them in due course. They have no choice but to agree to that, and I am sure that they will not walk away from something as potentially significant as this. So I don't think that we have lost anything in that respect at this stage."

Ray nodded, realising that he probably didn't need to thank Professor Sharpe again, although at the same time sensing that part of a great weight had just been lifted from his shoulders. Sharpe now glanced at his watch, a cue, thought Ray, that the meeting was over. He stood up.

"I'll get on with that ethics submission straight away, and wait to hear from the trial monitoring committee about any data required. Would you like to meet at the same time in three days?"

Sharpe nodded, gathered his papers and headed back over to his desk. Just as he reached it, however he stopped and smiled.

213

"I have to say it is nice to have some involvement, no matter how small, in real research again. You are very lucky to be at the beginning of your research career. Make the most of it ..."

Ray nodded again and, for the first time in a while, smiled himself.

CHAPTER 47

The next round of patient assessments was due to begin in three days. Ray found himself incredibly busy again. Since Carter was 'gardening', Ray's clinical workload increased a little, although one of the other neurology consultants had taken on responsibility for Carter's patients. The ethics amendment had to be written and submitted; a suitable psychiatrist had to be identified as they would have to be named in the submission, and so on. However Ray took to all of this with a new sense of energy. The review meeting with Sharpe came round quickly. It was brief and businesslike, but friendly. True to his word, Sharpe had activated the process to convene the study monitoring group and had forewarned ethics that a rapid response on the amendment would be appreciated.

Ray also had a long chat with both Emilie and a briefer chat with Paul. Paul had been contacted by the chair of the monitoring group to provide them with all the scan data. He, of course, remained blinded at this stage as to which patients had undergone active treatment, but the monitoring committee had access to that information which would inform their decision on how to proceed. For a few days, Ray was able to immerse himself again in the operational issues of the study. There were even spells in the day when he didn't think about Carter at all; until the letter fell through his door ...

Dear Dr Shepherd,
The Medical Practitioners Tribunal Service of the General Medical Council requires you to attend a hearing on 24th inst at 1.00 p.m. in our London Headquarters. You are being called as a witness in a case of alleged medical malpractice involving Professor Gerard Carter ...

Ray briefly scanned the rest of the letter. So this was it. He focussed first on the practicalities. At least with a 1 p.m. start he could make the trip within one day by catching an early flight. After he had booked the flight, he e-mailed Dr Singh to advise him on the date and time. He wasn't sure whether Dr Singh would be there or not, but he had asked to be advised. He sent a text to Paul giving the bare bones of the message. Only then did he allow himself time to think about the implications. He felt his chest tightening in the way it had when the whole thing initially blew up. The university still had not made any decision in terms of its investigation, although it had taken evidence in writing and at interview from a number of people, including Paul and Emilie. Somewhat to his surprise, he hadn't been called himself yet, although they did of course have his statement and a copy of the video. Sharpe hadn't mentioned the investigation at any of the four meetings they had had by now, and he thought it wasn't appropriate for him to bring it up. The implication from the way in which Sharpe dealt with him was that he had done nothing wrong and he remained the university's key person in terms of the study, but until the whole thing was resolved, he couldn't be absolutely sure about that. Anyway, he had seven days now until the GMC hearing, during which he would be able to complete most of the current round of visits. He suspected that the visits themselves were going to be pretty emotionally draining.

His fears were confirmed on his very first visit to Chris Higgins, one of the non-responders. Kath had answered the door as usual. She was as polite as ever, but he sensed a new level of anxiety and even an undercurrent of hostility this time.

"Well, Kath, how are things?"

"I've not been able to move him through at all today. He seems to have another one of these chest infections. We've had the GP in and he's on antibiotics. He's hardly able to eat anything at all now without a lot of coughing and spluttering. The GP mentioned something about a PEG tube – I think that's some sort of tube into the stomach that can be used for feeding, although he didn't think it was often used for MS patients. We've heard rumours about some people being much better but your trial is just letting Chris waste away. Sometimes I wish ... well, you shouldn't really wish that, should you ...? You know the worst thing ... he can't even be bothered with the dog these days ..." she burst into tears.

Ray held her forearm for a minute.

"Look, Kath. I can see how hard this is for you. What I've got to do today is to go through the usual tests with Chris. I don't want to give you false hope, but it's only fair to tell you that some people in the study have done very well and are much better than at the start. We think they had the active treatment although we can't be sure until the study code is broken. Although the trial is not officially finished yet, we've asked an outside group of doctors to look at the results and consider whether patients who had the dummy treatment should be given the active treatment now."

He saw her eyes light up a little.

"How quickly would that happen?"

"Could be within 3 weeks ..."

The light in her eyes went out ... "Oh ..."

As Ray entered the bedroom, he could see why. Chris looked terrible, as near to death as other patients Ray had looked after. He was barely able to speak and the effort of doing so provoked a paroxysm of coughing and gathering of foam around his mouth. Kath rushed forward to wipe his mouth and kissed him lightly on the forehead.

"There, there, Chris." She spoke to him like a child. "Dr Shepherd's just going to do some of the usual tests. He thinks that he might be able to give you some new treatment soon. We just have to hang in there until we can get it ... it might be two or three weeks."

Ray could see that it was very unlikely that Chris would last long enough to have the injection, let alone the lag period after it until it took effect. This would create a new dilemma. Suppose the trial monitoring group agreed that the placebo patients should have active treatment? Should Chris be put on life support, i.e. a ventilator and artificial feeding, to keep him alive until the injection might take effect? Patients with end-stage MS were never usually considered for this as the outcome was inevitable, but it was possible that the prion treatment had become a game changer. This very scenario might repeat itself over and over again once the treatment was out there for patients with severe MS. He made a mental note to discuss this with Professor Sharpe at their next meeting.

Once he had completed the examination, he packed up his equipment and made to leave. He felt he had to tackle the issue head-on with Chris.

"Look, Chris. I know that things are pretty bad with you at the moment. As I said to Kath, we will know within two to three weeks whether we can give you the active treatment. It does appear that the active treatment is effective although it takes a wee while to work – a few weeks at least – that means that we need to keep you as fit as possible during that time. I'll be contacting your GP today to let him know about that and I'll keep in close touch with you and Kath over the next wee while. In the meantime, you try to keep your strength up."

As he headed out to the door with Kath he said: "The same goes for you … try to keep your strength up. In some ways this is even more difficult now than it was before. Up until now, we would have had nothing else to offer Chris and our big effort would be on keeping him comfortable and helping you both prepare for the inevitable. Now we might have something that will help but it might be too late for him – I realise that puts an extra strain on him but more so on you, and there's not an awful I can do other than to ask you to contact me or Emilie any time if you need to talk anything through, or if you notice any more change in Chris. I'll talk to his GP and emphasise the importance of taking all active measures at the moment to deal with infections and so on …"

"Thanks Dr Shepherd, I know you're trying your best … we'll try to do our bit …"

With that, she touched him lightly on the hand and turned back into the house.

Chapter 48

The next visit proved to be a lot easier. One of the things he had noticed among the responders was that they were delighted to answer the door to him, but also probably to anyone. The simple act of being able to walk to your own front door, open it, and shake hands with or hug the person standing there was something that the able-bodied took for granted, or even tried to avoid. How many times had he been in a house where the doorbell went and everyone tried to look busy in the hope that someone else might answer? For the MS patients who had come back from the brink however, it seemed to be one of the ways in which they could demonstrate that they were back, fully in the world again.

Lisa was no exception. Almost as soon as the doorbell had rung, the door flew open and there she was, standing tall, beaming all across her face.

"Hi doc. Great to see you. Hope you've brought your walking shoes ... remember that promise."

Ray laughed. "Did I promise to walk out with you? I thought that was going to make tongues wag."

"We're quite used to tongues wagging you know! If you don't fancy walking, you could try a dance with me."

With that she spun around on her tiptoes and pirouetted in the small hallway.

"I used to do some ballet at school you know. Was never much good, but gave it my best shot. I'm thinking I might take it up again ... well on second thoughts I'll maybe just stick to a bit of Latin and basic ballroom."

"That's strange. All my female patients seem to want to dance with me. They've obviously not seen me in action. I take it things are going well?"

"Why don't you ask Lucy?" Lisa pointed into the sitting room and Ray went through.

"It is truly a miracle," said Lucy. You won't believe the things we've been able to do, even since we last saw you. Some of them you might not even want to hear about, but they're all good," she laughed.

"OK. Message received. I just want to do the usual questionnaire and physical examination. You know the routine by now ..."

It took about twenty minutes to complete the exercise and Ray had to admit that he couldn't now find any abnormality in Lisa's nervous system function. Power, tone, coordination, cranial nerve examination and all her higher mental functions such as memory were absolutely normal. It was as though she'd never had MS.

"If I wasn't a doctor, I'd say you were cured," he said as he completed the paperwork, "but of course we never use that word, we leave it for others. You mentioned before that you were having some mood disturbances. How is that now?"

"Oh, there's no doubt I am a stroppy bitch from time to time, but maybe I was always that way ..."

Lucy nodded in the background.

"There are times when I get angry with everything. It seems irrational. What have I got to be angry about? I've been rescued from certain death thanks to you, and yet ..."

Ray chipped in. "I think that is quite a normal reaction in people who've been through stressful experiences. Recovering can be a stressful experience just as much as getting ill. But I should tell you that we will be asking you, along with all the other patients who've had the treatment, to have a psychiatric and psychometric assessment. It's not compulsory, of course, you can refuse and there will be the usual consent procedures to go through."

"Oh, that's fine by me. Sounds just like the movies. I've always wanted to lie on a couch and pour out my inner thoughts to someone."

"I thought you already did that every night," said Lucy.

"Listen to her. Just because I'm well again she thinks she can take the piss. Well, OK, if that's the price of being healthy than I can live with it, I mean with her ... ha ha."

"That's good," said Ray. You'll hear about that from us in the near future. Otherwise I think you should just go about getting back to normal. What about work?"

"I've been giving that some thought. Engineering, particularly renewables engineering, has moved on quite a bit while I've been swanning around pretending to be ill, so I'm thinking of enrolling for a six-month refresher course. It'll ease me back into the idea of doing something useful as well as getting my theory and practical knowledge back up to date. My old company is still expanding so I hope they might take me on again. I haven't contacted them yet, as I thought we should wait for the OK from you, but if you think it's all right, I'll go see them this week. I guess they might freak out since the last time they saw me I couldn't get around on my own feet. Maybe I should tell them I'm a clone or something."

"I'm sure they'll be pleased to see you. I would suggest that you have the chat with the psychiatrist before you make the final decision on the course and going back to work, but from my point of view, I can't see any reason why you shouldn't. I guess the findings of the trial are going to become public knowledge fairly soon, but I'd be grateful if you could be a bit discreet for a little longer. Apart from anything else, you might be at risk of getting caught up in some sort of press circus once the news gets out. Of course we won't release any identities or personal details of patients involved in the study, but once your wider circle of friends and acquaintances know about this, it will be difficult to keep a lid on it."

"Gee, I hadn't really thought that through, but I suppose you're right. I'll be careful. After all I don't want to be thought of as some sort of freak."

"Just be careful, and, as ever, if you have any concerns, let me or Emilie know. In the meantime, I'm off before I have to do that *pas de deux*, or whatever it is ..."

Buoyed by the success of this visit, Ray felt he had enough strength for one more that day. This he knew was not going to be such a happy one.

Sandy Main had turned out to be one of the non-responders. As his mother ushered Ray through to see him, it was clear too that he was continuing his slow decline, though he was not in quite such desperate straits as Chris Higgins.

"Hello, Dr Shepherd. Back for the check-up again? I don't think I'm going to have much to report to you. If that was the treatment, it doesn't look like it worked for me."

"OK, Sandy. We'll talk more about that in a wee while. First can I go through the routine stuff?"

Ray completed the questionnaire and the examination. There had been no real change in Sandy since the start of the trial; no better, no worse. It was clear though that he couldn't go on like this indefinitely. Just as he completed the examination, Mrs Main came back through, carrying a tray with tea and biscuits.

"Sandy and I were just due for one, so I thought you might want to join us, if you have time, Dr Shepherd."

"Thanks, Mrs Main, That's kind of you. I wanted to talk to you both anyway."

He saw the look of panic flit across the old lady's face. Sandy was impassive.

"There hasn't really been any change since I first saw you, Sandy. However, we do know that some patients in the study have made very great improvements. It seems most likely that the treatment does have an effect, and that you probably had the dummy treatment, the placebo, but as you know, the way this study was designed, neither you nor I know that for sure. We have asked the external trial monitors, who do have that information, to look at all the information from all the patients in the study. If they confirm that, they might advise that all the patients who had the dummy treatment are given the active treatment now. We should have a decision on that within the next two or three weeks. I don't want to raise your hopes too high yet, but I thought I should let you know what we are thinking."

Both mother and son lit up.

"That's great news, Dr Shepherd. We've been praying that something like that might happen. We have heard rumours that some people were doing well; the MS society meetings can be a bit of a gossip shop, you know …"

"Well, as I say, I don't want your hopes going too high, but I thought you should be aware. You'll probably be hearing from us well before the next scheduled review."

Ray knew that he probably shouldn't be telling them this right now, but in some ways he needed to boost his own spirits, and forewarning them that they might be approached about active treatment didn't seem likely to compromise anything. He finished his tea and stood up. He couldn't really place the look in Sandy's eyes; it seemed to be a mixture of everything: hope, fear, resignation and elation, all at once. Sandy would have been through all of these emotions many times before and would be again, he was sure. As he left the house, Ray realised he was going through the same feelings himself.

CHAPTER 49

The evening of the 23rd was the longest of Ray's life. He looked at the letter from the GMC over and over again. He tried to visualise himself giving his evidence. Of course, they already had his written deposition and they had the video evidence. Dr Singh had been very helpful, explaining that the format of the hearing was most likely to be an examination of his written evidence, seeking clarification and expansion of some points, maybe challenging some of the assertions he had made. In Dr Singh's view, his deposition was reasonable and measured, factually accurate and supported by the video evidence, so he should have little to fear. However, he couldn't rid himself of the sick feeling in the pit of his stomach; what he was about to do was to end the career of a distinguished scientist. He didn't really feel any malice towards Carter, only a general sadness for him but more generally for his profession. Somehow having got involved in this seemed to debase everything about medicine and research, although his rational self said that this was not of his doing, and that it was his duty to support research integrity. He set the alarm, though he knew that it wouldn't be necessary. He wasn't going to sleep.

Sure enough, he dozed fitfully, but was awake for a full hour before the alarm was due. Despite being awake, he let it ring a couple of times before pressing the off switch. He dragged himself from bed, showered and put on his shirt, tie and suit ... the executioner's garb. He made himself a slice of toast and a cup of coffee, finished neither, and set off for the airport, throwing his mobile phone on the passenger seat.

"... and now the morning traffic report with Louise ..." the announcer's voice said over the radio jingle.

Louise sounded cheerful but business like. "We're getting reports of a road closure on Airport Road close to junction 6. Not many details, some sort of police incident. Those of you heading for the airport are likely to experience delays. You should consider taking an alternative route if possible."

"Shit," thought Ray, "that's all I need." He pulled up behind the car in front, leaving enough of a gap to make a U-turn as he gathered his thoughts. As he tried to think of another route, his phone rang. He glanced across at the screen. 'Incoming call. Unknown number.' He decided to ignore it. The message changed to one missed call. He pulled the car around, drove a hundred years or so and made a left turn. It would still be possible to make the airport on time. He'd only gone about a mile when his phone rang again … same number. Could it be someone from the GMC? Better answer it …

"Dr Shepherd … can you help me? Something terrible …"

"Who's speaking?"

"It's Susan Strother. Eric's got a gun … I don't know …"

"Where are you?"

"He's at the shop … the general store … he's inside … the police are here … they can't get in … there's kids inside …"

The penny dropped for Ray. He wasn't far from the Strothers' house … the police incident… Airport Road … the general store …

"OK, Susan, keep calm. I'm on my way. Can you tell the police I'm coming?"

He swung round again and re-joined his original route. This time he headed up the outside of the queue of traffic. He was aware of people shouting at him, fists waved, lights being flashed and so on. But he kept going. He turned his own headlights on full beam. Oncoming traffic pulled to the side. Maybe they thought his white car was a police vehicle. He didn't really care; he just needed to get there. He began to hear the wail of police sirens in the distance. They got gradually louder. He realised there was a police car behind him, but he carried on regardless. As he swung into the car park for the general store, the police car drew up beside him, a young constable jumped out and banged on his window. Ray wound the window down.

"Sorry officer, I know I broke a few rules there, but the man with the gun in the store is a patient of mine. His wife just called me. I think I might be able to help."

"What's your name, sir?"

"Sorry, I should have said. I'm Dr Shepherd. I work at the university medical school." Ray showed his university ID badge. "The man in the shop is a patient in a clinical trial that we are running. I think the treatment he's on might have something to do with how he's acting at the moment."

"I see. You'd better come with me."

The constable led him through the melee of parked cars, some with flashing lights, past an ambulance and on towards a small knot of people, some in uniform. Among them was the familiar but anguished figure of Susan Strother. She was wearing jeans, a T-shirt and sandals. Over her T-shirt, one of the police men had draped his jacket. Her face was red and puffy with tears rolling down her cheeks. As she saw Ray, she ran towards him.

"Oh, Dr Shepherd. Thanks for coming. Eric seems crazy ... not himself ... can you speak to him?"

One of the policemen approached them.

"I'm Inspector Redmond, the incident commander. I assume you are Dr Shepherd. Mrs Strother told us about you."

"I'm Ray Shepherd. I'm running a clinical trial in which Eric is one of the patients ..."

Ray went on to explain quickly about Eric's MS, about the remarkable physical improvements that the treatment had caused, but also about the concerns over mood changes, which in Eric's case seemed to be particularly extreme.

As he spoke, Susan sobbed quietly to begin with, then more violently as he came to the bit about mood changes.

"I didn't want to tell you, but recently he has become quite violent. He has hit me a few times. That's not him at all ..." she said. "This morning we had a terrible row, he just strode out of the house saying that he'd had enough. I've no idea where he got the gun from."

Redmond then explained that Eric was inside the shop. He had a handgun, and so far as they could tell, there was a woman with two small children and the shopkeeper inside the shop. He hadn't threatened them directly, but neither would he let them leave the shop.

"Could I talk to him?" said Ray.

Redmond looked sceptical. "We have a trained negotiator on the way. Our usual policy in this kind of incident is to allow the negotiator to handle things."

"I know him, though, and I know more about the treatment he's on. I think I could persuade him to give himself up. He obviously needs medical help at the moment ..."

225

Redmond thought for a bit. Susan didn't say anything, but her body language suggested that she wanted Ray to have a go.

"OK. We'll let you talk to him. I want you to wear one of these, though." Redmond held out a bulletproof vest.

Ray hesitated for a moment and then put it on. As he did so, he thought to himself how bizarre it was that within the space of a few weeks he had worn a concealed camera and now a bulletproof vest. It was like something from the movies.

He walked toward the shop. His legs felt like jelly but he tried to keep a calm voice.

"Hello, Eric. It's Dr Shepherd here. Can we talk for a bit?"

Nothing … no response …

"Eric. I was meaning to come and see you shortly anyway. I need to talk with you about your treatment. Could you come out of the shop for a few minutes?"

The shop door opened slightly, then wider, and Eric stepped out into the early morning sun. He was wearing a blue striped shirt, jeans and brown shoes, quite smart, actually. If it hadn't been for the gun in his right hand and a wild expression in his eyes, he might have looked like he was just coming back from the squash club. From a physical perspective, he certainly looked very fit now. Ray remembered the young athletic rugby player from the photo in their sitting room and saw the same man looking back at him now. All excepting that expression. Through the window of the shop he could see a man, woman and two children peering out from behind the display. He motioned to them to stay in the shop.

"Don't worry, doc, I haven't touched them," said Eric.

"Susan called me. She was worried about you …"

"She's always worried about me ... worry, worry, worry … nag, nag, nag … slowly driving me nuts." he said.

"Listen to me, Eric. I was going to contact you anyway about the treatment. For you, and for some of the other people, it has certainly worked, made you fit again, able to walk, able to do all the things that you wanted to. But it does seem to have affected some people's mood. Some of the other patients find that they're getting depressed or getting angry, or sad. How about you?"

"Well, how would you feel if your head was full of worms? That's what you did, wasn't it. You put worms in our heads ... burrowing about … getting into our thoughts … Oh yeah,

everybody looks at me and says how great I am. Parents, friends …
'Oh Eric, how well you look. It's a miracle. You must be so happy'
and on and on and on. Well here I am: worm-head. There's nothing
I can't do now, apparently. And all these people have come out to
see me. Isn't that nice for them? Let's go and see the worm-head.
Used to be a cripple you know. Look at him now. Just look at him
now …"

Suddenly, there was an almighty crash. Ray thought the roof
had fallen in or something. Then he realised that Eric had fired a
shot into the ground.

"OK, Eric, just stay calm. You don't have worms in your head.
It's just a bit of protein that helped to rebuild your nerve cells.
That's why you can do a lot of that stuff again. It's not a miracle,
it's just a treatment. And like lots of treatments, it might have side
effects. We didn't know when we started this what the side effects
might be, but it does seem that one of them is to affect your mood.
We'll be able to help you with that. In fact it's one of the things I
was going to talk to you about on my next visit."

"Just a bit of protein, eh? Just a bit of protein … You know that's
what my dad used to say when you swallowed a fly or got a
caterpillar on your lettuce … just a bit of protein … well I know all
about your protein. I live with it. At night I can feel it moving about
inside my head. Sometimes it moves to good places, sometimes not
so good. But I know how I can fix it …" With that he waved the
gun around.

Ray thought he was going to fire it, but instead his shoulders
dropped a little and he seemed to calm for a moment.

"Oh, don't think I'm not grateful, doc. We all have to be
grateful, don't we? If it wasn't for the worm I'd probably be dead
now. Instead I've been able to do it all again, and I mean it all. She
doesn't like it, you know …"

Ray looked puzzled …

"Sex, normal sex. She'd forgotten what it was like. She'd got
used to being in control, so when Eric the cripple took up his bed
and walked, she didn't like it. But I've reminded her, you know …"
He laughed, an angry, horrible laugh.

"Is that what you fought about today?" asked Ray.

"Amongst other things … She cried you know. She's cried a lot
lately." Again, he seemed to deflate a little. "She doesn't deserve to

cry, not after all she's done for me. But that fucking worm just gets me so angry … I got this gun, you know. You'd be amazed how easy it is to get a gun these days. No certificate, of course. They wouldn't issue them to people with worms in their heads, but if you know the right people to ask, hey presto. And you know what I'm going to do with it?"

"I'm kind of hoping that you're going to give it to me. Then we can go home and see about getting you some more help. You're nearly there you know. Physically you're as strong as an ox now."

"Oh, I know that … it's just that I'm nuts, is that it?"

"No, you're not nuts. We can help to get your mood back to normal. You just need a bit more treatment."

"I think I've had enough treatment. One worm in your head is bad enough. But you know that they breed, eh? So, soon I'm going to have a head full of worms. What then, eh? No peace for Eric then. No, they'll be crawling about, all day and night, figuring out what I'm thinking, making me do things I don't want to do. I'm not going to have that. I know how to fix them …"

There was a long pause. Eric went on …

"What do you think the gun's for? Worms don't like guns you know. So I figured I'd give them a dose of lead poisoning. That should fix them …"

"Just keep calm, Eric. I've got other ways of dealing with this. We can get you properly healthy again. Remember the things that we talked about before that you wanted to be able to do? We can get you back to all of that …"

"It's too late, doc. You've done a lot for me, but I'm the only one that can fix this now …"

Eric stood up straight. Physically he looked great, in his prime.

Ray was aware of a terrible scream coming from behind him, like nothing he had ever heard. He swung his head away momentarily, realising that the scream had come from Susan. It was over in flash. As he turned back Eric raised the gun, put the barrel in his mouth and pulled the trigger…

A loud bang, a flash, and the window misted up with a mix of blood, grey matter and shards of bone. Eric's body, minus most of his head, slumped to the ground.

A second, even longer scream from behind …

Ray fell to his knees, all power drained from his legs. People ran past him. Some went into the shop to embrace the occupants, including the children who had witnessed the whole incident from behind Eric. They must have seen the back of his head disintegrate at close range. Luckily the bullet had carried on upwards and lodged in the wall about a foot above the window. Others, including Susan, ran over to the limp, lifeless body of Eric. Inspector Redmond, two other policemen and a paramedic came to Ray's side.

"Are you OK, Dr Shepherd?" asked the paramedic.

"Well, I've not been hit, if that's what you mean," said Eric.

CHAPTER 50

The paramedics helped Ray back to the ambulance for a physical check over. Once that was done, someone produced a cup of warm, sweet tea. He was joined on the back step of the ambulance by Susan and by Inspector Redmond.

"I'm sorry, inspector, I should have waited for the negotiator."

It was Susan who replied first.

"Don't be sorry. You did everything you could. Without you, he'd have been dead long ago. He wouldn't have listened to anyone." She took his hand. Ray wondered who was comforting who.

Inspector Redmond agreed. "You did the right things. I'm sorry it turned out this way." The latter comment was directed mostly at Susan. "We'll have to take full statements and so on, but we can give you a bit of time to compose yourselves."

Ray asked if he could make a couple of phone calls first and Redmond agreed. There was no way he was going to London today and he needed to let Emilie and Professor Sharpe know straight away.

When he rang the GMC, he was put through to the chair of the committee. He tried to explain as succinctly as he could what had happened that morning. The committee chairman was sympathetic.

"I am sorry, Dr Shepherd. That must have been a terrible experience for you. We will reschedule the hearing for another day, perhaps next week. Do you think you will be fit to take part then?"

"Of course, and thank you for your consideration. I think most of today will be taken up with police statements and so on, and I do have to admit that I feel pretty shaken up. I'm sure that by next week I'll be ready for the committee though."

"Thank you Dr Shepherd. We'll send through a revised date and time shortly."

Emilie was shocked and keen to come over to see him straight away. He reassured her that he was OK and that he'd be back in the office later in the day, once the police business was finished, and he had ensured that Susan had help on the way. He would have to sit down with Susan to talk this through but today wasn't the right time, not for either of them. They would both have trauma and grief reactions, albeit of differing kinds, to deal with in the coming days and weeks, maybe even years in Susan's case. As an immediate concern, it was important that Susan had family on the way to be with her. The police were already arranging that for her. In terms of the practicalities, there would have to be a police post-mortem and an inquest at a later stage. This incident would also now become another important part of the study outcome. Would it be enough to scupper the treatment going forward? Ray wasn't sure, but he knew he would have to let the trial monitoring committee know as soon as possible as it might influence their decision on offering treatment to the other patients who had received the placebo.

Professor Sharpe was supportive as Ray had expected, and asked if Ray could come over to his office once the police were finished with him. As it turned out, the purpose of that visit was simply for Sharpe to reassure himself that Ray was OK after the trauma of the day, or at least as OK as he could be, and to offer any help that he could. By the time Ray arrived, Sharpe had also arranged for someone else to take on his clinical duties outside the trial until such time as he felt able to take over his full role again. Sharpe's advice was that he should get the GMC business over and concentrate on finishing the trial data collection before going back to his full clinical role. He also offered further help with the trial if necessary.

Once the police statements were made, Susan had gone off with her family, and the visit to Sharpe's office was over, Ray headed back to his own building. Halfway back, he caught site of a news screen in one of the campus cafes. The channel was running a breaking news strapline 'man shoots himself in front of crowd, including children'. On the screen was an image of the general store and a melee of figures. Ray suddenly realised that he'd better phone his dad before he saw the incident on TV. He had no idea if he would be named – he imagined that the police would withhold such details until other members of Eric's family had been informed, but it was quite possible that his dad would recognise him from the TV images. As it turned out, he hadn't been watching it, but he was pleased to hear from Ray, and to know that he was OK. He was having a better day, or at least that's what he told Ray, whether it was true or not.

In the office, Emilie listened to Ray re-tell the story of the morning's events quietly, her head tilted slightly to one side and a look of concern on her face. She didn't say much, realising that it was probably better to let Ray talk this through. Eventually she said: "Do you think you'll be OK on your own tonight? You could easily come to stay with us. Of course you'd have to put up with the kids buzzing about but that mightn't be a bad thing."

"No thanks, Emilie. That's a kind thought. I'm sure I'll be fine. I might come in a bit late tomorrow though, depending on how I sleep, or not. We'll need to see Susan again, but I think we should step back a bit for the moment. Her parents were coming down today and she has other friends who will be supportive. Maybe next week though we should offer to see her if she wants to see us."

Emilie took over, practical and on the ball as usual. "I'll contact her early in the week. I suppose there will be a funeral to arrange but in the circumstances that might be delayed a bit. We'll also deal with queries from the other patients, if word gets out that this was something to do with the trial."

Ray headed home. He felt strangely relaxed during the evening. The television was showing a programme on Laurel Canyon, that fabled place where musicians had gathered in California and from which some of the great rock stars of the sixties and seventies had emerged. When that finished, Ray had a small dram and went to bed. He fell asleep quickly.

Suddenly, Eric was in front of him again. The gun fired, and in slow motion, fragments of brain and bone showered out. This time the window shattered. The children stood screaming, covered in blood with grey and white matter on their clothes. Something wriggled among the grey stuff …

Ray woke in a cold sweat … this was to be the first of many times that this dream came around. Sometimes he saw Eric's face, triumphant almost, before he fired the gun. Other times he saw the children, heard them scream. Always, he woke in a panic. He knew that this was a post-traumatic stress incident; whether he had full-blown post-traumatic stress disorder he wasn't sure, but apart from the dreams, he was able to function fairly normally, so he decided not to seek professional help. In time it would fade, but first he had something he must do.

The next few days were as unreal as any he had ever experienced. Inevitably word got around that Eric had suffered from MS and had been in a clinical trial which was still ongoing. Mercifully the identities of other participants in the trial did not come out. Emilie proved to be a tower of strength, contacting all the patients, checking that they were OK, reassuring them in as much as she could that this incident was a one-off. Fortunately, it had been such an extreme event that none of the patients or their carers seemed to think that it could be of relevance to them. The ones who had had active treatment remained delighted with their physical improvement while the non-responders remained desperate for something to be done, almost irrespective of the consequences.

Emilie also went to see Susan twice and returned to reassure Ray that she was coping as well as could be expected. Emilie was insistent that Ray didn't need to visit her just yet. Susan was content to know that Ray was thinking of her and had no criticisms of him, nor indeed of Eric having been in the trial, despite the sad and gruesome outcome. Emilie realised that Ray had probably been through enough psychological trauma for the moment, especially since she knew that the GMC hearing was imminent. She wasn't totally surprised when he said he'd be out of town for a couple of days.

CHAPTER 51

The air steward's voice came over the PA system …

"We will shortly be arriving at Logan International Airport. Could all passengers please now return to your seats, ensure that your tray table is stowed and your seat is in the upright position with your seatbelt fastened. All electronic devices should be turned off at this time. We would remind you that your seatbelt should remain fastened until the aircraft has landed and come to a complete standstill at the gate."

Ray looked out as the plane made the familiar sweeping descent over the water on its approach to Boston. He'd made the arrangements hastily. Liz had readily agreed to his visit, although he had sensed a slight reserve in her voice when he'd explained that he wanted to talk through something big with her, but had been reluctant to elaborate on the phone. Thinking about it afterwards, it did seem a desperate sort of request, especially given their previous history.

Nevertheless, as he came through the arrivals gate there she stood with a smile as wide as the ocean. No business suit this time … instead she was wearing a low-cut turquoise blouse, tight-fitting black trousers and high turquoise heels. She looked amazing, as ever. A white bag was slung over her shoulder, and her car keys dangled from her right hand.

"Well, Dr Shepherd. This is an honour and a pleasure. Your chariot awaits …"

"Liz, thanks for this. To be honest, I'm not sure …"

"OK, that's enough for now. It's good to see you. Let's just take this slowly. Back to my place, a shower and freshen up, a beer and some food and then we can talk. How does that sound?"

"Great."

As they headed off through the tunnels that connected the airport to the city centre a torrent of memories and emotions ran through Ray's mind. Of course the city had changed, partly due to the 'Big Dig', a huge civil engineering project to bury the main freeways below ground, leaving more space for development on the surface. As a result of this, the first part of the route was new to Ray. However, once they emerged by the banks of the Charles River, it all looked more familiar. As ever, there were rowers out on the river, couples holding hands and people walking dogs in the parks by the riverside. A lacrosse match was going on in one of the fenced-in college pitches. Ray was reminded that this could be a brutal sport, played by tough-looking guys in padded kit and protective helmets. They went past the old Howard Johnson hotel where he'd stayed on his first visit to Boston. Then they were in Harvard passing all the familiar landmarks.

"Hey, the old one-string violin player's not outside the bookstore today," said Ray. One of his abiding memories was of a Chinese one-string violinist who had played incessantly outside the Harvard bookstore. It was probably an acquired taste, but not one that Ray had ever acquired. It must have driven people trying to quietly study mad.

"He's not been there for a couple of years now. Things do move on you know." Ray wondered if Liz was giving him a not very subtle message. He fell quiet again.

Soon they pulled up in front of a brownstone building in one of the more expensive parts of town.

"Well, this is it," said Liz. "Come on up."

They went up the seven or so steps to the front door, through the secure entry system and past the concierge desk and took the gleaming old lift to the second floor. Liz opened the heavily panelled wooden door and ushered him in.

The apartment was stunning. The décor was mainly black and white but brightened up by occasional brightly coloured cushions and by some striking Caribbean artworks on the walls. The lighting was subtle, much of it recessed but with spotlights to bring out the best in the paintings. A world away from Ray's flat back in the UK.

"This place is fantastic," said Ray. "I'm glad you didn't come over to my place, it would have been a bit of a step down."

"Yeah, I like it. Although to be honest I'm not here all that much. I seem to spend most of my time in the lab and the library. It is handy for some good clubs and music venues though and there's always plenty going on. The washroom is through there, to the left. Why don't you have a shower and I'll make some food. Italian OK for you?"

"Great … and thanks, Liz …"

As he stood under the powerful jets of water, Ray began to relax a bit. But there was something very different about this whole experience. Boston and Harvard seemed familiar, yet not familiar. Liz was the same, or was she? He was the same … no he wasn't. Barcelona had been great … sharing that afternoon with Liz, the tenderness, the love making, it wasn't just sex, all of it. But maybe that had been the end for them. Now there was a distance. She had moved on. Maybe he had moved on too. He thought about Fiona. What would she make of this?

He stepped out of the shower, towelled himself down and slipped on some clean clothes and a splash of aftershave before heading through into the open-plan, state of the art, kitchen area.

"Good. You scrub up nicely. I've made some tagliatelle. There's beer in the chiller. I'll have one too."

"Thanks, Liz. This is great. I feel more human now."

"OK. Let's eat, and then you can tell me all."

Over the food, they chatted mainly about Liz: how she had found this place; how her job was going; how Harvard had changed; which of their favourite haunts had gone and which remained and so on. After the food, Liz made coffee and they sat over on the large black leather sofa, a slight distance between them. Liz, as ever, directed the conversation.

"OK Ray. Now that you've relaxed a bit you can tell me what's eating you."

Thinking about it afterwards, Ray couldn't remember how long he had spoken for. All he knew was that Liz had listened attentively and had held his hand when he got to the most recent part of the story, from which he left out no gruesome detail.

"Jeez, Ray. No wonder you look exhausted. I doubt if many of us will ever go through half of that in our professional lives. I'm glad that you've held it together though. You're a different man now."

"I was thinking about that in the shower. We're not the same people any more, are we? I mean, when we were together in Barcelona I thought at first it was like old times, but it wasn't. Don't get me wrong, it was great … great … but different, for me anyway."

"Me too. But it's good that we can talk like this and be close. I think you should get some rest now. There's only one bed here, so you'll have to join me ... no, that didn't come out right ... you're welcome to join me ... well, you know what I mean ..."

The bed was typically American – huge. They could easily have slept together without being within three feet of each other. But they found they naturally cuddled together. It felt good ...

★★★

Ray awoke to the sound of a distant siren. He'd no idea what time it was, though some shafts of light were coming through the blinds in the room. He rolled onto his right side. Liz was facing him, beautifully naked, her head propped up and resting on her left hand.

"You looked so comfortable. I didn't want to wake you. Don't worry, we've plenty of time, Your flight's not until 8 p.m. and its only nine o'clock now. I thought we might go into town, maybe eat at Quincy Market this afternoon and then I'll get you back to the airport."

"Liz ... you've been great. A friend ... is that what this is?"

"That's what this is ... and it's nice."

There had been no sex this time, but a different kind of tenderness, love, friendship, companionship ... whatever. Ray knew now that their relationship was over ... well not over, just changed. They would surely always be friends, maybe even colleagues again, but never lovers ... and it felt right. He had also regained some strength to face what was ahead.

A few hours later found them upstairs at the wooden tables in Faneuil Hall. They had both always enjoyed Quincy Market with its mix of quirky shops, restaurants varying from the cheap and cheerful to quite upmarket, and, most of all, the street entertainers: musicians, clowns, jugglers, storytellers and generally wacky people. Having now resolved the future of their relationship, they talked long and freely about all sorts of things, including their future plans.

"For me, it's all up in the air at the moment," said Ray. For one thing, I've got this GMC hearing still to face, and then who knows what will happen after that with the study. Still, at least I've got good leadership from Professor Sharpe and everyone else has been supportive. I can't get Eric out of my head though. If it hadn't been for me...."

"If it hadn't been for you, he'd have died a lingering death, probably before now. I know it must have been awful … well actually I can't even begin to imagine how it was, but you shouldn't beat yourself up. That does no one any favours … not you, not the other patients, not your friends, not your future lover …"

The last bit threw Ray a little, though he realised that Liz would sense something of that other relationship that up until now had been something and nothing.

"Oh I know that. I've seen gruesome sights before working in emergency rooms and on the rapid response unit; road accidents, industrial accidents, suicides even … but it's not happened right in front of me before. I guess I know a little more of what soldiers must go through now. But yes, I'll hold it together. I know that now. I'm still not sure about future lovers, but I suppose that might happen too."

"That will happen, and you will be enriched by it. Take it from me, a woman."

"An amazing woman …"

CHAPTER 52

Two days later found him facing that very GMC hearing. This time the journey to London had been uneventful. The large wood-panelled room was forbidding; it seemed to ooze the memories of past misdemeanours and the playing out of professional and personal tragedies. But the experience of giving evidence was not as traumatic as he had expected. Dr Singh sat to his right. The panel had clearly read his statement and viewed the video footage. They had obviously also been well briefed on the events of the previous week, or perhaps they had just watched the television news, since Eric's very public suicide had been well covered, as well as Ray's failed role as negotiator (portrayed in the media as the doctor's brave attempt to reason with a deranged man). There had been some mention of the treatment trial but no direct attempt by the press to link the treatment trial with Eric's behaviour and gory death.

Before the taking of evidence began, the panel chairman went to some lengths to thank Ray for coming, and to express their concern that he was coping with the events of the previous week. He, in turn, thanked them for their concern and for postponing the evidence session until today. As Dr Singh had predicted, the actual proceedings focussed on refining the statement he had made, confirming details where necessary, and so on. He sensed that the panel had reservations about the use of covert recording, but they acknowledged that it had provided useful evidence, particularly when Dr Singh made it clear that Ray had only made this recording with some reluctance and on his express advice. At the end of the hearing, the chairman once again thanked Ray for his attendance, particularly given the recent circumstances. There was no specific mention of when or if Ray would be informed of the eventual outcome of the panel with respect to Professor Carter, and he didn't feel it appropriate to ask at this stage. To be honest, he was just glad that it was over. As they left the room, Dr Singh touched his forearm.

"Come on, I'll take you for a coffee," he said. "We don't do that for all our members but I think you've been through more than most in the past couple of weeks."

Over coffee, Dr Singh asked Ray about the progress of the trial and the next steps. Ray updated him without mentioning patient names. Of all those involved in the active treatment limb, the only really serious psychiatric issues appeared to have been in Amanda and Eric. Amanda, of course, had a previous history of psychiatric problems which may be relevant, but Eric had had no such history. Among all the others who had reported mood disturbances, these did not seem to have progressed although the formal psychiatric reviews were still ongoing. The trial monitoring committee, now fully appraised of the circumstances around Eric's demise and in possession of all the documentation from the trial, was due to meet the following day to make a decision on treating those who had most likely had the placebo. Among that group, Chris Higgins was giving most cause for concern, though both his GP and the hospital medical staff were primed to give all active treatment at least until a decision was made by the monitoring committee. Decisions were still required to be made on how they should proceed if the monitoring committee decided that the trial should end prematurely, but Professor Sharpe was being very supportive and was proving to be a superb senior investigator under whom to work.

Dr Singh, in turn, told Ray that he would be notified in due course about the outcome of the GMC proceedings. There was a slight chance that he might be recalled to give further evidence, though Singh thought that this was unlikely, even if Carter opted to challenge the charges, which, incidentally, he also thought unlikely. His final piece of advice was also helpful.

"Once this is over, you should have a break; that is, a complete rest and holiday. That's my prescription, speaking as a doctor… I still am one, believe it or not … but also as your Defence Society representative. Tired and stressed doctors are not what we need on our books, although we do have plenty of them …" He smiled and held out his hand.

CHAPTER 53

Professor Sharpe waved him into the room and directed him towards what had become his usual chair. It was three days after the GMC hearing. As ever, he was pleasant but business like.

"Raymond, thank you for coming in today. I wanted to share two pieces of information with you before they go into the public domain. The first is the report from the trial monitoring group. This copy is for you. It's a thorough document as you will see, but the gist of it is in the executive summary. I'll give you a moment to scan that while I order some coffee for us."

Ray picked up the document which he guessed probably ran to about ten pages. The front page had the university logo above the title and strapline:

PRIons in Severe Multiple Sclerosis (The PRISMS trial)
Interim Report of the Independent Trial Monitoring Group

He flicked open the booklet, not without some anxiety. He could see the faces of Chris, Sandy and the others as clearly as if they were in the room with him. This document was going to seal their fate one way or the other. The summary was mercifully short and to the point:

Executive Summary
The PRISMS trial is a double blind, randomised, placebo-controlled trial of the administration of a single injection of prion solution versus placebo in severe multiple sclerosis. In this interim review, the trial monitoring group has been asked to consider whether the trial observation period should be curtailed to allow active treatment of patients within the trial who are deteriorating or approaching the terminal stage of their disease. Twenty-four patients are currently enrolled in the trial, of whom twelve have received active prion solution and twelve have received placebo. Clinical observations and MRI scanning have been performed at monthly and two-monthly

intervals respectively throughout the observation period. Review of those data demonstrates the following:

1)   Patients who have received active prion solution have shown remarkable reversal of the demyelination process. Symptom scores and functional scales have improved and clinical findings have returned to normal or very near normal in all patients. MRI scans also now show normal or almost normal appearances in all patients.

2)   Patients who received placebo injections have remained stable or continued to deteriorate, both clinically and in their MRI scan appearances, which show progression of demyelination to varying degrees in all patients.

3)   Among those who received active treatment, there has been a significant incidence of mental health problems. A number have experienced episodes of depression or sudden mood swings. In two cases these have been severe. One patient, who has a previous history of depressive episodes, took a drug overdose during the review period. Psychiatric assessment confirms that she has made good progress following that episode with continuing support from mental health services. Another patient committed suicide by shooting himself, having demonstrated some psychotic delusional features in the period immediately preceding the shooting.

   Conclusions

Prion treatment has been associated with a dramatic reversal of demyelination in a remarkably short timescale among patients who had advanced disease. Functional recovery associated with this has been complete or virtually complete in all subjects. However, treatment has been associated with a significant incidence of mental health problems, severe in some cases.

   Considering potential risk and benefits, the trial monitoring committee's view is that the trial should be stopped, the investigators unblinded, and following appropriate analysis, the findings should be published. However the observation of all patients should be extended for a further two years, and should include psychiatric and psychological review as routine, as well as continued neurological surveillance. Repeated MRI scanning is not necessary in those whose scans have returned to normal.

   Patients who received the placebo injection should be offered the active treatment, subject to full informed consent which should include an explanation of the potential risks of mental health problems.

A future larger scale trial of prion treatment in patients with milder symptoms of MS is justified, subject to scientific and ethical approvals.

Ray took a moment to let the substance of this sink in. Effectively the committee was saying that the treatment worked and that the trial findings could now be released and put into clinical practice, at least for patients with end-stage disease. Of more immediate importance to Ray was that the placebo group could now have the active treatment. Of course they would have to stay alive long enough for it to take effect, and that was by no means certain, especially for Chris Higgins and one or two of the other patients, although he would ensure that maximum effort was now made for them, up to and including intensive care, artificial feeding and ventilation until such time as an effect of the treatment could be expected. This would be a difficult time for them and for those looking after them, but at least there was hope. After all, most of them were relatively young people with potentially many years of productive life ahead of them.

As he was musing on all of this, the door reopened and Sharpe came in carrying two coffees.

"I assume that's the result you were hoping for. Congratulations. You have done a wonderful thing, Raymond." He smiled as he laid the coffees down and formally shook Ray's hand.

"Thank you, Professor Sharpe. But as you know, lots of people have put effort into this. It's not just me. And without your support, I don't think I could have carried on."

"That brings me to the other thing," said Sharpe, his face taking on an altogether different look. "I wanted you to see this document. It's going to be issued at midday today. I think you should assume that our friends in the Fourth Estate will take an interest and might well try to contact you. My strong advice to you at the moment is to make no further comment to the press or anyone else."

Ray took the piece of paper from Sharpe and immediately recognised it as a university press release.

The university has today accepted the resignation of Professor Gerard Carter with immediate effect. Professor Carter had recently been on leave from his post following allegations of research misconduct and

243

a breach of university procedure. These allegations relate to an ongoing clinical trial. Following a thorough investigation by university authorities, Professor Carter has chosen not to contest the allegations. As a result of swift and appropriate action by other University staff, we can confirm that there has been no impact on the integrity of the clinical trial, nor on the safety and wellbeing of patients involved in the trial, responsibility for which has been transferred to the university Senior Vice-Principal, Professor Derek Sharpe. No further statement will be forthcoming from the university pending a parallel investigation of Professor Carter by the General Medical Council.
End of Statement

Ray slumped a little in his seat. The elation he had felt at reading the first document had suddenly turned to a leaden feeling in his legs and a sick feeling in his stomach. Sharpe was the first to speak.

"I have spoken to Professor Carter. I have to say that he has been quite dignified. Of course he wasn't in any position to contest the allegations in the face of the evidence. I don't think he will contest the GMC process either. They will almost certainly strike him off the medical register, perhaps permanently, maybe temporarily with a possibility of limited re-instatement at a later date. If the latter, at the very least I doubt that he will be permitted to ever undertake clinical research again. He did ask me to convey his apologies to you. He realises that what he did was unacceptable. He wishes you the best for the future ..."

"Could I ...?"

"I don't think it would be appropriate at the moment," interrupted Sharpe, anticipating Ray's question. "Professor Carter has left the country for the meantime and I think we should accept that as an indication he doesn't want to face anyone else at present. It is sad that his career has ended in this way, but greatly to your credit that you were strong enough to do the right thing in the face of severe pressure. I think the message that we should all take from this is that the end doesn't always justify the means; indeed in research, the integrity of the process is paramount. The results may not always be what we want or expect, but that is science. If we lose the integrity and rigour of the process, then all of science, and particularly clinical science, falls ... but I don't really need to tell you that. I suggest that you go home today and rest. I've already drawn up the information sheets for the placebo patients who will be offered active treatment. While I was out of the room I contacted Emilie and asked her to begin arrangements for contacting these patients, taking the most advanced ones first. So there will be plenty happening today without you being involved. Try to get some rest and come back refreshed tomorrow."

"Thank you Professor Sharpe. I don't know ..." Ray's voice tailed off ...

"Just go ... rest ... come back refreshed. Consider that an order from your Senior Vice-Principal" said Sharpe, breaking out into a smile.

"Yes, Sir" said Ray, "... and thank you." He picked up the two documents, slipped them into his satchel and headed home.

CHAPTER 54

Once home, he quickly read the full text of the monitoring committee report. It was detailed, but as Professor Sharpe had said, the gist of it was in the executive summary and he didn't learn much more from reading it, except to confirm for himself that the committee had been thorough. As he finished, a profound tiredness came over him. He bunched the cushion up under his head, kicked his shoes off, swung his feet up onto the settee and drifted off.

He awoke to the shrill ring of the telephone. As he rose to answer it, he glanced at his watch. 3.45 p.m.

"Hello. Am I speaking to Dr Shepherd?"

"That's me. Who's calling?"

"My name is Peebles. I'm from the *Morning Examiner*. I understand that you are a colleague, or were a colleague, should I say, of Professor Carter. I want to ask you a few questions about the press release we've had from the university today."

Ray woke up rapidly. "I'm sorry, I can't make any comment on that."

"You were working on a cure for multiple sclerosis. You had a lot of coverage a while back for some mice studies, as I remember. Is this related to these studies?"

"I am sorry Mr Peebles. I can't add anything to the university's statement at the moment. Thank you for calling." Ray hung up.

This conversation, or some variant of it, repeated itself about twenty times over the next two or three hours. Ray couldn't believe that there were so many news outlets. Every time he tried to be polite but gave the same response: no comment.

Around 6.30, the doorbell rang. Ray opened it. A pleasant young woman, blonde hair tied back, trench coat and notebook in hand, stood there.

"Hello, Dr Shepherd. I'm Jackie Rigsby from the *Weekend News*. I've come about Professor Carter. We understand that you are the whistle-blower whose allegations led to his resignation. We'd like to run a story on your brave stance against corruption. Would you answer a few questions for me?"

As she spoke, he heard the unmistakeable click and whirr of a camera in the background and spotted a photographer a few feet away.

"Oh, don't worry about him. That's John, our photographer, just a few routine shots ..."

"Look, Miss Rigsby, I'm sorry to have wasted your time but I'm afraid I can't make any comment on this at present beyond what the university has in its press release."

"But ..."

"As you know from the press release, there is an ongoing GMC enquiry. I'm afraid there's nothing else to be said at present." Ray stepped back inside and gently but firmly closed the door.

Half an hour later ... another similar episode: this time an older man. Ray didn't even catch his name, but gave the same response. As he closed the door, he wondered if he should pin a stock reply to the door.

About 8 p.m. , the doorbell went again. He was losing patience now. He strode forward and opened the door.

"Look ..."

"That's a fine welcome!" said the young woman, a grin spreading across her face.

"Fiona ... am I glad to see you ... I thought you were another bloody reporter."

"I saw the evening television news and I guessed you might want some company."

"Great, do you want to ...?"

"No," she said firmly, glancing down at the small holdall by her feet. "I want to come in. I brought my toothbrush."